STILL AND ALWAYS

P.S. MERONEK

Copyright © 2018 by P.S. Meronek

All rights reserved. In accordance with the U.S. Copyright Act of 1976, the scanning, uploading, and electronic sharing of any part of this book without the written permission of the author is unlawful.

The story contained in this book is a work of fiction. Names, characters, places, and incidents within the story are the product of the author's imagination or are used fictitiously.

www.ponytalepress.com

ISBN: 978-0-9883790-5-3
ISBN: 978-0-9883790-6-0 (ebook)

Printed in the United States of America

Author's Note

To everyone who has a dream, and the temerity to live it. In the end it matters. I wish to acknowledge the tremendous help I received on this project. Keith Glenn and Janet Gerber did an absolutely amazing job on the editorial process.

Keith Glenn offered unparalleled insights during the course of the two years it took to write the manuscript. A true professional in both the department of management and friendship. You gave a wonderful, tireless effort. I thank you a million times over and know I could not have accomplished this without you. Thank you, my friend. On with Billy Anvil!

James Falkener was also instrumental. I may be the messenger, but you will always be the guide. Peace out, and I know, carrots in.

Thanks to the original Peter and Laurie for their inspiration in the creation of this wonderful tome.

Steve Meronek

I hope you
enjoy this as
much as I did
writing it!

Chapter 1

"YOUR FATHER DID something, and had to leave."

I didn't understand. "When is he coming back?"

My mother had her back to me. She stared out the kitchen window as she absentmindedly rinsed another plate. I followed her line of sight out the window and into the backyard. All I could see were chickens pecking the ground among what used to be cornstalks. It was cooling down these November nights in Memphis. Christmas was right around the corner. We were halfway between ghosts and goblins, and the birth of Jesus.

"What the hell did he do this time?" I demanded.

"Watch your mouth Peter," she shot back.

"Hell isn't a swear word Ma. It's a place," I defended myself, not really knowing the meaning of my own words. I'd heard Preacher Thomas say it a couple of Sundays ago, when everything was as normal as normal could be. All that changed two nights ago when the Sheriffs came looking for my old man.

Our whole world, as small and insignificant as

it was, seemed to be caving in around us and all Ma could think of was me cussing the hell word. I looked at her closer, thinking she hadn't been right in the head for longer than I cared to remember. Now, obviously, she was in survival mode.

I knew what Senior had been up to. He'd gotten me to help him enough times when I was too young and dumb to know better.

I'd turned twenty-one this year, and suddenly it came to me. I'd do hard time when we got caught. That had happened to Senior for the first time when I was thirteen. He was finally paroled from the State Penitentiary two years ago, in 2011.

With my help, the old man had a fully functional lab up and running in the old trailer deep in the woods on Uncle John's farm, just three weeks after he'd gotten out of prison.

In the terrible August heat, on my birthday, I let him and Uncle John know I was quitting. When I looked at them, I saw myself in the not too distant future. In the meth game it wasn't a matter of if you got caught, or murdered, or had to kill someone. It was only a question of when one of these inevitabilities would happen.

"Did they come with a warrant?" I was calmer now.

Linda Lou just kept staring out the kitchen

window. A sparrow landed for a moment on the ledge outside, nervously twitched, and then flew off again.

"Ma, did they have – "

"I don't know," she cut me off sharply. She stacked the last plate with the rest of the dishes beside the sink, and turned around to face me.

"They would have said something if they did," I said.

"Give me a break Peter," she said, halfway between defeat and frustration. I suddenly realized it couldn't have been easy for her being married to Peter Senior all these years.

"They didn't tell me a whole lot. I think maybe they were… they wanted to talk with him. Maybe they wanted to take him in for questioning. I don't know."

"He must have known they were coming," I said more to myself than to her. Then, with resolve, "This doesn't change anything Ma."

She took the apron off, wiping her hands with it before folding it across the oven handle.

"I didn't expect it would," she said flatly.

"I'm not going to feel guilty, even if he and Uncle John both go down. I made these plans in the summer. I won't feel bad about leaving," I repeated. "You guys chose this life. You can't say you didn't, or that you couldn't say no to him. I told both of you I want no part of it anymore. I told everyone, and now I'm leaving next week. I can't – I won't – miss this gig Ma. I can't stay."

Maybe I was looking for absolution. I couldn't really say what I was thinking. I knew, as much as I said otherwise, I did feel guilty. I couldn't help it. I guess that's the way I was wired.

"There's something else Peter." Linda Lou began what I knew was going to be a confession.

"They wanted to talk to you too," she added.

"And..?"

She sighed deeply. "They found something back in the woods."

"The lab?"

"No. There wasn't any lab. That's gone."

"What then?" A cold iciness clamped around my throat. I think a part of me knew what was coming.

"They found a body." Ma said matter-of-factly, as if she was discussing the weather.

I felt like I was suffocating. My breath came in short gasps.

"Out behind Johnny's old house trailer, down near the old wellhead."

Chapter 2

IT'S ALWAYS STRANGE when you deal with law enforcement. Almost nothing is predictable. Invariably they know more than you do, and this usually works in their favor. Usually. Two things are expected though. Cops never tell you everything they know, and they always lie to you. Knowing this going into it gives you a counterbalancing advantage, but you must always be careful. They are dangerous. I kept telling myself this over and over again, not saying a thing until the detective finally broke the silence, and I won.

"Are you thirsty?" Detective Lynch looked up at his partner from where he sat on one of three metal chairs in the spartan interview room. He sat across from me, both of them separated from where I sat by a solid steel table. Everything – even the door – was all heavy, impregnable steel. Like their personalities, I thought.

"Coke? Pepsi?" Lynch looked back at me with fake, bemused interest.

"You got an Orange Crush?"

"No. We don't have that. Sorry," he feigned disappointment.

"Pepsi it is then," I said, smiling back, reminding myself not to trust these snakes. Nothing I had to say could help me. It would only lead to disaster.

His partner, Bubba something, hesitated before he knocked on the metal door. Someone on the other side of it let him out. The heavy door clanged shut behind him.

"He's really a nice fellow when you get to know him."

I stared through Lynch, thinking about his name.

He shrugged, tapping on the metal table, rotating his fingers like some kind of stationary slinky. The nervous silence continued. Again, I wasn't going to volunteer anything. I continued to eye him.

Finally Lynch said, "Thanks for coming in kid. Detective Barry, that's my partner, was pretty sure we were going to have to bring you in. You know, find you."

"He's entitled," I said.

"Well, just the same, thanks for saving us the trouble."

I started to think that maybe Lynch wasn't

a half bad guy, and then just as quickly caught myself.

"What is it you want from me Detective? If it's about what's behind my Uncle's trailer, I'm sorry but I can't help you with that."

"So you don't know anything about it?" he said flatly.

"That's right," I ignored the hint of sarcasm in his tone.

"What do you know?"

"Nothing."

"So why'd you come down here to see us, then?" his brow furrowed.

"To save you the trouble of coming and getting me. To tell you I can't help you, and I don't know anything you might think I do."

"And what might that be?" There was no hiding the contempt in his voice now.

We were both diverted by the latch of the steel door clicking open. It sounded like the lock and load of a firearm. Detective Barry was back with my Pepsi. Wordlessly he set it on the table in front of me. I didn't touch it.

Barry looked like a throwback from an old sixties crime series. He wore a cheap, grey polyester suit, devoid of character. He was built like a running back, and wore his blonde hair in a tightly-cropped crew cut, perfectly flat across the top.

His partner was the taller man. Lynch probably stood at six two, about my height. He was thin, also like me, but with an abnormally protruding Adam's apple that made his face look a bit like a turkey.

Both men were probably in their mid-thirties, and both of them, I was quite certain, thought I was guilty of knowing more than I was letting on.

Barry sat back down in the room's third metal chair, only backwards this time. He corralled the back of it like some kind of gorilla, and stared at me in what I thought was a pretty lame attempt at intimidation.

"Tell us what you know Peter," Lynch grunted.

I focused in on his dark eyes. Then I switched my gaze to his partner. Then I smiled.

"All right. I will." They seemed surprised.

"Drink first?" Lynch was suddenly far more congenial.

"Nah," I said. "For some reason I'm no longer thirsty." I leaned forward, my arms spread onto the table.

"I know," I began, "that I came into your police station out of respect for you. I know that you guys have treated me like I am guilty of something from the moment I walked in here. I know I'm not some kind of douchebag who's got anything to hide. I also know that I don't have to sit here and allow you two assholes to treat me like one, either." They both visibly stiffened.

"And lastly, I know I have no information that will help you in your investigation into whatever it is you're investigating. Oh, and there's one more thing I know. I'm leaving. Now. Unless you want to arrest me for something you can conjure up. Then I'll no doubt be able to sue the shit out of you."

I stood up, to back it up. They didn't look so sure of themselves anymore. "If you find my old man, or his brother, tell them to call me." I stepped around the table, making for the door. "I'll be in New Orleans."

Chapter 3

"THERE WAS A body all right. But, it wasn't your Uncle John's or Senior's. That much I do know." Linda Lou steered straight through the dirt washboard of the gravel road. She was doing the perfect speed to hit the top of every one of the mounds of dried clay.

"Ma, either speed up or slow down, or use the other side of the road," I implored her.

"There's turns ahead Peter. You never know how fast another vehicle could be coming around a corner. They're blind curves too. I don't want to risk a collision. I can't see around the trees. The leaves are thicker than they've been in years." The old Buick Le Sabre Senior bought on his way out of prison two years ago was solid. It could hold its own up against most of the newer automobiles, but she was right. It wasn't worth the risk of using the other side of the dirt road. I knew she wasn't going to go any faster. She slowed up just a bit, though. It was enough to at least ease the rattling.

"Thanks," I said. "Was it fresh?" I asked her, hoping it wasn't.

"I don't know about that. Eleanor couldn't say. Those two detectives you met with weren't saying a whole lot." She steered right a bit to let a half-ton have more room to come through. It was pale white and the color around the headlights seemed more like dried blood than rust.

"See, I told you," Linda Lou backed up the logic of her earlier statement. I had to agree with her. As the winding dirt road snaked through the forest, the oncoming traffic seemed to jump out in front of us from nowhere.

Eleanor worked as a nurse, and everyone knew everyone in this part of Memphis. The nurses knew all the doctors. One of them, of course, was the coroner, and that's who eventually got all the bodies.

"But it wasn't – "

"No," she stopped me from asking. "That much Eleanor knew."

"How did she know that?"

"It was a female's body." She pulled up, and braked for the stop sign where the asphalt met the dirt of the county road. She turned left toward downtown Memphis. The Buick sputtered and coughed as she hit the gas. "So they're looking for your father and Uncle John. They're calling them persons of interest."

"Senior's not a murderer Ma. You know that."

"Neither is your uncle," she agreed. "They would defend themselves if they needed to, but that's not murder."

"Maybe something happened they couldn't control. Maybe the woman – "

"Was what?" She shot me a look I hadn't seen in quite a while. It wasn't a pleasant one.

"Peter, your father may be a lot of things, but he was never a womanizer. On top of that, he would never do business of any kind with a woman. Ever. Neither would John. They didn't believe in it. There was a clear line there. He wouldn't even talk about it with me. You told me more than he ever would, and even then, I really didn't want to hear it. That woman wasn't a hooker, and they weren't business partners. My guess would be Senior and John didn't even know about it. It's dense brush back there near that wellhead. They wouldn't have a reason to go back there. It could have been a while back, too. When he was in prison, would be my guess. Maybe she had something to do with a grow op. Who knows?"

I nodded without saying anything. What she said made a lot of sense. Senior was in prison, and Uncle John was drunk a lot of the time. It wasn't more than a few years back you could smell the pot all around just driving down the back roads near harvest time.

"I'm still leaving," I said, staring up the road.

"Don't you think that's obvious Peter? You go on. We'll be fine. They've done this before. Left, I mean. It won't be the last time either. We'll do just fine," she reassured herself.

"I'll call you when I get a place."

"I know you will. You've always been a good boy," she forced a smile. I could tell she was worried though.

Chapter 4

A LIGHT, DREARY mist draped the Greyhound Bus station as we steered past some huddled conclaves of people, and parked near the entrance to the terminal.

"We're running late," I admitted to my mother. I hesitated as I watched her stare through the front windshield, even though the only view was the rain-blurred stucco wall of the bus station.

"We'll say goodbye here Peter. I won't go in with you."

"Ma, I…"

Linda Lou smiled. "Don't worry about saying goodbye. We've never been much good at it, but that's okay. We got it here," she touched her chest where her heart was, "Where it counts the most. I love you son. Just not in the same way the movies say it's supposed to be."

"That stuff isn't real," I agreed with her.

"No, it isn't. What we Jacksons have is a whole lot better. We don't always have to say it for it to be so."

"I guess I should get going," I said.

She suddenly grabbed onto the sleeve of my jacket, to stop me from getting out. "There's something else I want to say to you." She stared into my eyes. "You've got spirits, Junior. You're just like your father in that respect. They're inside of you, on either side of your heart, and they're as real as the air we're breathing. Make no mistake about it. Some of them are good spirits; they mean no harm. But the bad ones are demons. They are at war with each other. You're off to follow your dream, and that's a good thing. But, I'm here to tell you if you can't figure out which ones are talking to you, there'll be nothing but trouble and terrible disappointment for you in the Big Easy. New Orleans can be cold. It's an unforgiving place. I know you have talent, but they won't care. Not unless you do. So respect yourself Peter. Always do that, no matter what happens, and you'll likely come out the other end in one piece. If things don't go the way you expect them to, just come on back home. This thing with Senior and your Uncle Johnny is nothing. So don't worry about it. Any time you want you just come on back son. Memphis is your home. It will always be your home. We'll always be your kin. You'll always be my baby boy."

She was blabbering now, but I appreciated it

nonetheless. "Thanks Ma. I know. We'll see what happens."

She nodded then, still watching me. "We'll see what happens," she repeated my words slowly and deliberately. "Be careful out there Peter."

I leaned over and kissed her on the cheek. I got out and grabbed my Stratocaster and suitcase from the back seat of the Buick. I told her one more time that I'd call her once I got settled somewhere. I headed inside the bus station without looking back. An hour later we were headed south down the Interstate, toward the Louisiana bayous.

I must have dozed off, what with the rhythm of the rain and all, probably about four hours into the trip. The last thing I remembered seeing before the screaming woke me up was the green sign saying we were fifty-three miles out of Jackson.

I sat bolt upright at the same moment the bus driver was killed. I was lucky because I had sat near the back of the bus, close to the bathroom. I was looking down the aisle at the driver when he disappeared, moving in an instant sideways blur from where he had been sitting behind the steering wheel, out through the other side of the bus. I'd remember later, when I was able to process everything, how the driver had just sort of blown up – exploded. Like someone had dropped an open can of red paint from the top of a stepladder onto the floor right in front of him.

The entire bus began to spin crazy sideways.

Chapter 5

WHEN THE BUS shot out from under me to my left, the force violently threw me over onto the right side of the next seat. I figured afterward that's what probably saved me from getting seriously banged up, and maybe even killed. I was lying there when the back of the bus broadsided the Amtrak train. Like some contorted ragdoll I hurtled sideways, into the padding of the seats across the aisle.

Metal ripped and sheared off all around me. The Greyhound screamed as the unyielding diesel locomotive tore through the bus's flimsy sheathing. Windows exploded and glass danced into the air all around me. It felt like hail as it hit my scalp and arms. I was now crumpled in the aisle between the twisting chairs. I was completely at the mercy of the ongoing conflagration. The train kept dragging us down the tracks though, and just when I thought it couldn't get any worse, it did.

I looked up from where I was trapped in the aisle into the terrified eyes of a middle-aged woman. She had been sitting across the aisle from me, in the seat next to the window. Everyone always wants a window seat. Well not this time, and never again, I thought ruefully. She was now wedged between those two seats next to me. I wanted to reach over to her and somehow help, but I was frozen. There was too much noise. The human screams mingled together with the mechanical shrieks. Both became indistinguishable from one another as we barreled on down the tracks, the diesel locomotive locked in a macabre death dance with the Greyhound. The bus was shredding apart as it was being sucked under the train.

The woman in the seats near the window reached out to me. Her fingers trembled like an old, dying person's. I don't know what she thought I could do for her. She was a moment away from oblivion as the sheet metal, which formed the side of the bus, suddenly ripped open near the ceiling. In a flash of sparks it was gone, sucked under the iron wheels of the train beneath us. I stared past the woman. The cool moist air was like a tornado as it suddenly filled the now-open side of the bus. Her terrified eyes brought me back. I knew in a few seconds she, and the seats, would be next. Not more than three feet separated us. Her eyes pleaded with me.

Something deep inside me stirred. In that

instant, for the first time in my life, another human being became more important than me. Suddenly I had to do something – anything – to save us both. I struggled desperately to raise myself up off the floor of the bus.

I couldn't move. The train's lateral forces had pinned me the moment I'd been thrown to the floor. It was like crouching inside a giant, tightening vise. All my strength was not enough to break free.

Unbelievably, I became conscious of the train beginning to slow. Something below us, call it fate, tore at the bottom of the bus just as I was making one last superhuman effort to free myself. Like an invisible claw reached up from the grimy dirt between the railway ties, the seat near the window jerked sideways and downwards. I sprang free and grabbed the woman's outstretched arm.

She popped out from between the seats where she'd literally been slipping away. I flung her with all my strength over my shoulder to the side of the bus farthest from the train. Her arm came out of its socket with the sound of a gunshot. She screamed and lost consciousness, now lying on the same seats I'd been on moments before.

The claw struck again, somehow snagging itself onto the bottom of the seat nearest the window. It, and the seat beside it, vanished, sucked beneath the churning wheels of the train. The bus lurched sideways, more of it disappearing under the train. The scraping of metal-on-metal was deafening, but lessening. The diesel still sounded like a monster.

It looked as if I could scramble up the aisle toward the front of the bus and save myself. The sidewalls of sheet metal on the bus a few rows up were still intact, now one with the side of the diesel. The rear of the bus was taking the hardest hit. I started forward and knew right then and there that I couldn't leave her for dead. Maybe I thought my own life would be worthless if I did, or that she was worth more than just leaving for dead. Ma's words came into my mind, and I understood more about respect than I ever had before. It was what she'd tried to explain to me. I understood now what she'd meant when she told me if I didn't respect myself, no one else would. And I knew in that instant that this was one of those odd, incomprehensible moments in life where a not-so-simple choice would change everything.

I grabbed her limp form and somehow found the strength to hoist her over my shoulders. I felt the aisle floor give way beneath me as I took my first step, and then another, death chasing us both down the aisle. But then everything began to stop. The locomotive, the bus, the horrible sounds, the screaming and shrieking, all of it finally and mercifully stopped.

I carefully laid the limp form of the woman on a couple of still intact seats about five rows up from where the two of us had been sitting. Completely spent, shaking, I collapsed in the chairs opposite her. I looked back to where we had been sitting. There was nothing there but a giant, gaping hole.

Relief washed over me, in spite of the carnage around us. The respite lasted for only a few moments. Then I heard a sickening sound above the rumble of the diesel engine. It was like the sound the towels made after they came out of the dryer. Ma would snap them in the air before she folded them. Only the popping I heard now was more like a muted explosion, a dull cannon thudding across an open meadow. I could feel the heat instantly as the gas in the shredded tanks beneath the floor of the Greyhound ignited.

Chapter 6

OF THE HALF-FILLED busload of people, most of us had survived the terrible impact. I could hear people moaning, and hysterically screaming near the front of the bus. Some had no doubt sustained some god-awful injuries.

The woman I'd rescued stirred to life across the aisle from me. We made it, I thought to myself. Only now we were going to be burned alive. Already flames licked up the sides of the bus, fed by what must be an ever-widening lake of diesel fuel directly beneath us. I coughed to clear my lungs as the cabin quickly filled with smoke.

It was now or never. I got up to get the hell out. The woman moaned pitifully as she began to regain consciousness.

There wasn't enough time I thought with angst. I'd already saved her once. Surely that was enough. I coughed again, it was quickly becoming harder to breathe. My eyes started to sting and my vision blurred as tears filled them.

I only had a second or two to decide. Again, I found I just could not leave her. A will I hadn't known existed welled up from somewhere deep inside me. I re-hoisted her onto my back, and gasped a couple of deep breaths.

Holding onto the woman with one arm, I staggered back to where we had been sitting. I looked for a foothold to climb the two feet or so down to the ground. I spotted a piece of gnarled metal that would have to do. At the same instant flames shot up from the lake of burning fuel spreading out under the Greyhound. I reeled back a step or two, startled by the sudden flare, but there was nowhere to go but forward. Behind me I heard the blood-curdling screams of people who were being burned alive. Ahead of me lay salvation across what was now a fifteen foot sea of fire.

I would be burned too, but if I didn't trip and fall headlong into the inferno, I might make it out alive. It would be a hell of a lot easier without a hundred pounds of dead weight across my shoulders, I lamented.

Was I looking for an excuse to dump my burden? Maybe, but if it was just me my odds were much better. Then again, the woman didn't stand a chance without me and I'd spend the rest of my life knowing what I did. Cowards didn't choose to be cowards – they just were. I guess heroes are the same. I was no hero, but in that moment I was more afraid of the guilt I would carry than of dying.

I adjusted her weight to even it out across my back, took a couple of huge breaths, and climbed down into the furnace below.

I gagged on the smell of burning fuel as I took my first step off the torn metal. By the time I'd taken three or four steps my pant legs were on fire. I stifled a scream because it immediately felt like I was getting stung by a thousand angry bees.

I kept moving forward. I knew I was committed from the moment I stepped off the bus and into the fire. Chillingly, the screaming behind me had stopped. No one had to tell me what that meant.

I was about three-quarters of the way through the fire when the unthinkable happened. I took what I thought might be the last five or six more determined steps through hell when my ankle turned sideways on something under the flames. My weight, with the woman on top, pitched forward and sideways. We were going down into the fire.

In a last desperate attempt born of pure instinct I reversed my grip on the woman and shoved her off my back toward the edge of the fiery lake. It was all I could do with what little failing strength I had left.

The weight was gone, but now there was no saving me.

Chapter 7

MY FACE WAS inches from falling into the fire. Suddenly I stopped, suspended just above it. The flames licked across my face and ears, and all I thought of was how putrid the smell of burning hair was. Then the flames receded as I was jerked upwards and out of the fire.

"I gotcha!" a strained voice said from somewhere above me. I was being lifted from death.

"Grab hold of me! I gotcha!" he repeated, his voice a little more under control this time. "You're out. You're gonna be okay."

I clung to the man as we escaped the edge of the inferno. Behind us the flames were already a good eight or ten feet high. Whoever this was, he had just saved my life.

I was hacking and coughing uncontrollably when he laid me down some forty yards from where the Greyhound was now completely engulfed in flames. I looked down and saw black all over my legs where jeans had once covered them. No cloth there now, just what used to be skin, now blackened like burnt toast. Wisps of smoke, like the smoldering of a cigarette on the edge of an ashtray, wafted up from my burned, bare flesh. The pain was strangely absent in my legs, but getting worse by the minute everywhere else. I heard sirens in the distance, lots of sirens.

"Lie still son. I know it hurts, but help's coming."

I looked up at him then. Immediately I recognized the stripes of his coveralls.

I coughed, a spasm overtaking me. When I could finally speak I said, "You're the engineer."

He nodded, anxiously explaining, "I hit the brakes the moment I saw you. The bus, I mean. It's a dangerous crossing right in the middle of a curve. They need better signage. I've always said that…" he trailed off. "You're gonna be okay. You'll be all right."

"What happened to the woman?"

A quizzical look appeared across his weathered face, and my heart sank.

He shook his head slowly. "I'm sorry. I didn't see anyone else. As far as I know, you were alone." He glanced off in the direction of the holocaust. He looked back at me. "You're the only one. Everybody else, well… I don't think they made it kid. They're all gone," he said. It was obvious he couldn't believe what had just happened.

"That isn't possible," I was incredulous. "I carried her through the fire. She was about forty, with blonde hair, maybe a hundred pounds. I tripped and threw her off my shoulders just as I fell and you grabbed me. You couldn't have missed her. She was right there with us."

He stared at me.

"I'm not making it up," I protested. I looked back toward the pyre of flames that used to be the Greyhound and shivered, recalling the horror. I thought of all those other poor souls on the bus. I looked back at the engineer. "I carried her out of that," I whispered hoarsely.

He shook his head; his eyes wide open and clear. "I didn't see anyone besides you," he assured me. "There was no woman. I jumped off the engine the moment the train stopped. The whole thing happened so fast." He glanced back at the burning wreck. "The front of the bus was in flames so I ran to the back. You came out through it, but you were alone kid. There was no one else. You kept walking through the fire like some kind of ghost. I grabbed you near the edge just as you tripped on something."

We stared at each other, the engineer thinking no doubt I was in shock, me wondering what the hell was happening. There was no way I hadn't carried her out of the bus. Of that much I was certain.

The emergency vehicles arrived then, just as the pain began to take over. I think I must have finally gone into shock then, because everything right after that was pretty much a blur to me. I woke up in the burn unit at the Jackson Baptist Medical Center two days later.

Chapter 8

"GOOD MORNING MR. Jackson," the nurse smiled at me. Her teeth were perfect rows of white pearls. The drab rain of previous days was gone, brilliant white sunlight flooded through the small, private hospital room. I was groggy, my veins no doubt filled with powerful painkillers from the IV bottle suspended on the chrome stand beside the bed.

"I'm sorry if I woke you," she said cheerfully.

"It's okay," I said. Everything was coming into focus, but not fast enough for my liking. "Where am I?"

"Jackson, Mississippi. You're in the Baptist Medical Center."

"I'm alive then."

"You're alive Mr. Jackson. From what I've been told you're also very lucky."

"Please," my head was clearing, "Call me Peter. Mr. Jackson sounds strange to me. It's what they sometimes call my old man. I'm twenty-one years old."

"Peter it is," her smile was effervescent. "How are you feeling?" I could tell she was sincere.

"You tell me." I looked down at my bandages. All of my clothes were of course gone, replaced by endless wrappings of white gauze.

"I don't remember a thing," I admitted.

"I'm not surprised. You've been very badly burned. You were in shock when you came in."

"I'm still in shock," I stated in a matter-of-fact tone. "And by the way, what do I call you?"

"I'm a who."

"With an obviously wonderful sense of humor. Seriously, are you going to be taking care of me while I'm here?"

"I'll be coming in and out while you convalesce. I believe Doctor Nathan Silverstein will be taking care of you. He's the physician on record for you."

"At least you'll be helping out." I smiled for the first time.

"Patty," she smiled back. She was a looker, but clearly unavailable. "That's my name."

"How long have I been here Patty?" I asked, taking a more serious tone.

"Two days. We kept you sedated so they could work on you and assess your condition."

"Am I going to need some kind of surgery?

How badly burned am I Patty? No bullshit. I can take the news."

"I'm not supposed to be talking to you about your injuries. That's the Doctor's job. He'll be dropping in to see you later this morning."

Her smile was gone. I couldn't even feel my legs through the yards of white gauze wrapped around them. That could mean a lot of things.

"You'll get me canned."

"No I won't. This is a private conversation," I conspired with her.

She glanced at the open door and hugged the clipboard closer to herself. She'd been standing near the bottom end of the hospital bed. Now she moved closer to me, positioning herself between the bed and the door.

"You're the luckiest patient I've seen in the three years I've been working here," she confided in a whisper. "From everything I've heard you should be dead Peter. No one should have survived what you went through out there on those railway tracks. From what some of the people who were there said, you should be a whole lot worse, but having said that, you'll be here for a while. For the next few months…"

"Few months?" I stammered.

"For the next few months it's wait and see.

It depends how quickly, and how well you heal. Peter…" she spoke haltingly. She stared at me. It was the same look I'd gotten from the engineer. "Twenty-nine other people didn't make it out of that bus. It's horrible. They all burned alive. The driver was killed instantly."

I shuddered at the memory of the exploding can of red paint. One second the bus driver was there, and then he was gone, just like that.

Patty continued. "No one should have lived through that crash, but one person did."

I swallowed hard and suddenly felt cold all over, like the temperature in the hospital room had dropped twenty degrees.

"What about the blonde-haired lady I carried out?" I demanded.

Puzzlement washed across her face. "Everyone died out there except you Peter."

It was the same thing the engineer had told me. I slowly shook my head in disbelief. Could I have been hallucinating? I knew in times of extreme crisis the mind could play strange tricks on a person. Now that I thought about it, I had to admit to myself that I couldn't really recall any finer details of what she looked like. Just that she was probably in her early forties, and that she had blonde hair.

"You look tired," Patty said. I could tell she had become nervous.

"I just slept for two days," I waved it off. "I'm not nuts if that's what you're thinking. Perhaps I wanted someone else to live through it as well. Maybe I wanted that so badly I invented someone to save."

"Could've been," Patty seemed relieved. I didn't sound so crazy anymore. I'd come up with a plausible explanation. Even as I said it I hoped it was true, because we both got a small degree of comfort from the idea that I'd made it up. Could it be I was feeling the guilt of being the sole survivor? I'd heard people who lived through plane crashes often felt they should have died with the others. Maybe as the whole thing was sinking in I was feeling something similar? If I was, saving a person who never was there made sense.

"My mother!" For the first time I realized this thing would be all over the six o'clock news. By now my family would have seen it back in Memphis. Hopefully they knew the sole survivor was me. I had to call home.

"Do you want a phone in here?" Patty offered.

"Can you do that?"

"Of course, but it does cost money."

"I did have a credit card…" I trailed off.

Patty said, "Admitting saved everything." She moved over to a closet next to the bathroom.

"Looks like your wallet is here. You'll have to call to set up an account. I'll bring you the unit phone."

"Thanks Patty… for everything."

"You don't have to thank me, it's my job."

"I know," I said, "But, thank you anyway."

She left wearing the same smile she came in with.

Chapter 9

ABOUT AN HOUR later I hung up the phone just as a doctor entered my room. He was a slender man in his mid-fifties. "Good afternoon Peter. I'm Dr. Silverstein. How are you feeling?"

I cut right to the chase. "How bad is it Doctor?"

"Not as bad as it should be. It's amazing you escaped that inferno. Your shoes protected your feet, but your legs and parts of your torso, all the way up to your arms and face, were badly burned."

"What does that mean?" I was anxious.

"That means you'll require surgery. Tomorrow morning. Don't worry," he smiled for the first time to reassure me. "I'm an excellent surgeon."

"I don't get it. What are you cutting?"

"Your skin is damaged beyond repair. We have to remove the destroyed tissue and replace it with skin from another part of your body. It's called grafting. We'll take good layers from wherever we can find them to replace what we have to scrape and sand away from the parts that were burned.

Don't worry," he repeated. "You'll be completely under anesthesia, you won't feel a thing."

I wasn't entirely satisfied with his explanation. I looked down at my bandaged body. I felt a slight throbbing under my knees. "Maybe I'll heal on my own," I ventured with skepticism. Scraping and sanding didn't sound so good, and taking healthy skin from parts of my body that were fine sounded ominous.

He looked at me with renewed interest, trying to figure out if I was serious or just that ignorant. Good luck with that, I mused. The meds were still doing a pretty good number inside my head. I imagined I was going to be doing a lot of hurting when they finally weaned me off them.

"Timing is critical when it comes to burns Peter. We're operating as quickly as we can, and hope scarring will be minimal. Depending how deep the burn is, we may have to scrape two or three times. We'll know more after the first time. I'm not going to lie to you. Your situation is serious. There will be pain along the way. We'll manage it though, and do our best to make you comfortable throughout your ordeal."

"It sounds complicated and scary," I said. "And expensive. I'm afraid I don't have any medical insurance Doctor."

"I'm not an administrator, but I don't think payment is going to be an issue," he assured me. "From what I've heard the hospital isn't worried. Greyhound has deep pockets. Everyone will be paid Peter. Including you, I suspect."

I seized on what he said, "Can you recommend a good lawyer?"

"No, I can't. It would be a conflict of interest. I think you could use some sage advice and honorable guidance right now." Doctor Silverstein glanced at the open door of my room. Just the usual foot traffic of orderlies and nurses in the wide hallway outside my room. "But, I'm afraid I can't give you any."

"I get it," I said. Even through the haze of painkillers I knew he wouldn't put his license on the line to help me.

"I have another question," I spoke politely, but with reservation. I wasn't sure if I should bring it up again. "Out there, on the tracks…" I hesitated.

"Ah," he interrupted me. "The phantom passenger you rescued. Patty told me," he answered before I could ask.

"What do you think Doc? To me she was as real as we are. Am I crazy?"

He winced, "I would say not, but you are

traumatized. Everyone who was out there says there was no blonde-haired lady. You were the only one who made it out alive."

"It was so real," I stared at him. "I can still feel the weight of her across my back. If I was making it up – hallucinating – she was one hell of an apparition."

"If she was real, if you rescued this person, then where is she Peter? Why didn't anyone else see her?" He paused to let me think about it.

"I guess you, Patty, and the engineer are right," I conceded. "Do you think I made the whole thing up to explain why I was the only one to survive?"

"Quite likely. There can be a lot of guilt associated with what you've been through. We see it a lot in these types of tragedies. Those other passengers didn't die so you could live, they just didn't make it out alive. It's the luck of the draw. In this case, like many others, it came down to seat selection."

"Is this going to bother me later on? As I get older, I mean."

"That's up to you. How much does it bother you now?"

I took a deep breath and let it out slowly. I looked up at the bare, white ceiling. "Which part?"

I asked. "Those poor souls on the bus. Have you ever heard dying people screaming inside a crematorium Dr. Silverstein? They're human sounds, but not really human, if that makes any sense to you. Or the passenger I imagined?" I looked back at the Doctor. "Either way it feels like I'm losing my mind."

"There is no standard by which to measure these things," he said.

"Great," I lamented. "So none of it really happened. I dreamed the whole thing up, is that it? Well these burns I got are pretty damn real. So was the pain I felt walking through that fire. Why are they real, but the woman is just a figment of my imagination? Maybe none of those people whose bodies they're still dragging out of that oven they used to call a bus were real, either. You might not be real Doctor. Did you ever think of that?" I was on the verge of hysteria.

"I want to assure you Peter, that everything you're feeling right now is normal. Your thoughts, your doubts, all your fear and anxiety are to be expected. The train hitting that busload of people was horrific, an abomination. It would overwhelm any normal human mind. It's going to take time for you to assimilate all of what happened. The burns on your body are bad enough, but I believe they will prove to be the least of your concerns. There's no way of knowing how long it will take you to mentally work through this. For your sake, I wish I knew. There's help – "

"Counseling?" I intercepted him.

"When and if you choose to avail yourself of it. For now you need more rest."

I had to admit I was suddenly exhausted. It was like I was waking up only to go back to sleep. I supposed it was normal, given my circumstances.

"I'll check in on you in the morning, before the surgery," the doctor was about to leave.

"Thanks Doctor," I said. "For everything. Sorry for the freak out about reality."

He smiled. "It's all right Peter. Get some rest. You look tired."

He was right. I didn't even remember falling asleep soon after he left, but I sure as hell remembered waking up.

Chapter 10

MY HOSPITAL ROOM was dark and grey, save for the hallway's ethereal glow, which slipped in through the crack under the closed door.

When I first opened my eyes everything seemed normal. The clock on the wall in front of me said it was five minutes after two. I'd been out for at least twelve hours. Things were kind of hazy, like how the low-lying areas where we lived looked when the fog rolled in and you couldn't see more than fifty feet in front of you. I shook my head with the irony of it. The pharmaceuticals I was on were as powerful as the meth I'd cooked with Senior and Uncle Johnny.

My mouth was parched and dry. I gagged and coughed as I swallowed to moisten the back of my throat. It felt like somebody had stuffed a fist back there.

I needed water. No sooner did I think it than I found myself in the room's bathroom, with no notion whatsoever of how I got there. A wave of high anxiety coursed through me. How the hell had I gotten out of bed, unhooked the IV from my arm, and gotten in here? Normally I would have to roll the stand with me around the bed, and into the bathroom. But there was no stand, no IV bag, and no needle in my arm. In fact, I couldn't see any trace of it ever being there. I looked up and into the mirror. I gasped and staggered backwards. My knees almost buckled under me. I steadied myself with my hand on the wall. There I was, only it wasn't me. There was no mistaking my eyes, but it was a different man staring back at me. Most of my nose was gone, only bone remained where flesh used to be. Everything else was blackened, like a marshmallow that had caught fire and crusted over. I gaped at myself, my white teeth exposed along with the lower part of my jawbone where flesh had melted away. I was grotesque. I recoiled from my horrible reflection. My breath came to me in short, suffocating gasps. My head spun in different directions as I fought desperately to keep from collapsing onto the floor. I wanted to scream, but didn't have the breath for it.

A sickening nausea almost overcame me as the putrid smell of burnt flesh assailed what was left of my nostrils. It had to be some weird retroactive thing. The crystal meth still inside my brain from bygone years was no doubt combining with the potent meds to produce the mother of all nightmares. Science was fucking with biology, and I was suffering the dire consequences. I had to wake up before I went insane.

I closed my eyes so tightly they began to hurt. When I opened them again I was standing over myself lying on the hospital bed. Then the creepiest thing I've ever experienced in my life happened. The person on the bed – me – suddenly woke up and stared back at myself. With this, suddenly, mercifully, my out-of-body nightmare ended. I was back in my bed, staring across the dimly-lit hospital room. I looked this way and that and saw nothing but walls.

As I regained my senses I couldn't help but notice how itchy the burned parts of my body felt. It wasn't painful, but uncomfortable like a rash from stinging nettles. The itching quickly grew worse until it became maddening. I needed more drugs like I needed a heart attack, so I used all my willpower to not push the panic button for the nurse. Somehow I had to see this hell through. I bargained with myself that if it got any worse I'd summon the nurse and take something to quell the torture. I remembered having read about burn patients, but none of the articles mentioned such a hellish itching.

I pushed the button that worked the recliner

so I could sit up. I clenched my teeth and stared at my bandages. The white gauze seemed to emanate an eerie, white glow in the darkness of the room. I wondered if this was just another page in one of my nightmare's chapters.

After I'd watched the clock for fifteen more minutes and nothing had changed, I realized I had to do something. I still didn't want to call anyone, and I certainly didn't want to risk a repeat of the scene in the bathroom.

To hell with it, I finally thought to myself. I decided to scratch the itch. Dr. Silverstein said he was going to scrape and sand me anyway. Scratching myself seemed a superfluous exercise that couldn't cause more damage to my skin than it already had.

I leaned over and grazed the outer layer of the bandages on my right thigh with the tips of my fingers, lightly at first, and then harder as the itching immediately gave way to exquisite relief.

Chapter 11

"HOW DID YOU sleep last night?" It was Patty, her usual bubbly self. She moved to the windows and opened the curtains, and a cloudless, blue sky appeared. She turned to me to see why I didn't immediately answer.

I was thinking about it. "I had one of the more interesting evenings of late," I admitted. I added, "Are burns supposed to itch Patty? Is that usually the case for what I'm going through?" I pushed the button to raise the back of the hospital bed as I spoke.

"Itch?" Concern flashed across her face.

"Yeah, worse than you could possibly imagine."

"Do you itch right now?" Worry now flooded her features.

I shook my head. "No, not now, but last night. Let's just say the devil himself couldn't have slept through what I dealt with."

"And what exactly might that have been?" a familiar voice asked from the hallway door behind me. I turned to see Dr. Silverstein enter the room.

"Good morning Patty," he acknowledged the nurse.

He took a moment to scan my chart before he scribbled something onto it.

"How are you feeling Peter?" He searched my eyes as he walked over to me. "Did I hear you say something about itching?" He stood over me, watching carefully.

"Maybe it's nothing to worry about," I began. "But there was a time last night when my burns began to itch like hell. I think I also had some kind of a really weird hallucination. Either that or a bad nightmare that seemed as real as it gets. Those painkillers you pumped me full of yesterday should have knocked me clean off my feet last night, right?" We both glanced at the tube leading from my arm to the IV bag.

"Everyone is unique Peter. We all have a similar physiology, but trauma to the body can cause different symptoms in individuals."

He shrugged, "All right, no more bullshit. You're right. Itching in a burn such as the one you sustained should not have occurred. Especially as severe as you've just described, and certainly not this early. Pain, maybe, even likely. We do our best to manage it, but I'll be the first to admit medicine isn't an exact science. We're still learning.

So, I think we should lightly sedate you and have another look under your bandages. We'll put off surgery until we know what's going on."

I was worried about being too groggy to call home again. Several times I'd tried on the bedside phone they brought into my room. All I'd gotten was a 'try your call again later' each time I dialed the number. Maybe Senior forgot to pay the phone bill, but that didn't explain why Linda Lou hadn't hooked it back up by now. None of them had ever had a cell phone either. It was disturbing I couldn't reach anyone. I couldn't help thinking in the back of my mind that something was wrong up there in Memphis. It was frustrating that I couldn't do anything about it right now.

It was even more upsetting that no one called me. The story about the wreck and all the grisly details had been splayed out across all the major news networks for days. I'd watched some of it on the room's television, yet as far as I knew no one had called the hospital to ask about me.

"All right, we'll have a closer look then," said the doctor. "Patty?" He turned to the nurse, "Why don't you see to the details? Prep Mr. Jackson and I'll have a look, say in one hour. That should give me enough time to complete my rounds."

An hour later a gurney with me on it was wheeled into a sterilized operating room.

Immediately after cutting away the yards of white gauze that covered my right leg, Dr. Silverstein gasped under his mask. His eyes bulged open widely, astonishment written across his face. I saw something else on his face as well. It was fear.

Chapter 12

MY HEART WAS racing as I tried to sit up to see what he was looking at.

"No, no. Just relax Peter. Let me do my job please," he spoke with clinical professionalism. "It won't do any good you moving around like that while I'm examining you." I noticed the strain in his voice.

Patty put a hand on my shoulder. I looked up at her and she nodded. It was instantly reassuring, but I was still worried. Gangrene came to mind.

I spoke to the ceiling, "How bad is it? Am I going to lose my legs?" I couldn't believe I was even asking him the question.

"No," he spoke tentatively, still cutting away the gauze from my leg. The snipping sound of the scissors made me remember a warm summer evening out in the backyard when Senior figured he could cut hair. He'd used me as a guinea pig, and it had gone badly. That was the end of his barbering days. Snip, snip, snip.

"I've never seen anything like this before," he

spoke to no one in particular. His voice was an astounded whisper as he thought out loud.

"What the hell is it?" I demanded to know. In another minute everyone was about to find out what I could be like when I was really pissed off. Yeah, try and hold me down, see how far that gets you.

The doctor tossed the last of the gauze from my leg into a basin. "Tell me if you can feel this," he instructed. He appeared to be prodding and poking the bottom part of my leg.

All I felt was a slight bit of pressure every time he poked, and I told him as much. "I don't feel any pain, if that's what you mean," I elaborated.

"All right. That's to be expected. The pharmaceuticals are doing what they're supposed to do. Scissors," he spoke to Patty, who handed them back to him. He immediately began to cut away the bandages from my other leg.

"Same thing," he whispered, again seeming to talk to himself. "This is absolutely astonishing."

"What is it Doc? I have to know."

He gaped at my legs, now fully exposed. Then he turned his head and stared at me.

"It's incredible Peter! When you came in here you had third degree burns. It wasn't a matter of if you needed an operation. It was a matter of how many times we were going to graft, and how bad the scarring would eventually be."

"I don't get it. Has something changed?"

"Everything has changed," he said haltingly. "What I'm looking at now is no worse than a bad sunburn. I'm looking at a miracle. There is no way this could have happened, and yet it has. It would appear that your body has healed itself! Your legs…" I could see he was confounded. "They're basically fine. You walked through a lake of fire and there is absolutely nothing wrong with them. At your current rate of healing, you'll be walking out of here by dinner! I'll check, but I can only assume the rest of your body is the same."

All I could do was gawk at him. I barely refrained from asking him, "Are you sure?" Instead, I said lamely, "Well I guess that's good news then."

Dr. Silverstein composed himself quickly. He spoke to Patty, "Take Mr. Jackson off the painkillers slowly, just in case." Still in awe, he shook his head. "I want you to stay here for another couple of days Peter. I'd like to call some of my colleagues in to assist me. I'll call an emergency meeting to brief them. I want them to look at the photos of your legs from when you were first brought in, among other things. Then, tomorrow morning,

I want all of us to run a thorough examination. Nurse, after you remove all of the gauze, I need photos taken of Peter's burns every half hour. Make that every fifteen minutes. Starting now. From this moment forward I'll need everything fully documented. I want Peter's heart monitored, and I'll need his blood."

"We drew samples when – "

"Draw them again," he cut Pattie off mid-sentence. "Retrieve every bodily fluid – period. Also gather up these bandages. Throw nothing away. Do you understand? Gather the sheets from his bed, and the towels from the bathroom. I want everything Peter has come into physical contact with. Gather it, bag it, and catalogue all of it. Put everything into a sanitized storage locker. This changes everything we know about tissue regeneration. If we can isolate and duplicate what has happened, we can revolutionize everything we've come to know about human tissue. Peter, for whatever reason, you may have altered the future of medicine."

I must have looked bewildered. All I could think to say was, "All because of an itch?"

They started laughing.

I gave them another three days of my life. That was how long it took before Sedgewick Harding III came calling.

Chapter 13

"WHAT KIND OF guitar are we talking about?" He'd begun to wheeze a bit. He held up his left index finger, a gesture I assumed meant he needed a moment. His other hand exited the inside of his suit vest with an object that he quickly brought to his mouth. It hissed as he depressed the trigger mechanism, the finger of his other hand still suspended in the air between us. The inhaler only took a few seconds to work. Then he was fine again.

"I've had it pretty much my whole life Peter."

"Asthma."

"Correct. It has tried unsuccessfully to kill me on a number of occasions, most notably on my wedding night, if you can believe it. Just before I passed out, my new wife, God bless her, found the inhaler. We went on to consummate the marriage, of course. Conceived my first boy, I'll have you know. We had fun with that inhaler too. The damn thing is all-purpose. At least, it was on that night. That was thirty-five years ago. We still laugh about it, you know. The irony. I almost kicked the bucket because I couldn't find it, and then we used it as, shall I say, a bit of a catalyst to bring forth a new life," he mused. He elaborated seriously, "It wasn't like it is now back then, you know. They didn't have any of those sex toyshops. Of course they didn't have a lot of things back then they have now," he spoke somewhat wistfully.

I couldn't help but get drawn into his yarns. Sedgewick Harding was a master storyteller. An old-style southern gentleman, and one of the best trial lawyers in the south. People loved to watch him while he talked. He was a living, breathing, one-man reality show. An entertainer.

He saw the train wreck on TV, then heard about the 'cure,' as everyone was now calling it. Smelling an adventure, he came calling to see if I might be interested in hiring him as legal counsel. At first I didn't think I'd need it given the fact my burns were gone, but in his inimitable style, he swayed me. Pointing out there were other important things to consider. Like, for instance, my guitar.

"It's called a Stratocaster," I changed the subject.

"How much did it cost you?"

"It was a collector's item. It's rare. I mean it used to be rare."

"How much would you say it was worth?"

"A guitar like that?" I thought about it. "I'd say at least five thousand."

"I'll get you ten."

I examined him. He wore his pure white hair in a ponytail. He looked every bit of his sixty or so years, with a frame that carried thirty pounds more than it should have. His blue eyes twinkled at me. He was serious all right.

"You're hired Mr. Harding." I decided as we spoke, I probably needed him.

"Why don't you call me what my friends call me? And my enemies, for that matter. The Wedge. Or, if you like, just Wedge."

"Done," I said. "Mind if I ask how that came about?"

He chuckled. "Early on my colleagues realized that if they gave me the slightest opening, just the thinnest place for a wedge, I'd have them for dinner. It wasn't much of a stretch to go from Sedgewick to The Wedge. Wedge, for short."

"I like it," I grinned at him. I liked Wedge too. "What are we looking at here Wedge? It seems there's nothing wrong with me, you know."

"No, I don't," The Wedge replied with sincerity. "And neither does anyone else for that matter. All the experts have admitted as much. Right now, the only thing everyone can agree on is they don't have a clue what happened to you. I don't want to scare you Peter, but think about it for a moment.

Whatever happened to heal your burns could just as easily reverse itself. You were badly burned through the gross negligence of the bus company and their driver. The pain you felt right after that horrendous accident was unfathomable. The sights, the sounds, and the smells will haunt you for the rest of your life. How could you ever forget those helpless, screaming souls as they burned to death all around you? Are you feeling me Peter?" He smiled knowingly.

I was beginning to understand him a bit more. The Wedge, I was certain, was just warming up.

"We have a case," I stated.

"We have a case," Wedge agreed, the confidence never leaving his smile. "Have faith in me, and you won't ever have to worry about the rent again."

My jaw must have dropped. "That big?" I mused.

Wedge nodded. "Big enough that I will advance you, say, how's twenty-five thousand sound? That ought to be enough to replace your guitar."

My heart was racing. I'd made some decent loot in the meth business, but this was different. For starters, it was legal. I knew the guys who insured the bus line had deep pockets. If Wedge was fronting me twenty-five grand on a settlement, I could only imagine what the end amount would be.

"What do you think you can get out of these folks?" I had to ask.

"I like you Peter. You're a personable young man, just starting out. Life isn't always easy. Witness what you just went through. I'd like to see you come out of this a millionaire several times over. I take forty percent, you get sixty. Believe me when I tell you, I'm worth it."

I let out a quiet whistle.

"I would also like to guide you through the medical end of things. Obviously what happened to you is anything but normal. All the records at the hospital, the samples they took, the tests they performed, everything, is owned by you. Therefore, you should be the beneficiary of whatever is discovered. A new kind of drug for instance. You ought to benefit if it's a result of your unique physiology. At this stage we can only guess where everything might end up, but if you make a difference you should benefit, as will other burn victims. Your rights and ownership of discoveries relating to your injuries must be preserved. I can help you with this."

"I signed some forms at the hospital," I remembered.

"Don't worry about it," The Wedge assured me. "All you did was give them permission to poke around inside of you a bit."

I took a deep breath. "Is this where we shake hands?"

The Wedge took my outstretched arm. His smile was infectious.

Wedge came to the hospital one more time to bring me some clothes, and coach me through a police statement. If they needed me later, they would reach me through him. I used the phone in my room one more time before I left, to try and reach Linda Lou. There was still no answer, and I was worried. Saying goodbye to Patty was hard. She really cared about me, and I was going to miss her.

I dealt with the red tape to get my advance. Now I had to decide which way to head. North, back to Linda Lou's, or south again, to the Big Easy?

The decision tore at me, but in the end I reasoned there wasn't a whole lot to be accomplished by retracing my steps. Whatever was going on back in Memphis would be dealt with. They were grown adults. I'd grab a cell phone in New Orleans, and try to reach them again. By now they would know I was alive and well, and would have heard about the miraculous healing. I would fill in all the juicy details when I was finally able to speak directly with my mother.

I bought another ticket on a southbound Greyhound bus. I thought about the old cliché about getting back in the saddle. I was nervous as we took to the Interstate, but we finally pulled into the New Orleans depot with no further incidents. I cabbed it into the French Quarter, and paid for a week's lodging in advance at a reasonably-priced hotel.

I was exhausted. Everything I'd been through took its toll on me. I laid down on the comfortable, double bed and stared up at the ceiling fan, taking stock of the last week. Wondering at how, and why I now found myself here, in this room, in this place.

I opened the second-story window; it was a beautiful evening in the City. I listened as the sounds from the street below wafted through the window, and into my room.

I heard music laced between the edges of people talking, laughing, and occasionally arguing. It was the distinctive sound of the jazzy blues that only the Big Easy could so effortlessly serve up.

I was so ready for this. Tomorrow I would find myself another guitar, better than the last one.

Chapter 14

I WAS UP early the next morning feeling rejuvenated, and full of anticipatory energy. I bought a laptop, and returned to the hotel to find a music store that sold new and used guitars. I'd learned a long time ago that used guitars, especially Stratocasters, had their own unique sound. You didn't always need to pay top dollar to get a good one that suited your playing style.

Although it was a good forty-five minute hike from the hotel, I decided to walk to the music store, appropriately called The Big Easy Guitar Works.

The walk over there was a trip. This was my first time in New Orleans, and I was impressed. As I trudged across the French Quarter it was the architecture that drew my attention first. A lot of the main floor establishments were open to the street. Restaurants and bars with no windows to interfere with the aroma of the fresh seafood as it cooked in the kitchens. The music could spill freely into the cobblestone streets. Of course the vibrant sounds would have to compete with the next venue, sometimes right next door, but no one seemed to mind.

Then there was the obligatory seedy side of the French Quarter. I was offered every drug known to man from the nameless, faceless dregs who lived in the alcoves and fed off the hapless addicts. I was street smart so I ignored most of the low, sidelong queries of "Whatcha want?" When pressed, I stared them down. They left me alone as I wasn't shopping, or competing with them.

The music store, when I finally arrived, was larger than I imagined. By the look of things, it had originally been some kind of warehouse.

I meandered across the wooden floor, eventually making my way to the guitar section. Again, I was impressed. There were a lot of instruments. I knew only a small percentage of them would be really good ones. Some of them would come with a pretty sizeable price tag, but if I liked something that turned out to be expensive, I knew I could now afford it.

I sidled up to a group of four guys and a girl, all about my age, who were listening to an older, balding guy trying one out for size. He sounded pretty good, but also a little dated. I stood off to one side of the group, politely listening to his licks. He went off on a tangent when he saw I'd joined his small audience. He finished with his best a couple minutes later, and everyone applauded, myself included. The guy nodded his appreciation to the small audience, and replaced the guitar in its stand. He wandered off in the direction of another display wall. The five other young people, duly impressed, meandered off in opposite directions. I looked closely at the axe the guy was jamming with. It was an average guitar, ergo the average sound.

"See anything you like?" someone behind me casually asked.

I turned to see the girl who'd been listening to the impromptu concert. I shrugged. "I just got here. I really haven't had much time to look around yet," I admitted. "But what I do see, I like," I was being honest. "They've got some cool stuff in here."

"I've always thought so. Do you play?"

I smiled. "Once in a while."

"A closet musician," she smiled. "Or maybe a hobbyist looking to buy his first guitar?"

Not wishing to offend her or be impolite, I offered my hand instead. "I'm Peter."

Her eyes sparkled as she took my hand in hers. "I'm Laurie," she introduced herself. "I work here."

"Wow. You're a bit young to be selling these guitars aren't you? No offense," I quickly added, "But usually they hire someone with a bit more experience."

She let go of my hand, but not her smile. "Well, you wouldn't be the first to underestimate me Peter."

"Appearances can be deceiving," I admitted. "Have you worked here long?" There was something about her. She was fun to flirt with, and I had nothing to lose. Maybe she could help, but I was here to buy exactly what I wanted.

"About a week," Laurie was candid with me.

"Have you sold many instruments?"

"A few. This store helps. It's the best one in New Orleans," she explained further. "It's kind of a musician's music store. There's been some pretty amazing talent walking through the turnstiles. Amateurs don't often shop in here. I don't want to kill a sale," she lowered her voice, "but if this is your first guitar, you'd probably get a better deal in a larger chain store. The Guitar Works is more of a one-off kind of place."

"Quality over quantity," I mused.

"I'm afraid so."

"And of course that translates into a more expensive guitar."

"Right again Peter."

I smiled. "Good thing this won't be my first instrument."

She concentrated on me. Her smile was gone,

replaced by a cautious curiosity. She'd caught the double entendre.

"You look kind of familiar. Have I seen you playing somewhere?"

I laughed. "Not yet."

"But you're talented," she accused me.

I shrugged. "How about I let you decide? Why don't you help me find a guitar? I'll play a little something, and you can tell me what you think."

Her grin returned. "I've got a funny feeling this is going to be one of my more interesting mornings."

"I saw something over there," I glanced over her shoulder to the array hanging on the feature wall. "Why don't you show me a Stratocaster Laurie? I want something with a unique sound. Something special. If I like one that turns out to be expensive, I can afford it, so you won't be wasting your time on me."

"You seem to know your guitars," she said.

"I know what I'm looking for," I agreed.

She nodded, "I don't doubt that for a second. Let's see what we can find for you."

She led me over to the wall where some of the most amazing guitars I'd ever seen were proudly displayed. I followed her, totally unprepared for what happened next.

Chapter 15

"THAT ONE?" LAURIE pointed to the Strat I was in love with. I was watching her, and she knew it. She sashayed over to the wall of guitars. Her hips moved in a rhythm. Up, down, up, down. One, two, three, four.

"Yeah, that's something I'd like to try out," I admitted.

She plucked it from its hanger and brought it over to me. "Do you want a strap?" she asked.

The guitar felt supernatural as I cradled it in my arms. I glanced around and spotted the amp and chair the older guy used earlier.

"This will be fine, thanks." I sat down. The instant I plugged in the guitar I felt the faint edges of a weird tingling – an itch – as it spread up from my feet and into my legs. It happened quickly. Not like the itch I'd felt in the hospital. More like someone running their fingernails softy across the flesh under my clothes. It spread up into my arms, and finally into my fingers. It took only a few seconds, but seemed a lot longer. Finally it sparked out through the end of my fingertips, like when

I shuffled across the carpet back home in winter and touched a metal doorknob. Snap, crackle, pop. I flicked the fingers of my playing hand and noticed that it suddenly seemed awfully warm in the store. I brushed a bead of sweat off my brow, frowned, and turned my attention back to the amp. Leaning over the guitar in my lap, I flicked on the power and it jumped to life. I was too close to the amp and cursed silently at the rookie mistake as the shrill squeal of feedback pierced my ears like a needle.

"Sorry," I apologized to Laurie as I quickly moved the Strat and adjusted the amp. It was something a kid would have done, but the damned itching had rattled me. It was mostly gone now, but had coursed through me in a way I'd never felt before. Something to do with the amplifier, I reasoned. It couldn't be anything else, but I couldn't escape the weird uneasy feeling that came over me. It was fear, but not the ordinary kind, like unexpectedly coming across a rattlesnake. It was more a nervous tension, like working your way up to copping a feel after some heavy French kissing.

I ran my fingers up and down the strings across the fret board. Something felt different, that was for sure. I looked up and saw Laurie had noticed something too. I could see a quizzical concern cross her face.

I smiled to reassure her. The weirdness translated into a supreme, otherworldly confidence I'd never felt before. It was show time! I leaned over the guitar and began to play.

I got lost in it. I had no earthly idea where the notes came from. Time became meaningless. I could have been playing for a moment, or years. The Stratocaster became a living, breathing thing as I cradled it in my arms. I made love to it, oblivious to all else. It was like I was having waves of orgasms, in a world only the guitar and I could ever know. Finally, spent to my very core, with a tremendous, longing angst, my hands fell away from the strings. As the world around me came back into my focus, I became aware of the tears pouring from my eyes. An almost suicidal sadness enveloped me. The music that had mysteriously come to me gave way to a horrible sound. A rush of falling, broken glass, and screeching, tearing metal. I looked up – I was back in The Guitar Works. There were thirty or forty people around me, cheering and screaming at the top of their lungs. Their applause was like a wave of thunder. In the midst of them all, mouth open in utter disbelief and wonderment, I spotted Laurie. She covered her mouth, then took her hands away and began to applaud with the others. She beamed at me, her eyes dancing with glee. She began to laugh, and then cheer with everyone else who had come from every corner of the store to hear me play. The sadness evaporated, and I began to feel an overwhelming sense of gratitude. Until I spotted the woman, standing alone at the edge of the crowd, who I rescued from the train.

She stared at me blankly. She nodded, almost imperceptibly, then turned and began to walk away toward the exit door.

I flew off the chair and screamed to Laurie above the cacophony of yelling and applause, "I'll take it!" My eyes were still focused on the woman's back.

"What's wrong?" Laurie could see my shock.

"I have to go – I'll be back later. I'll explain everything then." I shoved the guitar into her arms and moved past her and through the crowd.

"Who are you?" she almost pleaded.

There was no time to answer. I didn't want to be rude to anyone, least of all her, but I had to talk to the woman from the train. I had serious questions I knew only she could answer.

I made it past the crowd just as I saw the door close on the woman's back. I scrambled through the aisles, finally flinging open the door.

I looked up and down the street in a panic. Damn, I thought. Which way had she gone?

There she was! Again, I saw only her back, but it was enough. She rounded the corner a couple of buildings to my left. I sprinted after her, hoping in a few seconds I'd have some answers.

Chapter 16

I COULD SEE it was a one-way street even before I rounded the corner. Someone had parked illegally, too close to the stop sign. My momentum carried me into it. As if blocking a tackle, I pushed off the side of the vehicle. I straightened out, eyes scanning for the mysterious woman. I spotted her immediately. Her blonde hair stood out in stark contrast to the age-stained buildings lining both sides of the narrow street. I could see parking was at a premium. Cars were stacked up along both sides of the street. I kept running – she wasn't more than fifty feet in front of me now, and I was closing fast.

An SUV with heavily-tinted windows pulled out into the street as the blonde-haired woman hurried past it. Everything seemed to slow down then, as I noticed a mother with a baby carriage. She came from between two parked cars across the street as the black SUV left its parking spot. The roar of an engine somewhere behind me overpowered all other sounds. Still running, I stole a glance over my shoulder. In the same instant I heard the first of two cracking noises – gunshots.

I was confused, but was putting it all together on the run. Something bad had gone down behind me. Gunfire was erupting in the normally placid streets of New Orleans. A car suddenly accelerating the wrong way down the one-way street was obviously involved. The driver was doing his best to avoid being shot, or someone inside the vehicle was shooting back at someone. It really didn't matter, because the car would ram the SUV head-on. There was no room for them to steer past each other in the narrow car-lined street. To make matters worse, the baby carriage and the woman pushing it were in the middle of it all.

More on instinct than anything else, I diverted my headlong sprint after the blonde-haired woman. I bounced off the front bumper of a parked car, and scrambled into the street, not knowing what I'd do. If I did nothing, at least two innocent people, one of whom was a helpless baby, were likely going to end up dead. Once again, I could not let anyone die if I could help it. I also knew there would be absolutely no margin for error.

The engine behind me roared louder, punctuated by yet another gunshot. My eyes locked onto the baby carriage, now a mere five feet in front of me. The mother was frozen in the middle of the street staring in horror over my shoulder at certain death. The SUV stopped, the driver not knowing what else to do. The roar of the other car's engine thundered through my skull.

My hand came into view in front of me, followed by forearm and then elbow, all in slow, exaggerated fragments of motion. My outstretched fingers closed and tightened around the frame of the baby carriage.

Never breaking stride, I lunged even with the side of the carriage and wrenched it from her hands. She awoke from her trance and screamed, "My baby!" She pivoted in my direction, and started to run after me. I made the gap between two parked cars, carriage in my hands, in three more strides. The explosion of the colliding vehicles behind us reverberated between the buildings on either side of the street.

I carefully set the carriage down on the sidewalk. The mother scrambled up on the other side of me, and retrieved her now-crying baby. As soon as I saw they would be all right, I looked back into the street behind us. The word carnage immediately came to mind. I moved swiftly back between the parked cars and over to the crash to see if I could help. My street smarts kicked in, and I looked back from where I knew the gunshots had originated. I saw them immediately. There were two of them, and they were both staring at me. They were stopped on the sidewalk on the street corner. They were saying something to each other, but never took their eyes off me.

People were spilling into the street to ogle. I became conscious of the not-so-distant wail of police sirens. The cops would be here in moments, I thought with relief. I turned toward the wreck, and peered over the crumpled black hood and into what was left of the SUV.

The airbag had deployed on impact, its shroud draped over a dazed, middle-aged woman. She was confused, but she would be fine. There was no one else in the SUV. I turned my attention to the other vehicle. The older-model Mustang hadn't fared nearly as well as the bigger SUV. Its entire front end was completely destroyed. Smoke and steam billowed from what was once a sleek silver-colored hood. Keeping in mind that someone, maybe even one of the Mustang's occupants, was armed, I moved carefully around to the driver's side door. My senses were on high alert. I sniffed the air for the smell of gasoline as I peered through a hole where the window used to be. Shattered glass was everywhere. That, and a lot of blood.

Chapter 17

THERE WERE TWO of them, both black teenaged males by the look of it. The passenger wasn't moving. Neither one of them was wearing a seatbelt. As a result, their injuries were severe. The driver groaned, followed by a wheezing, gurgling sound. At best, the gurgling meant there was blood in his throat; at worst, the sound was coming from somewhere deep inside his chest. In either case, if the paramedics didn't get here in the next few minutes, I was probably looking at a dead man.

I knew instinctively if I tried to move either one of them I might kill them. I looked helplessly from one to the other. They were kids, maybe not even old enough to drive. Fast car, fast life, and more than likely, a quick death, I thought sadly.

For the first time I noticed the widening patch of darkness across the driver's chest. The grey hoodie couldn't hide the small hole in the middle of the spreading blood. He'd been shot. I sighed deeply, understanding the gurgling sound that grew louder as the kid vainly fought for his life. Angst filled my heart because I knew he was dying in front of me, and there was not a damn thing I could do to save him.

His eyes opened and stared up at me. Tears spilled down his face. He was scared.

"Hang on," I said lamely. "Help is coming." The sirens sounded close, only a street or two away now. He coughed suddenly, and blood spewed out across the front of the hoodie.

"Do you believe Jesus died for us?" I don't know where the question came from, it just did, and so I asked him.

He could barely breathe, but it must have meant something to him. As much as he could, he nodded. His eyes were wet, black rocks. "Do you love him?"

Again, the barely perceptible nod.

"He loves you too, and he forgives you."

His eyes stared past me then, to somewhere over my shoulder. It seemed my words gave him a little comfort. There was one last gasp for life. Then, nothing more. He was gone.

My angst became overwhelming sadness. I reached through the window. Ever so carefully, I placed my hand across his face, over his eyes. I lowered my hand, feeling his moist tears, and closed his empty eyes. Somewhere this boy's mother was going about her day-to-day affairs. All too soon her routine would be ripped open, like the senseless violence that tore open her son's chest.

I was glad the boy had not died alone, that in his last moments he knew someone cared. I glanced at the other boy, the one in the mangled Ford's passenger seat. I couldn't tell what kind of shape he was in. He was silent and motionless, I hoped for the best.

I looked back up the narrow street as the first cop car rounded the corner, siren screaming and lights ablaze. If I stuck around, I could be here for hours talking to them. I reasoned that I could add nothing by my presence, and so I stepped back from the wreckage and melted into the surrounding crowd. I silently wished all of them luck as I began a slow, introspective walk back to the hotel.

It wasn't that I was heartless, it was just that I had seen it in one form or another before. I recognized that death was always a part of life. There was no arguing this fact.

I was a child of the meth business. Senior had seen to that. I left on my own volition, in large part because I saw where that kind of lifestyle inevitably led. Those boys back there knew where their lives would probably end up, and this knowledge hadn't even slowed them down. Did I feel sorry for them? Absolutely. Could they have changed their destiny with wiser choices? Sure, but then they wouldn't have been themselves. For most of us, death comes like a proverbial thief in the night, but decisions – good and not so good – can affect the timeline. To ignore this was foolish.

As I trudged along the Big Easy's cobblestone streets my mind drifted back to the blonde-haired woman. I was absolutely certain she was the very same woman I'd first seen on the Amtrak train. I felt a sudden chill as the thought occurred to me that I may have actually been led by her to the terrible crash. Then I shook my head and told myself to get a grip. To what end, I wondered? Was I supposed to save that woman and her baby? Talk about a messianic complex. I just wasn't that important I told myself.

And that religious thing back there! It was like I read that kid his last rights or something. That was just plain weird. I was the most unreligious person I knew. Why the hell had I said those words to that boy? Where had they come from?

I danced around a couple of unsteady drunks as they exited a pub. This whole day was insane, I thought.

What had happened back at The Guitar Works? What was that all about? I didn't even remember how long I'd been jamming, but I couldn't forget the response from the people who'd been listening. The odd thing was how their reaction seemed to mirror what I'd been feeling. It was like I was some kind of conductor to their collective emotions; able to touch somewhere deep inside their souls, where even they rarely got a chance to go.

Then there was Laurie. The chemistry we both felt was undeniable. I was already looking forward to the next time we would meet. Maybe she could explain a few things to me. At the very least she could tell me how long I'd played that guitar. Maybe it was the instrument itself? Perhaps it was some kind of supernatural guitar? I wondered who had owned it before it ended up at the store. Or was it brand new? She would know.

After what seemed like an eternity of internal dialogue, I rounded the corner down the street from the hotel. I was exhausted. Clearly the events of the past few hours had caught up with me. Even so, I didn't feel like going up to my room. I decided I needed a drink instead. Some live music wouldn't hurt either.

Three doors down from the hotel, I ducked into what in another time would have been called a speakeasy. Now it was known as a dive. I sat down and ordered a double shot of whiskey. The house band was excellent. One drink turned into a bunch. I had no recollection of leaving when I woke up in my room the next morning. I had one of the worst hangovers of my life. I never was much of a drinker, and the way my head felt reminded me of this in no uncertain terms.

Chapter 18

"YOU DON'T LOOK so good."

"Yeah, well I don't feel so hot either."

I'd slept until noon. Actually, I passed out until then. Somehow I managed to grab a shower. My hands were shaking so bad that shaving was out of the question.

The clerk at the front desk wasn't being condescending, he was making a simple observation, trying to be friendly.

I focused in on his eyes. "Normally I don't drink as much as I did last night Franklin."

"Hey, I ain't judging you Peter," he peered at me across the top of his glasses.

"Where's the best place near here to get a coffee?" I asked him.

"That would be TJ's Beanery, about six doors down on your left, directly across from The Winery."

"Thanks Franklin," I waved at him on my way out. "I appreciate it."

"Anytime Peter. Hope you feel better."

I liked Franklin. We met when I checked into

the hotel. He lived his entire forty-odd years in the French Quarter, so he knew a lot about what went on around here.

I called Laurie at the guitar store halfway through my second cup of coffee.

"You don't sound like yesterday," she noted right off.

"I had a rough night after I got back here," I explained. "I'll be fine in a couple of hours. I'm not much of a drinker."

"New Orleans has a way of turning you into one," she noted wryly. "I wasn't sure if I'd hear from you again Peter," she said tentatively. "The way you left yesterday was odd to say the least."

"I'm sorry about that. I saw someone I knew, an old friend," I lied. "I didn't want her to get away."

"I see."

"No, you don't," I corrected her.

"Did you catch up with her?"

"I ran after her, but there was an accident at the end of the block."

"Two people died," her voice was strained.

"I spoke with one of them. They were kids. I'm sorry the other guy died too. I thought he might make it."

"The passenger died from trauma. The other guy was shot." Laurie sounded worried.

"I know," I admitted.

"You talked with the guy who was driving?"

"More like to him," I said. "He couldn't speak, but he understood what I was saying."

"Oh no! That's so sad," her tone changed. "What did you say to him?"

"I told him everything would be all right." I didn't tell her the rest. Even now as I remembered my own words, they sounded strange inside my head. "No one should die alone. Especially not the way he did. As far as I know the guy who was with him never regained consciousness."

"That may have been for the best," she said. "Peter, I…" she hesitated, not certain of her next words.

"You're not sure what happened yesterday," I guessed. "Neither am I," I admitted. "It isn't just yesterday either."

"What do you mean?" she asked.

"If I told you last week what the next week of my life would look like, you'd probably think I was crazy."

"All right. You have my full attention. Good crazy, or bad crazy?"

"More like just plain batshit crazy. What's

happened to me is something I can't explain. I've also got a funny feeling there's more coming my way."

"That sounds ominous," she sounded anxious.

"It might be – I don't know. I do know I felt something special when we met, but I'm worried about involving you in my life right now. I still want the guitar though," I added after a couple of seconds.

"Oh wow. Am I ever relieved," she said sarcastically.

"I didn't mean it that way."

"Look Peter, I felt it yesterday too. How 'bout we wait and see. Neither one of us can see the future. I like you, a lot. You tell me I'm wrong if I think you like me too."

"No, you wouldn't be wrong. It's just – "

"Just what? You're going to protect little old me from things you can't explain? Well here's a newsflash, I'm a big girl."

I thought about what she'd said. Then I asked her, "If I come over and see you again, do you have any aspirin? My head hurts like hell."

Chapter 19

I LIKED EVERYTHING about the Marigold, the hotel I was staying at, except the size of my room. Franklin and I were getting to know each other. We liked each other, and it was obvious he didn't want me to leave.

"I may have a solution before you go looking for another place," he volunteered.

"You know of somewhere?" The six aspirin I'd taken after coffee this morning made life more palatable, but I still felt like shit. I vowed for the hundredth time never to drink like that again.

"Maybe, depends," he offered.

"Don't worry, I can handle the rent," I assured him.

"Rent's free," his glasses hung low across the bridge of his nose. "If you agree to keep an eye on the place while I'm gone, that is."

"I'm not looking for a job Franklin," I said back to him.

"I'm not offering you one."

"I don't get it," I said.

He plucked his glasses off his face, and

massaged the bridge of his nose. "You know I'm living in the cottage out back of the hotel?"

"I do now."

"Did I tell you I also own this place?" He slid his glasses back on and stared at me with serious intent.

"I'd be lying to you if I told you I didn't have my suspicions," I admitted. "Has anyone told you that you do a lousy imitation of a desk clerk?"

"Down here in The Big Easy black people don't usually own property, and especially not hotels."

"Wait a second," I stopped him. "Are you trying to tell me you're black?" I grinned at him.

He smiled too. "You're a fish out of water kid, and it shows. From the moment you walked in here and opened your mouth, I knew there was something different about you. I sense you're an honest man Peter."

"It's a lie!" I played with him.

"I need someone to watch the place, when I'm not around." He was serious.

"Are you going somewhere?" I looked across the front desk at him more carefully.

He shrugged. "I'm originally from New York. My family is still up there. I have to go back for some family business. I don't know how long it will take this time."

"Are you coming back?" I read between the lines.

"You're as smart as I thought you were."

"Why me Franklin? You don't know anything about me."

"I'd have to be blind, deaf, and dumb not to know about you kid. I recognized you when you first came in here and rented the room. You're that kid who survived the bus crash up in Jackson. It was all over the news. I'm talking to you because I don't have anyone I can trust down here. Believe me, that's another thing about The Big Easy that's not unusual. This place is a den of thieves."

"How do you know I'm not any different? Never mind the fact I don't know the first thing about running a hotel."

"I'm not asking you to run the place, just look after it for me. Make sure no one rips me off. I'm not leaving tomorrow, and I'll show you the ropes before I go back to New York. There's not a whole lot to learn. I know you won't rip me off," he declared.

"You say that after knowing me all of a week. Me and responsibility don't always do well together."

"I'm calling bullshit on that one. I know you're smart, and I saw the lawyer you hired on TV. The Wedge is famous, he's the best, and he's known for his huge settlements. You're going to be rich kid. So, I repeat, you don't need anyone else's money. Soon enough you'll have plenty of your own. Come to think of it, The Wedge probably gave you some sort of an advance."

"Maybe," I was being coy.

"Why did you come here Peter?" Franklin asked suddenly.

"I came for the music," I conceded. "I play guitar and I sing a little. I'd like to get into a band."

"Then you're not in any hurry to get out of here." It was a statement.

"Not really," I agreed. "I just got here."

He smiled. "Think about it. This might be the perfect fit. The cottage is separate from the hotel; it's got more than enough space to practice. You could get a whole band in there. No one can hear you with the windows closed. Tell you what," Franklin proffered me a deal, "I'm not leaving for about another month. Let me show you how this place works. You can help me hire a desk guy. I'll introduce you to the staff. In a month or so, if you don't like what you see, you can walk away. But, if you think it might work for you, you can live in the cottage, and watch the place for me while I'm gone. Best of all, you can play your music all night long if you feel like it. No one can hear you back there," he repeated.

"I don't know," I hedged. "It sounds like a lot of responsibility."

"You could handle it in your sleep. At least let me show you the cottage." His face broadened into a clever, winning smile.

He was a good judge of character. I would never rip him off.

"I'll think about it," I finally capitulated, wondering what I was getting myself into. "We'll keep talking. Right now I have to meet someone."

He stuck his arm out across the top of the front desk and I shook his hand. His grip was strong and sure, but so was mine.

Chapter 20

I MET LAURIE for an early dinner a half hour later in a seafood restaurant a few blocks from the Marigold.

"You look great in jeans," I complimented her as we sat near the back, away from the noise of the street beyond the open front windows.

"Thank you," she smiled warmly. The anxiety I was feeling for the past few weeks lifted slightly, like the lazy delta tide going out across the bayou in the early morning.

"I could have come to you." I'd offered earlier, but she declined, instead agreeing to meet me near the hotel.

"It was easier for me to find you, I live here," she stated the obvious.

The waiter came quickly. I ordered an unsweetened iced tea for starters; she opted for a sweeter glass of Riesling. We each ordered something to eat, and then got back to our conversation.

"When you came into the store I thought I recognized you as a musician, but you're not."

"Thanks for the accolade," I commented lightheartedly.

She frowned. "You know what I mean. I was thinking you were famous. You still look like someone I've met before. Have we? Ever met, I mean?"

"Not unless you've lived in Memphis, but you've probably seen me recently on television. Last week I was in the news a lot."

Her brow wrinkled, then it came to her. "Of course! You're the bus guy. The one from the accident," she stammered.

"That would be me," I sighed. "I'm the bus guy all right."

Laurie realized I wasn't happy. "I'm sorry Peter," she immediately apologized. "I didn't mean it that way. It must have been horrible for you. They said you had been badly burned?"

"I'm fine," I sipped my tea. "No need to apologize either. I suppose the whole mess will die down soon enough, and people will move on. But I have to admit, I'm not getting a real fuzzy feeling about being called the bus guy. If this moniker sticks, I'm going to look seriously at getting plastic surgery," I joked.

"You're not – "

I started to laugh. "No, I'm not," I allayed her fears.

"Are you all right?" she was concerned. "I mean, you look fine and all."

"I'm okay," I assured her. "Physically, that is. Mentally, that's another story."

I elaborated for her. "Some weird things are happening around me. Stuff that doesn't seem to fit."

She looked puzzled, "Stuff?"

"Yeah. For example, I've been seeing this woman. I know I told you she was a friend, but I didn't have time to explain. She was on the bus."

"She got on with you?"

I shook my head. "No, that's the weird part. I never actually saw her get on the bus. But suddenly she was there, sitting in the seat right across the aisle from me, *after* the train hit us."

"All the newscasts said you were the only survivor of the crash," Laurie spoke haltingly. "How is it possible you saw her again yesterday when everyone except you died? That doesn't make any sense."

"You haven't heard anything yet," I said. "I rescued her from that crash."

She stared at me. Her expression wore a hint of disbelief, and…fear?

"I'm not crazy." I was put off that no one believed me.

"Peter, if that was an old girlfriend who came after you, it's okay, but I need you to be honest with me," she said.

The waiter returned to the table just in time to interrupt us. He informed us dinner would be out in another ten minutes or so, and asked if everything was all right. I thanked him, and he left. I stared into Laurie's eyes.

"Laurie, no I saved a blonde-haired lady from that burning bus. I carried her over my shoulders out of that furnace, and I don't give a damn about any news reports that say otherwise. We were the only ones who made it out. She disappeared somewhere, but she was there."

"And you saw her again yesterday?"

"Yes, I saw her in the store right after I played that guitar. She was the one who led me around the corner where that gunfight and crash took place." It didn't make a lot of sense to me, I realized. What must it sound like to her?

"I know this must sound crazy to you," I vocalized my thoughts.

"You've got to admit, it is incredible," she said. "Why didn't she stay and talk to you?" Laurie asked the obvious.

I leaned back in my chair, fighting for control. To say I was frustrated was an understatement, to say I was scared was far more accurate. "I don't know," I admitted. Then, again, more quietly this time, "I just don't know." I felt spent. None of it made any sense to me. Who the fuck was that woman? More importantly, what the hell did she want from me?

Laurie leaned toward me and gently touched my hand. "I believe you," she said quietly. In that moment I felt more peaceful – more loved – than I could ever remember. "I'll help you find her."

Tears welled up in my eyes.

"You're amazing," I said.

Chapter 21

I BOUGHT MY guitar from her the next day, and spent the next three weeks getting familiar with how things worked around the Marigold. Franklin was doing his best to make the decision to stay easy for me. I bought a used amplifier, and he allowed me to set up in the living room of his cottage. The acoustics were actually pretty good. Franklin worked in the hotel all day, after I had lunch in the restaurant, I would practice in his cottage.

I got to meet the hotel staff, and I liked them. They were like Franklin's extended family. He treated them well; in return they respected him.

I still couldn't reach Linda Lou back in Memphis. Every time I tried to call someone to find out about her and Senior, I got busy. When I managed to find time, no one was home. I was more and more anxious every day, but the time I spent with Laurie calmed me. In fact, in a frighteningly short time, I was developing some very strong feelings for her.

"So, you've accepted his offer. When do you move into the cottage?" she asked.

"He's leaving for New York this Friday," I told her.

Laurie twisted around to face me. "Do you need my help with the move?"

I glanced up to see if she was being serious. We both knew aside from my Stratocaster, all I had was a couple suitcases.

"I should be able to handle it," I grinned at her. She had a wonderful sense of humor.

Laurie kept looking at me, a playful smirk on her full lips.

"Oh," I stammered, finally getting it. "Come to think of it, yeah, I could use some help on Friday. I'd say around eight o'clock. That is if you think you might be in the neighborhood?" I flirted back awkwardly.

"I'll be in the neighborhood. Eight o'clock will be fine."

"Good," I said, feeling more nervous than I'd felt in a long time. I'd been busy, so had she. We were together frequently over the past month, but it had always been for a meal or a meandering walk along the cobblestoned streets of the French Quarter.

Anything more than that with Laurie had just

not come up. The small, cramped room upstairs, I knew, wasn't the place for it. Now was obviously different, now I had Franklin's cottage.

Knowing what was next for us, I realized I needed to know more about Laurie. We talked, but it had been mostly about me. I was embarrassed at my self-centeredness, and I told her as much.

She immediately waved it off. "Don't give it a second thought," she said. "You've had a lot on your mind. I knew you'd come around when you were ready."

"You have a lot of confidence in me."

She laughed. "In myself too. You and your new friend Franklin aren't the only good judges of character."

"Well," I said, looking into her eyes as I drained the last of the beer I'd been nursing. "I think it's high time I shut my mouth, and let you do the talking."

"What do you want to know?" Her voice was suddenly a shade deeper. She slowly traced her index finger around the rim of her wine glass.

"Tell me about yourself. Where's home? Originally, I mean. Who are your parents? How many siblings do you have?"

"I'm not from here."

"What brought you to The Big Easy?"

She frowned, remembering something not entirely pleasant. "You mean who?" she enlightened me. "I'll tell you that one later, after another drink."

"That's fine by me," I wanted her to know I didn't care about her past. I signaled the waiter for another round of drinks.

"Tell me about your family then."

She drew a breath, "All right." She was still playing with her wine glass. "I was born in Jacksonville, Florida. I was too young to remember moving a half hour south, to the oldest city in America, Saint Augustine."

"Is that a fact?" I didn't know.

"What was St. Augustine like?" I was curious.

"It's a lot like any small, coastal town in the States, except St. Augustine has a lot of older tourists coming and going. Retirees go there because it's cheaper to drive there than to fly to the Caribbean. Younger people actually live there. St. Augustine has a ton of restaurants, bars, and hotels."

"It sounds like New Orleans," I mused.

"It's different," she immediately replied. "People come here. They leave St. Augustine. If they're smart, that is. A lot of girls end up pregnant before the end of high school. They drop out, get married if they're lucky. Of course that usually doesn't last. The women wake up at thirty on welfare with four kids. Then they end up working for tips in one of the bars. The men don't do much better, mostly they end up in prison, hooked on drugs, or whatever."

"It's sad."

She agreed, "The absence of hope always is."

"But you got out," I noted.

"Not before a few skinned knees, I can assure you," she replied. "I've often thought about it. Was I any more intelligent than those who stayed, or did I just get lucky?"

We stopped talking as the waiter reappeared and set a Heineken next to me, and another glass of wine in front of Laurie.

"Which one did you decide on?" I asked after he'd left.

"I've come to believe, it was a bit of both. I met a guy in my senior year of high school. He wanted to get out of St. Augustine. It was either Miami or here, we tossed a coin and came here. I don't know where I'd be if we hadn't met. I suppose we all end up doing what we find necessary."

"It wasn't necessary to follow your boyfriend, you had other choices," I stated what I found to be obvious.

She looked directly into my eyes. "When things in life happen, sometimes you don't have that luxury Peter. I was one of those girls who got pregnant."

Chapter 22

I LEANED FORWARD across the restaurant's small table, closer to her. I took her hand in mine. I felt the slight trembling she could not hide from me, or the world. I looked deeply into her eyes and saw the regrets for the mistakes none of us were immune to in the halcyon days of our reckless youths.

"It's all right," I assured her. "Everything is going to be okay. Did you have the baby?"

She searched my eyes as tears welled up in her own. She spoke softly, almost in a whisper, with reverence.

"Angelina, because I know she would have been an angel." Tears began to run down her cheeks.

"It's alright," I repeated, not knowing what else to say. I lifted my hand to her face and gently brushed the tears away.

"He left me. I was all alone Peter, I was abandoned. And now, every single day of my life I live with my decision. Sometimes I feel her, as if she watches me from somewhere beyond this place."

"She forgives you Laurie."

She leaned back, away from me, away from the soft caress of my hand across her face.

"How can you say that? You can't possibly know what it's like to do what I did. I killed her. I murdered my daughter." She was angry now.

I searched desperately for something to say to comfort her. I wanted more than anything to take away her pain, because in that moment I realized I was falling more deeply in love with her than I ever would have imagined possible.

"I could have put her up for adoption, and I have no answer for why I didn't do that."

"You were young, and you were by yourself," I protested.

"Yes, that's true," she fought to regain her composure. "And now, for the rest of my life, I have only myself to blame. I celebrate her birthday. She would have been four next week. I think I do it to somehow atone. It just makes me feel worse, but I do it anyway," she said tearfully.

I spoke with conviction, now knowing exactly what to tell her. "You're right," I said. "I could not possibly know how it feels to make a decision like the one you were forced to make. But there is one thing I do know. The burden you carry is far too heavy for you alone to bear. You need help to get through it. There's a reason we met. A million things had to go right," I emphasized the last word, "For us to be here.

"I know it hurts whenever you think of Angelina, and I saw what you do with it. You recoiled from me, and got angry with yourself. I believe they call that penance."

I saw she was about to protest, and I stopped her by continuing, "I'll say what I'll say, and then you can speak your piece."

She must have seen the fire in my eyes, because she closed her mouth, indignation written across her face. I knew I was risking a lot. She might just get up and walk out on me, but I figured it was worth the gamble, because I was just being honest.

"A few minutes ago, when I told you about the things that were happening to me lately, you told me you believed me."

She nodded, remaining silent.

"Well, I took that as you believed *in* me. When you told me that, I felt more…" I searched for the right words, "I felt that for probably the first time in my life I really meant something to somebody. So now it's my turn." I grabbed her hands and clenched them in mine. I noticed she wasn't crying anymore.

"You made me feel I wasn't alone. As far as I'm concerned, and I know you probably think it's a little early in the game for me to be saying this, but you're not alone anymore, either. You have me now, I believe in you. I can help you lighten this terrible load you've been carrying these last few years. You may never get rid of it entirely, but that's okay. As long as you don't have to lift it all by yourself, it will get easier. I'm here, and I'm not going anywhere any time soon."

"You really think you can help me?" It came out as a soft plea.

"Yeah," I massaged her hands between mine. "I can help you. I want to."

She stared into my eyes for what seemed an eternity. "I think I'd like that," she finally said.

"Good. That makes me happy," I smiled at her. "What about your boyfriend? Is he still around?"

"He isn't important. In retrospect he never was. The whole thing was a mistake, I was running away."

"From St. Augustine?" I asked.

"In part. I think it was more to get away from my parents, though my real father died when I was quite young. Mom got remarried a few years later. My stepfather didn't treat me very well, so when I got a chance to leave, I took it."

"What do you mean he didn't treat you so well?"

She let out a breath, more of relief than anything else I suspected. My intuition told me Laurie didn't have anyone she could talk to about these things. It was no doubt a part of why it was still bothering her years later.

"He didn't molest me or anything, if that's what you're thinking. He was just distant. He treated my mom the same way. She didn't seem to mind, though. I think she was happy to have the steady paycheck coming in. He was a dentist. I think he still is."

"You don't know?" I found it odd.

"No," Laurie said with no emotion. "I rarely talk to Mom, and almost never about Larry. That's my stepdad's name. We're not close. My mom and me, that is. We drifted apart after my dad died."

"I'm sorry," I said with sincerity. "It must have been tough."

She shrugged. "I had friends."

"They're not the same," I noted.

She agreed, "No they aren't, but they were better than nothing."

I now understood a lot more about her situation. It must have been easy for her boyfriend to convince her to leave with him.

"I think this is our food," I spotted the waiter making his way toward our table.

"Peter?"

"Yeah?"

"Thanks."

"You don't have to," I said, smiling.

She grinned back. "I know." She closed the gap between us then, and kissed me slow and hard.

Chapter 23

THE REST OF the week marched by in a hurry. Franklin and I spent time together every chance we got. He'd been right on both counts; I was honest, and a quick learner.

"Do you have a ride to the airport?" He was flying out first thing in the morning.

"I'm okay. How about you and the cottage?" he asked from across the table in the restaurant.

I shrugged. "You probably noticed I don't have a lot of stuff. Most of it's already back there. I appreciate everything you've done for me," I said, for probably the fiftieth time this week.

He examined me from over the top of his glasses. By now it was one of his very familiar nuances. "I believe my trust is well-placed."

"It is," I agreed. "I've got your back. Don't worry. If I run across something and get in over my head, I'll call you."

He kept looking at me, not blinking.

"Is something wrong?"

"That's exactly what I was going to ask you," he said. "I've been around kid. I've learned to read people to stay alive. My instinct tells me you have a shady past. I'm hoping you didn't bring it with you."

I stared right back at him, letting the silence hang in the air like a man left to rot on the gallows.

"If you're worried about your place – "

"I'm not worried about my place," he cut me off. "It's insured, and like I told you shortly after we met, you're no thief. What you are is very capable. That's the part that has me concerned."

Now I was offended. "What? Do you think I'm going to set up shop in your hotel? Really? Maybe we should just forget about this whole thing. I think it's better if you find someone who's more trustworthy to mind the store while you're gone." I got up out of my chair. It made a hollow, growling sound as I shoved it backwards over the hardwood floor beneath it.

"Sit down Peter," he calmly said.

I glared at him.

"Please," he gestured with his hand for me to sit.

For a moment I wondered what I should do next.

"Please," he repeated. This time Franklin wore a faint smile of contrition. I slowly sat back down.

"What I meant to say is I think you have a lot on your mind," he said.

"And I can see that you're a little paranoid. Something that isn't always a good thing, I might add." I was calming down, thinking more clearly, yet still unsure where he was coming from, or in which direction he was headed.

He paused before he continued.

"You have me wrong. I'm okay with you. I have been since early on. We've spent a fair bit of time together over the past month or so. You've learned a lot about the hotel business, quickly too. That's not surprising though; you have a ton of street smarts. No one's gonna steal from you. You don't just suddenly pick up those skills out of thin air. You know it, and I know it. But in all this time we spent together, I can honestly say I don't know a damn thing about you personally. Other than I see some trouble around you. Not with regards to me," he held up both of his hands, waving off any protests he thought I might have. "All I know is what I've seen about you on television, and I've met Laurie…" he trailed off, never taking his eyes from me. "Are you running from someone? It couldn't be the law. They'd have grabbed you in Jackson right after the train wreck."

After a pause, I said, "You're a very clever man."

He nodded, "That makes two of us. What were you doing up there in Memphis? I could guess, but why don't you tell me?"

I sighed, "We had meth labs, off and on."

"Off and on," he repeated.

I elaborated, "Senior – my father – did some time in prison."

"He ran the operation?" Franklin asked.

I nodded. "He and my uncle. Senior taught me how to cook the stuff. That gave him more time for the marketing end of things."

"And you're not cooking anymore?" he said carefully.

"I quit. I could see where it was all heading. I didn't want to be there for the end of the ride. I guess I have my music to thank for that."

"So what's got you rankled? Surely your own father's not turning the screws on you?"

I shook my head, "No, I'm out. Forever. He and my Uncle Johnny know that. In fact, I haven't even been able to talk to any of my family since I left Memphis. But that isn't what you're seeing. There's something else." I drew a deep breath and leaned back in the chair. I cast glances around the restaurant. It was the middle of the afternoon, and mostly empty.

I turned back to Franklin and confided, "I think someone's been following me."

"How long has this been going on?" he leaned forward, and lowered his voice. "When did you first notice?"

I said, "Right after I got here. I thought at first it might be you."

His eyes narrowed.

"Hey, I wouldn't have blamed you."

"It wasn't me."

"I know that now," I admitted. "I'm just saying I wouldn't have been offended. I'm sorry, but I'm just being honest with you."

Franklin waved it off, "No offense taken. Do you have any idea who it might be?"

"Yeah, I think I might," I said cautiously. "The only thing is," I hesitated before I continued, "I'm not as worried about who's following me as I am about who led me to them in the first place."

Chapter 24

JUST LIKE I'D told Laurie, I told Franklin the whole story.

"You must think I'm certifiable," I finally said.

Franklin let out a low whistle. "Anyone else, yes, I would probably think that. But, in your case, I'll make an exception. Partly because I've seen some of it on the six o'clock news. Everyone around here knows your lawyer as well. The Wedge would not be representing you if it wasn't true. He certainly wouldn't be making sure that hospital coughed up all those records. You got everything? He took the sheets and towels, and even the gauze they wrapped you in?"

I nodded. "Everything in that hospital I came in contact with, we own. That's what The Wedge said."

Franklin smiled for the first time since I'd told him my story. "Son of a bitch, you *are* gonna be rich kid."

"It's not something I spend a lot of time thinking about," I told him pointedly.

He looked at me with something between

curiosity and admiration. "Somehow that doesn't surprise me," he said.

"I'm just happy I'm alive." I said. "If the scientists and doctors can use what they learn to help other people, that would make me even happier. If it was up to me, I'd probably give it to the world for free."

"The Wedge won't," Franklin pointed out. "Oddly enough, he's one of the few men who could find a way to make it available to everyone. If there even is a way – they have to find out what happened to you first. All that is out of your hands now Peter. You've got to be concerned with what's at hand," he warned me ominously.

"So you think it's related to the accident?"

Franklin considered his response carefully before answering, "The kid who took the bullet was in contact with you right before he died. Whoever shot him would have still been close to the crime scene. I'm fairly certain it was the guys you locked eyes with down the street, and I doubt they were alone. They saw you talk with the kid right before he died."

"I would have already gone to the police if he told me who did it," I protested, although I followed his train of logic.

"If they think the kid told you something

before he died, they won't be asking you about the conversation. They'll just get rid of the risk."

I slowly nodded.

"Whoever is coming after you won't know you're watching for them. That gives you a small edge, but it might be enough."

"What do you mean?" I asked. I was in over my head, but no one had ever put out a hit on me before.

"Avoid crowds. That's number one. They will be looking for an opportunity. A bunch of people around you is camouflage for them. Someone can sidle up right behind you and drive a shank through your heart. They would be gone before you hit the street. No one would remember seeing anyone, and wouldn't come forward if they did, for fear of the same fate."

"How long am I supposed to hide in the hotel? Sure, I live out back, and eat here and everything, but are you asking me to be a prisoner?" Sooner or later I would have to venture back into the real world.

"Don't look at it that way – this is temporary. You have a great future, but only if you live to see it. I've heard you practicing in the cottage. You've got something that most musicians can only dream of. There's emotion in your music that can't be explained. Pretty soon people are gonna find out about you, it's only a matter of time."

"And there might be some dumb punk kids who want to take it away before I even get a chance." I was angry now. I was also scared. Someone was coming after me for what they mistakenly thought I knew. They were assholes, and crazy enough to do it. I slumped back in my chair, feeling weak.

"That's right," said Franklin. "But we won't let them."

I frowned at him. "Uh-uh. No way. This is my problem, not yours."

"On the contrary." I couldn't see his eyes behind his glasses. It was as if they disappeared into his skull. The tiny slits reminded me of what I'd read about sharks. They always closed their eyes as they took out their prey.

"They've made it my problem – our problem."

"Did you forget you're leaving town tomorrow?" I reminded him.

His eyes reappeared. The dread I'd felt a moment ago eased up slightly.

"I didn't forget." He paused, and seemed to make up his mind about something. "I have to make a couple of phone calls. I'm going to introduce you to my associates. I want you to be here tonight. We'll have dinner at eight o'clock, at this same table."

I nodded, "Yeah, sure, absolutely."

"Good." He could see I was rattled. "Don't worry," he added. "We'll take care of this. You won't owe me a thing," it was as if he'd read my mind.

"All right," I agreed. "I've got one condition though." He tilted his head, questioningly. "When we get past this thing, you'll agree to be my manager."

His face turned into a scowl. "What the fuck do I know about the music business?" he growled.

"Probably a lot more than you're telling me. Besides like the old saying goes, it isn't what you know, it's who you know. I think you know some very interesting people. You trust me, I trust you. Deal?" I extended my hand across the table. He went from being gruff to bemused, and then he began to laugh.

He took my hand in his. He said, "Sure, why the hell not? I've got a funny feeling about you kid, but I've got one condition of my own. If it turns out I'm no good at it, you'll fire me."

Chapter 25

I RETURNED TO a half-filled dining room a few minutes before eight o'clock. The table we'd been sitting at earlier in the afternoon was strategically located. A direct view of it was obscured, but anyone occupying the table had a clear view across the room. Our table was coincidentally always reserved. Franklin and his associates were already seated when I joined them. None of them got up as I sat down opposite them.

"I see everyone's early," I commented, nonchalantly appraising the man and woman who sat opposite me.

The man was about Franklin's age, probably mid-forties. I could see there wasn't much fat on him, although he wasn't what I would describe as muscular either. In fact, everything about him was very average, forgettable. The woman was anything but.

She was in her late twenties. In spite of the fact she wore very little makeup, she was stunningly beautiful. I found myself fighting not to stare at her. We locked eyes for a brief moment.

I forced back a shiver, because what I saw was all business. Behind the façade was clear and chilling, ice cold. I knew immediately that both of them were dangerous. I looked to Franklin to make the introductions.

"Peter Jackson, meet Albert Sousa and Bonnie Bernier, two people I trust with my life." We all shook hands.

Albert spoke next, in a low, almost melodic tone, "Tell me about the blonde-haired woman you met on the train Peter."

"All right," I replied hesitantly, realizing there would be no small talk. There was more going on than had first occurred to me. They were here to learn what they could to help Franklin. They didn't know me, and couldn't care less about me. I instinctively knew neither of these people trusted anyone, which was fine by me. Senior and Uncle Johnny had taught me the same. It was a matter of survival.

"I didn't exactly meet her," I began.

"Did the two of you ever speak with one another?" Bonnie asked me. Her voice was low and husky. She spoke with a distinctive Acadian accent. Born and raised down here, I thought, wondering about the relationship between her and Albert.

I shook my head. "No, we never did."

Albert and Bonnie exchanged furtive glances. I couldn't tell what it meant, but it made me uneasy. I continued, "Actually, the first time I remember noticing her was right after the train hit the Greyhound."

"You didn't see her get on the bus?" Bonnie's brow furrowed.

"I didn't notice her, no. Believe me, I've thought about it many times since then. It's strange to me, how could I not notice someone sitting directly across from me? Try as I might to remember her getting on that bus, I always draw a blank. I think my mind was on other things, and the woman didn't matter until the accident. I guess it's kind of like when you're going somewhere, and can't recall the details of the drive over."

"What do you think happened to her after the wreck, right after you carried her out through the fire?" Albert asked.

Franklin had obviously told them every detail.

I didn't immediately answer.

I shook my head slowly from side to side. "I know what you're probably thinking. It's the same thing everyone has been accusing me of since the accident."

"What's that?" Bonnie spoke up.

"You're thinking either I'm crazy, or I made all this up."

"Did you?" Albert asked, raising an eyebrow.

"Why would I?" I frowned at him. "And even if I did make her up, how would you explain the other shit that happened? Do you think that one of the best attorneys in America would invest a nickel of his time if this was a load of bullshit?"

Albert slowly nodded. "That's what I thought," he conceded. "It's the credibility factor. No fucking lawyer would waste his time over something that didn't have at least some element of truth. Not on contingency, that's for damn sure. The one thing that's indisputable is your burns. No one called it a miracle, but they might as well have. It happened over a month ago, and the media is still talking about it. If you hadn't sequestered yourself at the hotel, they would have you on every talk show in the country by now. I get it, though. You're camera shy, or whatever. So there's something to it all, and I have to believe you about that blonde-haired lady. You told Franklin you saw her again at some guitar shop?"

"Yeah, that's right. It's called The Guitar Works."

Bonnie jumped in, "Tell us what you remember about that Peter. I'd like to hear it in your own words. Are you absolutely, one hundred percent certain it was the same woman?"

"Yes," I said. "There's no doubt. I recognized her the moment I saw her. She knew who I was too. I could tell from the way she looked at me that I was the reason she was there."

"She came to see you?" said Bonnie.

"Yes. I don't know if she came to talk with me, but she definitely was there to see me."

"Why?" Albert asked.

"I don't know. She took off before I had a chance to say anything to her."

They all stared at me. My mind was racing. "She never spoke to me," I said. "Not on the bus, or at the music store. That must mean she never intended to actually speak to me?"

"I don't get it," said Franklin, puzzled.

Bonnie said, "She was there so you could follow her."

We sat in stunned silence.

"She'll be back," Albert said knowingly. His voice was a hoarse whisper.

I gaped at him for what seemed a long time before I realized my mouth was hanging open. I stammered, "I could really use a strong drink right about now."

Chapter 26

"TO SAY SHE expected me to follow her implies she was leading me somewhere. But after the train wreck, she disappeared, she never led me anywhere," I continued, after the waiter delivered a round of drinks.

"That's not true," Bonnie observed. "Think about it for a second. If she hadn't been on the bus, you never would have noticed her in the music store. She would have been just another face in the crowd."

I nodded, "I see your point. So you think she wanted me to follow her out of the guitar store? Obviously her plans were interfered with, because I wasn't able to. I guess she didn't count on a gun battle, an accident, and two guys dying in the street."

"You're assuming a lot," Albert spoke quietly.

"I'm not assuming anything," I countered. I was frustrated. "But if I follow your logic, you're suggesting she wanted me to follow her into that gunfight. I was supposed to be the last one to speak with that kid right before he died? For what possible reason?"

"What did he say to you before he died?" Bonnie finally asked the question.

"Nothing," I said.

"What did you say to him then?" she pressured me.

"I wasn't taking notes," I was moving from frustration to anger, getting tired of the third degree.

"Try to remember. It might be important," her voice softened somewhat, encouraging me.

I took a deep breath, and exhaled. I took a healthy slug of the whiskey I'd ordered before I continued.

"I asked him if he knew God loved him or something like that."

They all raised eyebrows at me.

"Yeah," I admitted. "I thought it was pretty strange too when I thought about it later. I'm not very religious. I don't know why I asked him that. It was the first thing that came into my mind. I guess maybe because I saw he was dying."

"What did he say?" Franklin was fascinated.

I shrugged. "He just nodded. By then he had this far off look in his eyes. It was like he saw something behind me."

"Then what happened?" Franklin prompted.

"Nothing," I said. "He died. I looked at his

buddy in the passenger seat, he wasn't moving. I couldn't really tell if he was breathing. Then I got the hell out of there."

"Did you see the blonde-haired woman again?"

"I didn't see her, but I wasn't looking for her. I just wanted to get away from there before the police arrived."

Bonnie spoke up, "Did anything else happen? Anything you may have overlooked?"

I fought hard to remember. "I don't think so. Everything was happening so fast, I…" I paused, all of a sudden recalling the woman pushing the stroller.

"There was a woman," I said. "I'm sorry, I almost forgot about her. I was running to catch up to the blonde-haired lady. There was a woman pushing her baby in a stroller. She stepped out into the street from between a couple of parked cars. She was directly in the path of the accident." I shuddered, thinking about what might have happened.

"I didn't really have time to think. I just reacted to what I saw."

"You saved that woman and her baby," Bonnie said what I wouldn't.

I looked at her, into those once-cold eyes.

They were softer now, holding compassion that hadn't been there earlier.

I didn't know why, but I was uncomfortable agreeing with her, "Yeah, I guess I did."

A thought occurred to me, and I turned to Albert, "What makes you think the blonde-haired woman is going to be back?"

He said, "She has unfinished business, and a purpose."

"She appears to be changing things," Bonnie agreed. "She might be using you to assist her."

Albert asked me, "What was altered by your presence at the accident? What wouldn't have happened if you weren't there?"

I thought carefully before I answered, "I wouldn't have spoken with the driver. A gang of thugs wouldn't be coming to kill me. We wouldn't be having this conversation."

"And that woman, and her baby, would be dead," Bonnie added. "Your being there, or not, wouldn't have changed the outcome of the gunfight. Your conversation with the dying driver was inconsequential. What it inadvertently did accomplish was to set in motion an ill-conceived course of retribution."

"By that you mean the gangbangers coming after Peter?" clarified Franklin.

"Correct," said Bonnie. "Whoever witnessed Peter at the accident assumed the worst."

"That the driver gave up the bastards who murdered him," I finished her thought.

"Right again," Bonnie said.

"Isn't there some way we can reach out and let them know the kid didn't tell me anything?"

"If we found a way to communicate with them, they would feel vulnerable, and threatened at the same time. They would likely conclude they were being set up in some kind of police sting. That would give them all the more reason to eliminate the perceived threat, in this case the witness."

"Me," I said flatly.

"Yes," Bonnie stated with finality.

"So what can I do to stop all this bullshit?" I was exasperated.

"Option number one, you can leave New Orleans. Chances are they wouldn't try to follow you."

"A coward runs," I said.

"Maybe," Bonnie acknowledged. "But it would definitely prove to them that you're not cooperating with the police."

"It might make them think the cops are protecting Peter until he is needed," Albert pointed out.

"He'd be safe," Bonnie countered.

"With all due respect to everyone, I'm not going anywhere. In case Franklin didn't tell you," I looked from Bonnie to Albert, "I've had experience with people like these guys, and some of them were seriously dangerous. As you can see, I'm still here."

Albert said, "No one is doubting how capable you are Peter, but a wise man would have to concede it's sometimes smarter to go around a rock than through it."

"What about stepping onto it to get to the other side? I always thought Confucius, or Buddha, or whoever, could've done a little better in the options department."

Franklin couldn't help but smile. "Yeah," he agreed. "So leaving isn't an option then?"

"I'm not a coward," I said. "I can be very resourceful, and I'm good at looking after myself. For their sake, I hope they get me on the first try."

"You're quite the tough guy," said Albert.

My eyes hardened. "There's nothing tough about me Mr. Sousa. I would much rather not be involved in any of this, but I'm not running away from this problem. To me, that kind of living is being more dead than alive. I think…" I paused, considering what I wanted to say next, "That would not be a life I would be particularly interested in living."

"All right, then we go to option two," Albert didn't skip a beat. He reached under the table, and brought up the crumpled linen napkin from his lap. He placed it in front of him, and slid it across the space between us. "You're going to need this," he spoke casually.

I looked at the napkin, now directly in front of me. It was obvious what lay hidden beneath it. I looked up from the table, and into Albert's eyes.

"Why?" I asked. "Why are you helping me?"

He shrugged, and gave me the universal answer, "It is what it is. We owe Franklin. Any friend of his is a friend of ours, and we definitely take care of our friends."

Chapter 27

IT WAS NONE of my business why Albert and Bonnie were in Franklin Belanger's debt. In all the time I knew them I never asked them about it either. I figured if they wanted me to know they would have told me. Besides, I figured my relationship with them was probably a one-shot deal. They were here to protect me, and if necessary, kill for me. I didn't figure I needed them, but I wasn't about to turn down the help either. If we surmised correctly, and the guys who murdered the black kid were the ones following me, it wouldn't be long before they made their move.

So as not to be conspicuous, both Albert and Bonnie would pose as employees of the hotel. Albert would be a busboy in the restaurant, and I would introduce Bonnie as the new greeter for the dining room. The idea that Franklin wanted to add a little class by putting an attractive woman up front would be an easy sell. Both of them would have free access to the entire place, without arousing anyone's suspicions. If the gangsters sent anyone inside the hotel to case the place, they would report back that I was alone, and an easy target. Albert and Bonnie would take a suite upstairs. It wasn't unusual that some of the staff, myself as an example, lived at the hotel. They could hide incognito while still in plain sight.

To kill me they would have to do it inside the hotel, because I was no longer going outside it. We would wait, and watch. When they decided to hit us, we would be ready for them.

Chapter 28

FRANKLIN LEFT FOR New York the next morning. I saw him off, and assured him we would all be up to whatever tasks lay ahead. I tried very hard to hide my trepidation as I told him not to worry. Later that day Laurie arrived to help me move into the cottage behind the hotel.

The cottage was almost hidden from view by the dense foliage that surrounded it. It was flanked on both sides by the five stories of the hotel, and looked out onto a beautiful fountain in the center of the courtyard. Rising behind my new home was the back of another hotel. The cottage was effectively walled into the Marigold's courtyard. I carried one suitcase down the path and in through the secret front door. Laurie followed with my other, lighter suitcase. We entered, set the suitcases down in the bedroom, and came back out into the living room. Laurie collapsed onto the comfortable sofa next to my guitar. I got a bottle of Cabernet and a couple of glasses from the kitchen and sat down beside her.

"Finally," I said, as I poured some wine. It had

been a trying week to say the least. Before I had a chance to hand Laurie her glass, she grabbed my head between her hands and kissed me. My head was swimming by the time she drew back and gazed into my eyes.

"Welcome to your new home Peter." The look on her face stirred a passion deep inside me, and I moved toward her for more of the same. She held me still, and we gazed into each other's eyes, our faces and lips mere inches apart.

"Later," she whispered.

"Soon, I hope." I whispered back.

"Soon enough," she assured me. "We've got all night. Now, I want to talk."

I nodded, leaning back. She released my head from between her hands, her smile never abandoning her lips.

I said, "All right, but my guess is we have a lot more than one night." Her smile broadened.

"All the more reason to talk," she replied. "Could you please hand me my wine?"

"At your service." I retrieved both glasses, and handed one to her.

We clinked glasses. Neither of us spoke, but our eyes remained locked onto each other. It was a silent, strong testament to the feelings we had for each other.

Laurie sipped her wine, and set it onto the table. I did the same.

"What should we talk about?" I was curious.

The smile left her face. She was serious, and began in a deliberate tone, "I was watching you when we were walking through the hotel earlier. You didn't seem yourself Peter."

"I've had a bit of a rough week," I admitted.

"So let's talk about it," she leaned toward me.

"There isn't much to talk about," I nonchalantly waved it off. "I guess maybe I'm nervous about Franklin leaving. I don't want to let him down, he's done a lot of nice things for me." I waved my arm around the room. "Like letting me stay here, for instance."

Her brow furrowed. "Peter…" she hesitated. "Who is that woman?" She watched me closely. "The one who's greeting people?"

"You mean the one at the kiosk in front of the restaurant?" She didn't say anything.

"She's new," I continued. "Franklin hired her this week. He wanted to add some class to the place. At least that's what he said. I think her name is Bonnie. What makes you ask?"

"She's beautiful."

"Yes, she is," I admitted. I looked at her

cautiously. "Where are you going with this Laurie?" My tone was wary.

"The whole time we were walking around in there," she ignored me, "the two of you never once made eye contact."

I shrugged. "I guess we were busy. What's your point?"

"That woman could be a runway model, and you never even looked at her. You're her new boss, and she never once acknowledged you. Doesn't that seem strange to you? It did to me," she confessed with candor. She looked at me, eyebrows raised, waiting patiently for some kind of an explanation.

"Do you think she and I have something going on?"

"Yes, definitely, but," she smiled reassuringly, "not in a sexual way. Otherwise the two of you would have at least looked at each other. The fact you never even did that speaks volumes."

Silence enveloped the small room. I cursed myself. Why hadn't I at least put on some music? I must be more nervous about this whole affair than I'd thought. Wordlessly, I got up from the sofa and walked over to the stereo. A few seconds later Seal filled the air with his sonorous, soulful voice. I sat back down beside her. Her insight impressed and concerned me, at the same time. This was a woman, I realized, I would never attempt to deceive, nor would I want to.

After the meeting with Franklin and his two cohorts, I debated with myself how much, if anything, I would tell Laurie. I'd gone over every detail in my mind to convince myself that I was being paranoid. No matter how I tried to twist facts, I was always left with the same bleak prospect. A person, or persons unknown were determined to kill the only witness to a murder. To involve Laurie in something this nasty was not something I wanted. In fact, I would do everything in my power to avoid this. The only problem was, she was far too intelligent to remain on the sidelines. Ma had been right all along; I wrestled with demons.

Chapter 29

THE SEAL SONG ended, and another began.

"Why does it seem to me that people are always hiding something?" her voice punctuated the soft music.

"You think I'm keeping secrets?" Laurie's thoughts made me nervous.

"Are you?" she asked softly. "Does what's her name, Bonnie, think so? Who is she Peter? Is she somehow connected to that strange blonde-haired lady?"

I carefully tried to distract her. "Laurie, I've told you how I feel about you…"

She tilted her head, and I knew there was no use. "You know, you're way too smart for your own good."

"So I've been told," she agreed.

"You were right about Bonnie. She's part of something that's extremely important right now."

"Important?"

I sighed loudly. "All right. It's life and death important. Are you sure you want to hear more?"

She just waited for me.

So I told her everything.

Afterwards, she said, "I can accept the fact that Albert isn't really a busboy, but an assassin?" She involuntarily shivered. "And Bonnie; there's no way I would have thought she and Albert were a team. She really does look like a runway model. Of course if anyone wanted a perfect disguise, I guess hers would be the one."

"Beautiful, but deadly," I agreed.

"Why not go to the police?" she asked.

"And tell them what? That I suspect there's been a hit put out on me? Maybe someone connected with a gangland killing saw me talk to the victim right before he died? Then I'm a witness to murder. And then what? Protective custody? No thanks. Oh, and by the way, who exactly is after me? Do you know how many people in New Orleans fit the description of those two guys? Three-quarters of the city!" I realized I was being hard on her. Laurie knew a lot about certain things, but I had lived in a world of lunatics. I knew all about the kind of people who were involved. She didn't.

I explained, "The cops aren't exactly my friends." I remembered the two detectives I'd had words with back in Memphis. "There is nothing they could do to help me. Remember, there's a chance that I'm just being paranoid. The police might even think I'm making the whole thing up."

"Why would you do that?"

"People invent things all the time. They do it for attention, or maybe because they're just plain crazy. My point is, they may charge me for making a false police report; or use me as bait in some scheme to flush these murderers out into the open. They wouldn't give a damn about me. The way things are now I have a chance of living through it. We're far more effective handling this by ourselves."

"You and the assassins," Laurie glared at me.

I stared right back. "We'll never agree on this," I stated the obvious.

She ended the standoff. "Maybe the boogie man isn't really out there," the tone of her voice softened somewhat. "Maybe after a time we'll realize it was just that – an overactive imagination."

"Maybe," I said. "I hope that's true, but wishing it doesn't make it happen. I'm still alive because I've played it safe."

"Was it really that dangerous being in business with your father and uncle?" she asked.

I thought about it before I answered. "Yes. We had to be careful, just like we are now. It's why I got out of the whole thing."

"That, and your music," she ventured.

I looked tenderly at her. The tension between us evaporated. Even if Laurie didn't completely understand me, I could see I still had her support.

"So what's the plan then?" She was concerned.

"We wait," I replied. "We have more patience than they do. That will bother them. It shows disrespect in their world, like we're somehow better than they are. That we're not afraid of them. Their arrogance and anger will be their undoing. They'll make a mistake, and we'll make our move."

"How long do you think we have to wait?"

"Not long," I hesitated. "Two or three weeks at most, I suspect. Since the police aren't involved yet, they'll want to get me before I change my mind," I mused more to myself than to her. I was thinking like them – as a murderer would.

"Peter, you're scaring me, your voice didn't sound like you just now."

She interrupted my dark thoughts, and brought me back into the cozy living room of the cottage. I pulled her closer to me. "I'm sorry," I said as gently as I could. "I went to a soulless place just now." I looked deeply into her eyes. "I promise you, I won't let anything bad happen to either of us, but whatever happens, you have to trust me."

She nodded. Her eyes moistened, but she didn't

blink. "We'll wait for them together then," I could barely hear her words. Her fingernails dug into my back as she pulled her body against mine. "I love you Peter," she spoke very gently, but with determination.

"I love you too baby." I whispered in her ear.

We held each other for a while, gaining strength and warmth from the intimacy. She finally asked me, "Do you know what's going on with that blonde-haired lady? I mean she appears to you at the weirdest times, doesn't say a word, and then runs away. Why doesn't she talk to you? What's her problem?"

I shook my head and shrugged. "I think about her all the time. I totally agree with you, it's maddening. Who the hell is she? What does she want with me? Believe me when we finally talk, I'm gonna get some answers. Any normal person would just say what's on their mind."

"Do you think she wants money? You have to assume she's heard about that famous lawyer you hired."

"The Wedge," I nodded. "No, I doubt it's about money. If that were the case she would be doing the exact opposite. She'd be talking to me, not running from me. No, it's something else. Bonnie and Albert had an interesting theory.

They think she's here as some sort of guide, an intermediary."

"What does that mean?"

"It means she knows when something bad is about to happen," I struggled with an explanation. "She shows up, and stays just out of my reach, like some weird kind of apparition. Then she leads me somewhere, and just like that," I snapped my fingers, "I'm caught up in the middle of it, and she's gone. But why?" I asked rhetorically. "I don't know the woman. I never saw her until I got her out of that burning wreck."

"Maybe she knows you?" Laurie suggested.

"Then why not talk to me? Why all this bullshit skullduggery?"

Laurie sank into deep thought for a few moments. She finally said, "Maybe she can't talk to you. Or maybe…" she paused, "She isn't allowed to speak to you."

I felt a shiver run down my spine. "What do you mean?" My voice sounded hoarse. "Does she take orders from someone? Or is this just some kind of weird, sadistic game she's playing, using me like a pawn?"

"Pawn? I don't think so." Laurie chose her words carefully. "You're making decisions, not her; she's just there, acting as a catalyst. Once she got you there her job was done. You did the rest. If you think about it, she could have known about everything beforehand. Maybe getting you to that spot as it was happening was critical."

"How so? Those kids are dead." It was a sobering thought.

She looked at me closely. "You saved that baby's life. If you hadn't been there at that exact moment…" she trailed off. When she spoke again, it was with a reverential air. "It makes me wonder who that baby's going to be."

Chapter 30

SIX WEEKS LATER I was frustrated and anxious. We were on high alert, and constantly vigilant. But the stress, together with the boredom, were beginning to take their toll on me.

I was tired of the daily routine. Prior to taking over the Marigold, I had no previous experience in the operations of a hotel. I was surprised to find out how similar each day actually was. Different people came and went, but they tended to meld into one another. What I thought would be interesting became quite the opposite. In fact, if not for Laurie's frequent visits, I'd probably be climbing the walls.

It all became too much. I finally decided I couldn't continue examining every new hotel guest with a faked, casual air, while wondering if they had come to kill me.

"Have you changed your mind? Are you telling us you're leaving New Orleans?"

"That would make your job a whole lot easier," I pointed out the obvious.

Bonnie exchanged concerned glances with

Albert. We were meeting in their room on the second floor of the hotel, as we did from time to time, to compare notes.

"I'm sorry, I didn't mean it that way. I'm just stressed out. No, I'm not going anywhere. I gave Franklin my word I'd look after things while he was away. Where I come from, that's all we have. Our word. So leaving is out of the question. Besides, it seems less likely with each passing day that anyone is actually coming after me."

"They might be more patient than you think Peter," Albert cautioned me. "Maybe they're waiting for you to leave the hotel. We can't discount the possibility."

I shook my head, "I can't do this much longer. It's like I'm in prison. I'm really starting to think if those gangsters ever had it in for me, they've likely moved on. I don't think they're waiting outside the front door for me to finally make my exit. I honestly think I may have gotten it wrong when I thought I was being followed." I looked from one to the other, seeking their affirmation, because they were the professionals.

"Do you really think it's worth risking your life over such an assumption? What if you're wrong?" Bonnie asked.

"I could be," I admitted. "But I'm beginning

to think hiding out inside this hotel is worse. It's been six weeks already. How much longer do we keep this up? A better question would be how much longer do the two of you have? I'm sure you have better things to do with your time."

Albert leveled a benign stare at me. "Without going into details, no. Until we are instructed otherwise, protecting you is our job."

I nodded respectfully. "I can accept that. You and Franklin must have quite a history," I probed with subtlety.

They glanced at each other. Then Bonnie said, "Like Albert told you, the details are none of your business, but Franklin saved our lives."

"I get it. You owe him."

Albert spoke, shaking his head, "We owe ourselves Peter. We have honor. Where we come from, like yourself, it's all we have of value."

I sighed, "Franklin must think an awful lot of me."

"He values your talent," Bonnie confirmed it.

"He thinks you're a great musician," said Albert. He continued to eye me. It was unnerving. "You would be wise not to underestimate Franklin's abilities. He did not take the decision to manage your career lightly."

"Peter," Bonnie interrupted, "I've listened to

you play guitar and sing. The sound is muffled from inside the cottage, but you can still hear it quite clearly. You have that certain something that every musician longs for. Your destiny is attached to a comet's tail, and you seem to be the last one to see it. Franklin knows it even if you don't."

"I don't even think he's heard me play much," I was calling bullshit.

Albert waved me off, "He's heard you play enough. It's part of the reason he's in New York. He's arranging a few things as we speak. It's what he does."

He's probably arranging shit, I thought, but kept my doubt to myself. If these people thought I was the best thing to come along since Mick Jagger then who was I to say different?

"So you're both here to preserve Franklin's asset then?" I played along. I was beginning to wonder if all of them were a little bit nuts. I knew I was good, but I didn't for one second believe I was nearly as good as they thought.

"If that's how you want to see it," said Bonnie.

"Look, I appreciate the accolades, but I have to be honest with you guys. I think you might be caught up in some kind of rock star fairy tale." I held out my hands, palms down in a gesture that suggested they both come back to reality. "I'm just not that good. I came here with the hope of getting into a band, and playing some gigs in the local bars around town. I just don't want anyone to get their hopes up and end up disappointed. You, and more importantly Franklin, might want to tone down your expectations a bit."

Albert said, "We shall see, but please respect the contract you have with Franklin."

A flash of anger sparked inside of me. "Albert, did you just threaten me?" My eyes became narrow slits, like those of the rattlesnakes I'd run across in the deep woods of Tennessee. My question filled the air like a distant, rumbling thunder announcing bad weather.

"I only stated that you have a contract," he calmly replied.

I kept staring at him, aware that Bonnie remained silent while I did so. I slowly nodded. I knew from the moment I met them that Albert was the more dangerous of the two, but Bonnie had his back with a fierce loyalty. Now the relationship the three of us had was being sorely tested. We were all acutely aware of it. The tension in the room was palpable.

"I'm aware of the contract between Franklin and myself," I finally said. "The thing you may not be aware of, is that either one of us is free to walk away from it." I kept looking at Albert, the alpha male. I was being very careful not to offend anyone, but I was in no way backing off my position. "You might want to confirm it with Franklin before you say something that all of us may regret. I remind you, we are all on the same team." I felt hot all over. There was a loud ringing in my ears that was fast turning into something like a scream. My heart pounded, and the places I'd been burned began to itch like a son of a gun. I was burning up, but to Bonnie and Albert, I was calm and composed.

Albert slowly nodded. I would have missed the slight hesitation in his voice if I hadn't been looking for even the slightest nuance. A faint smile finally etched itself across his lips. "Either you're suicidal, or you're one of the smartest, cagiest kids I've ever met in my life. There's one thing I do know, though," he said.

"What's that?" I asked.

His smile got a little wider before he replied, "You have the guts of a half dozen slaughtered pigs."

Chapter 31

IT WAS THE next day, the second Friday in June, that I received an unexpected possible solution to my conundrum. It was from Laurie, who met me in the cottage for lunch. After checking through the peephole to make sure the knock was hers, I opened the door and invited her inside. The effervescent glow across her face had me curious.

"I have a surprise for you," she smiled. She floated into the living room, and set an unopened bottle of champagne on the coffee table. She turned back to embrace me. Her kiss as she fell into my arms was long and sensuous. Reluctantly, we finally separated, the passion still trembling through our bodies.

Her face was so close to mine I could feel her breath. "Wow," I said. "That was a nice surprise. Can I have another one?"

"Later," she pushed me away. "Could you pour us a drink? I have something to tell you, and it happens to be the surprise."

"Okay," I agreed. "But there isn't much that can top that kiss."

I opened the bottle and poured glasses for us both. We sat down on the sofa next to each other. She wore the mischievous grin of a pixie spreading her magic dust. I shook my head, smiling. "I have no doubt that what you're excited about is going to be interesting."

She nodded enthusiastically. Her eyes were sparkling.

"Am I going to have to wait long?"

She poked me playfully in the ribs. A few drops of wine spilled onto my jeans as I recoiled backwards.

"John Gant spoke with me this morning," she announced.

I was not familiar with the name. "Should I know who John Gant is?" I asked.

"I probably never mentioned his name before. He's my boss at The Guitar Works, actually more like my boss's boss. He owns The Guitar Works," she elaborated, clarifying any confusion. "He's hardly ever there though. He's one of those rich, older guys. He owns other stores and stuff around the country so he travels a lot. He just got back from California. Anyway, he called me into the manager's office because John doesn't have one in The Guitar Works."

"John?"

"He doesn't like anyone calling him Mr. Gant. He says it makes him feel older than he is. He doesn't like to be reminded of it."

"I see," I said with reservation.

"He's a sweetheart Peter. He's really cool for a guy his age."

"How old is he?" I became curious.

Laurie guessed, "No one really knows, but I'd say he's in his seventies."

"That's getting up there. What did he want with you?"

"He asked me all about you," she said.

"Me? How does he know me?" I was taken aback.

"He doesn't, he knows me." She was grinning from ear to ear. I was getting mildly irritated.

"Am I missing something?" I asked bluntly.

"He checked the invoices to find out who sold you the Stratocaster. Of course it was me. Luckily I got your cellphone number. There was no other contact info for you."

"Vixen," I teased her, smiling now, remembering how quickly we fell for each other. I spoke sincerely when I confided, "There was no way I was gonna pick up my guitar without giving you my number, and luckily I had just gotten that phone."

She beamed at me, and continued with her

story. "He saw you play. He heard every note, and saw everyone's reaction. He said in all his years he'd never seen anything close to what he witnessed. He described it to me as an otherworldly experience. He left for California that day, but hasn't been able to stop thinking about you. He was ecstatic when he learned in our meeting this morning that yes, I not only knew you, but I also knew where you were staying. I didn't tell him your address, of course. Not with what's going on right now. He wants to meet you."

"I don't get it," I was perplexed. "Why does he want to meet with me?"

Laurie's eyes twinkled with delight. "He knows some people who promote concerts."

"I still don't get it. What's that got to do with me?"

"He wants to put you on tour. Not as a headliner, but as a warm-up to someone else."

I grimaced. I wondered if she was playing some kind of joke on me. "I'm not even in a band Laurie!"

"I told him that. He said for now it doesn't matter, that it would be easy to put some guys together and start rehearsing some songs."

"Rehearse? What are you talking about? What songs? There's no band," I was incredulous. "No bar in New Orleans would hire an unknown musician, much less someone who plays their own music. This is insanity."

"John asked if you could get a set together of your original songs by the end of the summer. In a worst-case scenario, he'll pay for studio musicians to back you up. All you have to do is teach them your arrangements. You'll do the vocals."

I was hyperventilating. "This is absolutely crazy! John Gant must be some kind of lunatic."

Laurie continued. "There's one more thing you should know." She hesitated before she went on, "You won't be playing a bar in New Orleans. He was talking about you touring behind someone bigger than that. He mentioned a U.S. tour with an act that can sell out arenas."

A ringing in my ears was getting louder and louder.

She looked at me, suddenly concerned. "Are you all right?"

"I don't know," I spoke quietly. "I think I'm gonna be sick." I had just enough time to place the glass of wine on the coffee table before my mad dash to the bathroom. The good news was I made it to the toilet just in time. Even better, my problem of going stir-crazy holed up in the Marigold might be solved.

Chapter 32

AFTER THE WEEKEND, I called The Wedge. His secretary informed me he was in court, but that he would call me as soon as he returned to the office.

Too many things were happening way too fast. I didn't have the connections to find out about all the new people in my life. I needed help. I told Laurie I needed some time, and spent the entire weekend alone, ruminating. By Monday I realized I wasn't directing my own affairs. It was as if I was being skillfully manipulated by forces beyond my control. At the very least, I needed to know who these people were.

I was aware that, almost hypnotically, I had been going along with all of it. Maybe because most everything was positive. I liked the cottage, I was in love with Laurie, and I had money with more on the way. But there was also a darker, more dangerous undertone. The accident, the gangsters, even Bonnie, Albert, and Franklin. All of it, everything since I left Memphis, seemed way too contrived for my liking.

And who the hell was the blonde-haired lady? When I considered it carefully, I seemed to be the only one who'd even seen her. She was real enough; of that I was certain. I hadn't chased some figment of my imagination out of the guitar store.

But all of it was just too pat. I found myself wondering if it was all some kind of setup. Maybe these people were after the loot I was bound to come into when The Wedge finally settled all the lawsuits.

Then I realized that was impossible. Over and over in my mind, I played back the events of my arrival in New Orleans. No one met me at the bus station. Any conversations with strangers had been perfunctory, and of little consequence. No one directed me to Franklin's hotel. Walking into the lobby had been a purely random act, which I alone decided on. No one directed me to The Guitar Works either.

Out of everyone I'd met in these last few months, I trusted Laurie most. Granted, she stood the most to gain by her involvement with me, but I believed our relationship was based on love. What we could give each other, and what we wanted for each other. Not what we could get from one another. I was absolutely convinced she was genuine.

That's not to say that everyone else I'd met in the last while wasn't. I didn't believe this was the case, but most human relationships involve some kind of give and take. Unless they are based in truth and love, they usually involved money.

My relationship with The Wedge was definitely, unabashedly about the cash. Paradoxically, it was the reason I could trust him. He had everything to lose if he was being duplicitous.

"Sorry I didn't get back to you sooner Peter. I was in court," his voice boomed through the receiver. "Some guy figured it would be cheaper to bury his wife than divorce her."

"You're defending him on a murder charge knowing he did it?" I was surprised.

"Heaven's no!" The Wedge sounded offended. "Earl came for her one night with a loaded thirty-eight. Only problem was Jackie, his wife, was waiting for him with a shotgun. She got him before he got her. Now I'm defending her on second-degree homicide," he chuckled. "No worries though," he quickly added. "I'll take care of good old Jackie. I'll get her off. After all she is in her seventies. Earl should have just waited a bit, but that's life. Some people just don't have patience. What can I do for you son? Do you need some more dollars?" he changed the subject.

"No, I'm fine. That isn't the reason I called. Have you got a few minutes?" I asked him politely.

"I've got all the time in the world for you. What's on your mind? How's life in the Big Easy? Are you getting enough gumbo?"

"The food is fine," I assured him. "As far as New Orleans goes, I have to tell you Wedge, there's never a dull moment around here."

"That's good," he chuckled.

"It can be," I agreed.

He picked up on the nuance. "Are you in some kind of trouble?" His tone was sincere.

"I have a question. I've heard that lawyers sometimes employ private investigators when the need arises. Is that true of your firm?"

"From time to time, when necessary," he admitted.

"Can the ones you use be trusted?"

"Discretion is their hallmark. I would have absolutely no use for anyone who couldn't keep their mouth shut. That's a big part of the game we play. My guys are one hundred percent loyal to me. Think of what I have as a giant spider web."

"And you're the spider?" I guessed.

Wedge replied, "I couldn't do what I do if I wasn't. There isn't a gnat that lands on the web I don't know about. Most times the spider leaves these little gnats alone, but the next time might be different. So the gnats know they owe the spider their lives. Believe me when I tell you, this badass spider has a lot of gnats who owe me big time. I also have a great memory for this kind of thing."

"The spider never forgets," I complimented him.

"Now you've got it son. So what did you get yourself into since we last sat down with each other? How serious is it?"

"Serious enough," I said. "I need your help checking out some people I've recently met. I don't know a whole lot about them."

"Are they in a position to do you harm?" Sensing my trepidation, he got right to the point.

"Maybe, I'm not sure. I just don't know enough about them. I was hoping you'd be able to help me."

"Of course Peter. I was actually going to call you this week to update you on your case anyway, but that can wait. Suffice it to say everything is going well, and remains on track. It will take time, but if you need anything, all you need to do is call me."

"Thanks Wedge." I knew he was referring to cash more than anything else. This call had probably surprised him, but it didn't seem to bother him.

"I don't think I ever told you about this woman I met on the Greyhound. We never spoke, but I rescued her out of the wreck," I began.

Wedge interrupted, "I thought you were the only survivor?"

"No. That's what all the reports said, and it's what all the witnesses said, but I got her out. She disappeared afterward without a trace."

"I'll start with the manifest," his response was immediate. "All the bus terminals have closed-circuit cameras. Do you know where she got on?" he asked.

"That part I missed," I confided.

"We've already found out where that bus began its run. I'll just subpoena everything. I'll need a description of the woman."

"Blonde, shoulder-length hair, maybe in her forties. About five foot four in height, and weighed about a hundred pounds. I carried her out of the inferno, so I know."

"It's not a lot to go on, but maybe it'll be enough," Wedge spun it positively. "Is there anything else you can tell me about her?"

"I'm afraid that's it. There wasn't much time to take notes."

Wedge laughed. "At least you haven't lost your sense of humor. Did anyone else see or talk with her?"

"No one," I said with finality. "Not another living soul."

"Why is it so important for you to find her?" The Wedge was curious.

"Because I've seen her again, in New Orleans. And before you ask, no, I didn't get a chance to speak with her here either."

Chapter 33

I TOLD THE Wedge the story of how I didn't speak to the blonde-haired lady the second time I saw her. I also informed him about the kid who'd died, and the gangsters who might be after me. Then I filled him in on everything else. He was shaken – I could tell. He then told me he'd taken down the names of Franklin and his two associates.

"It certainly bears looking into," he stated, with a distinct air of concern. Left unspoken was the fact that if I came to an untimely end, so would the paycheck from the lawsuits.

"There's one final thing," I said after we'd spent over an hour on the phone. "I can't seem to reach my mother in Memphis. Her name is Linda Lou Jackson." I gave him our disconnected phone number. "Her friends don't even answer when I call. I'm worried something might have happened to her. She's alone at the house. My father and uncle disappeared shortly before I left Memphis. That's not unusual," I left it at that, "but a disconnected phone is. I would appreciate if your guys could find out what's going on for me. I know I'm asking a lot, but I'm afraid I have no one else I can turn to right now," I confessed.

Growing up, I had mostly been a loner. I suppose living on the outskirts of Memphis by the forest contributed to this. Early on I'd turned away from the city, and enjoyed long hikes in those woods. The company of birdcalls, scurrying rodents, and curious squirrels was preferable to people. I knew what to expect from the animals; it was the human beings that were not always so predictable.

"I'm happy I can be here for you Peter. And don't think you owe me anything for it. Everything's a part of the same package. We'll find out who they are, and what they're up to. Then we'll take it from there," he assured me.

"Thanks," I replied.

He got serious. "You not being able to reach your mother is indeed disturbing. Might there be something you haven't told me?" He paused, "Don't think I'm judging you though – I don't do that."

I suddenly became irritated, and defensive. I felt embarrassed at the same time; there was no way to defend my misspent youth. I calmed down as I reminded myself Wedge wasn't the enemy. He was just doing his job. I began to take more and more comfort at just how damn good he was.

"I started cooking meth when I was quite young," I admitted. "I quit when Senior, my father, got busted. I was in it just long enough to know I was making a big mistake. If I stayed in, I realized I'd end up paying."

"That means you're a lot smarter than he is," noted The Wedge.

"Maybe. I'm a lot like you in that respect. I don't judge folks, but I decided to go a different way in life. I'm out of it. For good. I've got my music."

"I believe you," he said.

"I appreciate it."

"I had to ask, now we're clear about it," he was almost apologetic.

"I've always been straight with you," I told him.

"How long have you had that chip on your shoulder?"

I could almost see the twinkle in that wily old spider's eyes as we said goodbye. The Wedge, I concluded, was a decent man.

Chapter 34

I FELT A lot better about things after my conversation with The Wedge. Like I took back some small amount of control over my life. I wouldn't necessarily call the lawyer a friend, that was probably not the kind of relationship either one of us really wanted. I was sure he could learn a few things about everybody. In the meantime, I'd keep my head down and make some observations of my own.

Coincidentally, Franklin called me later in the week. He was still in New York.

"Hello Franklin," I said.

"How'd you know it was me?" he was surprised.

"You're calling from a two one two area code. I've never had a call from the Big Apple in my life, but you'd have to be dead not to know that prefix."

"You may have to get used to it," he replied.

"What makes you say that?"

"I'm your manager, I'm working on things." He seemed like he was in a good mood. "How are you getting along with the team?" he asked.

"Better than ever. I trust you heard about the hiccup?" I was referring to the rather tense conversation with Albert and Bonnie the other night.

"Yeah, I heard about it. They were just looking out for my interests. They kind of overstepped their boundaries. Apparently you let Albert know that though."

"I like those two," I was being honest. "It was nothing, we got it all straightened out. We all got to know each other better, and I'm definitely glad they're on my side."

"They're good people Peter. I'm pleased you see it that way. Now they know you were right."

"About what?" I asked.

"The fact that either one of us can walk away any time we want to. We shook on it, and that's good enough for me." I could imagine him smiling on the other end of the phone. "Has John Gant been in touch with you?" he changed the subject.

"You know something Franklin? I've reached a point where nothing surprises me anymore. Albert told me you were arranging things. So you're the one responsible for that, it makes a lot more sense to me now. Laurie said he wants to meet with me. By the way, I threw up when she first told me about it. You owe me for that one."

Franklin was laughing. "I'll buy you both

a drink at the bar when I get back," he offered warmly. "Speaking of the bar... "

"The numbers are up across the board." I assured him. "We're having a good quarter." In what little spare time I'd had, I'd researched the hospitality industry. Inventory control was critical - knowing how to keep people from stealing from you. Coming from the meth business, I knew about keeping an eye on the product.

"I chose well then," said Franklin. "I'm proud of you. Thank you for looking after the store for me."

"Well, I appreciate you letting me stay in the cottage. It's a beautiful space. Don't worry about the hotel. I've tightened up the controls a bit; the staff seem to be respecting the changes. I've given a few people raises, by the way. Small ones, but they appear to really appreciate the gesture. It's getting more efficient, and everyone seems to be smiling a lot more lately."

"You're the reason, believe me. They like working for you, just like I thought they would."

"I hope you bought a lottery ticket," I wasn't joking. "You're either one of the most intuitive hotel owners in New Orleans, or you're just plain lucky."

"I'll take the luck when it comes my way, but

I saw something in you. And I'm not the only one. Speaking of luck, I'm happy John Gant heard you try out that guitar. He said you made quite a scene. It's too bad you had to make that hasty exit. He was dying to talk with you."

"How well do you know Mr. Gant?" I asked.

"Well enough," Franklin replied. "He owns a lot of stuff. The Guitar Works is a hobby for him. Music was always his first love. He still promotes some of the bigger tours across the country. John is getting older these days, but it hasn't slowed him down any."

"I think it's amazing he thinks I'm good enough to back up one of those tours," I said innocently. "What I still can't understand is how you got him to be there the same day I was trying out the Strat," I went for the jugular; I was no neophyte. Franklin needed to stop playing me. Somehow he knew John Gant, the music mogul. It was all too convenient, but then again there was no way he could have known I'd be in The Guitar Works that afternoon.

I fought hard to remember if I'd mentioned it to him in passing. All I drew was a blank. If I said anything, it was likely small talk, perhaps an offhand comment. That, I had to admit, was a possibility. But no one, not even me, knew I would be performing an impromptu concert that afternoon. Yet, in hindsight it would seem the enigmatic blonde-haired lady knew. It was all so confusing.

"It was a lucky coincidence." It was as if Franklin was reading my mind. If he saw through me, he didn't let on. More likely, he viewed my questions as totally innocent.

"You asked me earlier if I heard from him," I pointed out. "That would imply the two of you spoke about me."

"Absolutely we did. We're good friends. We go back a long way. Before I owned the hotel, I started out with a security company."

The lights suddenly came on. I felt sheepish as he continued his explanation.

"John started running statewide tours at first. Those early concerts needed security. Me and the guys I hung around with at the time fit the bill. John was the brains, and I supplied the brawn. I wouldn't be where I am today without the man's support. I learned most of what I know from him; he's my mentor. He's always had a brilliant ear for talent, and he's discovered some amazing musicians. It would appear you're next on his list.

"John called me, as he does from time to time. It didn't take long before he mentioned you.

He went on and on about this amazing kid he'd seen in The Guitar Works. He was raving about the most talented guitarist he'd heard in over a decade who picked the crowd up and shook them in the palm of his hand, as if shaking winning dice in Vegas. I asked him what the kid looked like not knowing it was you. As he described you, I couldn't believe the coincidence. I don't know if you recall, but you told me in passing that you came down from Memphis with the hope of putting a band together. Unless you had a twin, it couldn't be anyone else. I told John how you and I met, and that you were looking after the hotel for me. I also let him know I agreed to be your manager. I gave him the green light to call you."

Franklin and I talked about a few other things. He didn't know exactly when he was coming back to New Orleans, but said it probably would be soon. I thanked him again for everything he was doing for me before we finally hung up.

It was only afterward, when I had a chance to think about it, that I remembered Laurie told me that John Gant had located me through her. I never really did believe in coincidences.

Chapter 35

WITHIN A FEW days of my conversation with Franklin, John Gant came to the hotel to meet me. Usually people went to him, but in my case he made an exception. Albert and Bonnie felt it would be prudent to meet in the hotel's restaurant, as I expected. We made up a story about me having to stick around because of an audit. Gant bought it, and came down to see me. He wasn't what I expected.

The man who walked into the restaurant was a very average, humble man. A twinkle in his eyes, and disarming charm belied the titan he'd become. John was a slight, diminutive man. I thought he might have trouble maintaining his balance in a strong wind. His face was darkly tanned, in stark contrast to a full head of shocking, snow white hair. The only hint to who he was came from the large diamond in his right earlobe. He was dressed in blue jeans and a billowy, white cotton shirt, with sandals on his feet. I liked him from the moment we met, and he surprised me with a firm, youthful handshake.

We all sat down. I began, "I hope you don't mind that I invited my friends to join us for dinner."

"Of course not Peter. That was entirely your prerogative," his smile was infectious. "I'm pleased you could join us," he smiled across the table at Albert, Bonnie, and Laurie. His gaze lingered on Bonnie. "You look ravishing my dear. Please tell your mother and father how eternally grateful us mere mortals are that they brought such a lovely creature into this world."

As Bonnie smiled demurely, I could swear she blushed. John, albeit somewhat clichéd, had the charisma to pull this off. If someone like me paid her such a compliment, Bonnie might have considered it contrived. Not John Gant; one could tell immediately he meant every word.

"Mr. Gant, if I were a few years older, and you a couple years younger, I could definitely see us meeting somewhere in the middle," Bonnie gave it right back to him.

"It's John. Everyone please call me John. I've never been comfortable with this Mr. thing." He turned back to Bonnie, "I'm afraid my wife would probably take issue with you on that one. Deanne, the love of my life, happens to be thirty-two years old. When you get to the point I'm at in life, you stop counting everything except your blessings, one of which is Deanne. She couldn't be with us tonight, she had business to attend to back in California. She is the President of a record label we own out there. It keeps her very busy."

"You should have brought her with you," I suggested. "She might have appreciated the break."

"There's absolutely no chance Peter. She loves her work," he explained. "It would take a stick of dynamite to pry her loose from it."

"Deanne must be very talented," Bonnie said.

"She's definitely that," John concurred. He elaborated, "She is truly gifted, and very smart. Deanne received her MBA from Brown University. We met at a party in Bel Air about five years ago. To tell you the truth, I never thought she would be interested in me. Fortunately, I turned out to be wrong. We talked and realized that even with the age gap we had so much in common. Every time I went to California we spent quality time together. I'm forever grateful to the Pfizer drug company that brought us all Viagra," he confided with disarming honesty. "Don't look so stunned," he good-naturedly chided Albert and myself. "Give it some time. Sooner or later, you'll be grateful to them as well."

We all chuckled. The waiter I'd chosen to serve us arrived and took our drink orders. When John ordered a bottle of forty-year-old Taylor Fladgate port I knew it was going to be an interesting evening.

Chapter 36

WE WERE HALFWAY through a wonderful Creole-themed dinner, and most of the bottle of port, when John made an unexpected announcement. By this time, every one of us had a bit of a buzz on. Even Albert and Bonnie were far more relaxed than I had ever seen them. It was understandable, and certainly forgivable. We had been through a stressful time these last couple of months. Constantly vigilant, always on edge.

"A toast," John held up his glass. Another bottle of port had appeared seemingly from nowhere. The headwaiter was skillful and unobtrusive. We raised our glasses, not having the slightest notion of what was coming next.

John announced, "We are going to have a party." The tinkle of glasses wafted across the table, like wind chimes in a soft breeze.

"Actually, it's a concert," John elaborated. "Well, actually it's a bit of both. And you, Peter," he looked directly into my eyes, "will be the star attraction. You've already been in The Guitar Works, so you know it's a fairly large space. We planned on moving some of the displays around to make room for a sizeable dance floor. We were even going to build a stage for you and do it up right," he smiled broadly.

I glanced at Albert and Bonnie. They were completely sober now, listening to a plan that for them would translate into a security nightmare.

"We were going to," John continued. "Until I spoke with your manager and he suggested a far more grandiose location. Franklin has always had a flair for the dramatic."

"Mr. Gant," he raised his eyebrows when I spoke his name, correcting me. "All right, John then," I started over. "You barely know me. You've heard me play guitar, a few riffs, for a minute or two at the most. Suddenly you want me to play a concert? I'm sorry, but there's something not right about this whole thing. Don't get me wrong, I appreciate your enthusiasm. I'm happy you liked what you heard. But, and I hope you don't get offended by what I'm about to say," I paused to drive home my next point, "I think you all should maybe rethink this. Ah hell, why am I mincing words? I think you're batshit crazy, or you're trying to pull some kind of con here. No offense intended," I repeated.

The smile across John's face faded. But, to my

surprise, it had not been replaced by anything close to anger. Instead he appeared confused. I followed his line of sight as his gaze shifted in the direction of Laurie.

"Did I miss something?" Now I was perplexed. "Could someone please tell me what's going on?"

Laurie said, "How long do you think you were playing the guitar on that first day?"

"Like I said, I was jamming for two or three minutes. I was trying it out. You were there, you heard me. Why? What's this about?"

"Peter," John quietly got my attention. "Both of us were there. I was in the back, so I guess you never saw me. You played that instrument – and sang – for well over an hour. No one wanted you to stop. Everyone there agreed they had not heard someone with that caliber of talent in decades."

I looked at them both to see if they were serious. I chuckled uncomfortably. "That isn't what happened," I stated. "I tried out that guitar for a couple of minutes at the most."

Laurie ventured a possible explanation. "Did you smoke pot before you walked into the store? It can be really potent down here, and cause hallucinations. An hour can seem like a few minutes."

"Maybe," I acknowledged. "But I wasn't smoking any dope. I was perfectly straight when I tried out that guitar. And I know for a fact I only played for a minute or two. I also know I never did any singing. I don't sing, I can't sing, I have a lousy voice."

"You have an extraordinarily unique voice my boy. Those people in the store craved it like an addictive drug. Didn't you hear them screaming for more?"

I remembered the applause, and the cheers.

Laurie said, "You had to have been playing for far more than a few minutes. Think about it." She pointed out the obvious, "When you first sat down and plugged in the guitar…"

"I remember I got feedback."

"That's right. Do you remember how many people were there?" she asked.

"You mean where they had the guitar display set up?"

"Yes."

"I don't know," I fought to recall. "I remember that other guy, the older guy. He played for a while. There was a small group of people standing around listening to him. There might have been ten of them," I guessed.

"How many would you say were listening to you when you began to play the Strat?" asked Laurie.

I sat in stunned silence. Finally I heard my own voice as if from a distance. "There was you Laurie. Only you."

John asked, "How many would you say were there when you finished? How many were cheering at the top of their lungs, screaming for you to continue playing?"

"Over fifty," I whispered, not wanting to believe my own recollection.

"Everyone who was in the store came over to hear you," John declared. "I've never seen anything like it before, except maybe that one time," he mused more to himself than the rest of us.

"When was that?" I asked.

"It was a long time ago. He was just a kid back then. His name is Steven Tyler."

I shook my head slowly from side to side. "Aerosmith Steven Tyler?"

"He is now," John confirmed for me. "By the way, he thought his voice sucked too."

Chapter 37

"SOMETIMES THEY CALL it the zone," Albert was talking now. "It isn't as uncommon as you might think."

"What, is that like Michael Jordan scoring sixty points for the Bulls?" I asked. I was being flippant, but I had to admit he might be onto something.

"Sort of," said Albert. "That's one way of looking at it, an intense, focused concentration."

"Isn't that what I experienced?" I asked, not believing I was actually going along with what he was saying. It beat my other train of thought though; that I was as crazy as I had accused them of being only moments ago.

"Partly, yes, but in your situation there was also an element of time distortion. I think it's more like what people have experienced in a car accident."

I immediately thought of the fiery Greyhound bus wreck.

"Many people experience slow motion. As if things that played out over the course of seconds slowed down, and took minutes instead," said Albert.

"But this was the opposite of that," I interjected.

"It was more like an hour was shrunk into a minute or two."

"Fair enough," Albert agreed. "But tell me one thing in this universe that doesn't have some kind of polar opposite."

"So what you're…" I began slowly.

"You were playing the guitar Peter. You were there," Albert pointed out. "I wasn't, I'm only thinking out loud."

"And I'm absolutely delighted," chimed in John, "I happened to be there to see it. Were it not so," he smiled and raised a half empty glass poured from the latest bottle of port, "We would not be here enjoying each other's company. So Peter, can you simply relax and enjoy the moment? The explanation is a relatively simple one. Let us all accept it and move forward. We have new worlds to conquer, as they say."

I was dubious, but what other plausible explanation could there be for what happened? John, and especially Laurie, had to be right. After all, they were there. I just found it very difficult to wrap my brain around the idea that I missed over an hour of my life inside of some kind of weird, self-induced trance. Particularly since nothing like it had ever happened to me before.

John continued to speak. "Franklin suggested

we have the concert here, at the Marigold, instead of the music store. I thought it was a stroke of genius on his part."

"But there isn't enough space," Bonnie probably objected for reasons of security.

"Ah, but there is," John politely countered. "Right outside those doors over there." He pointed toward the French doors at the back of the restaurant that led to the courtyard. I could see the fountain at the far end of the open yard, in front of the cottage.

I saw immediately what Franklin envisioned. The courtyard would be perfect. A temporary stage could be constructed directly in front of the fountain. The marble floor in front of it would suffice as a dance floor. Tables and chairs could be placed all around. We could accommodate five hundred people or more; not counting guests who would be watching and partying from their balconies all along the perimeter of the courtyard. Of course, how the hell we would sell five hundred tickets for an unknown musician was a question for the ages.

As if reading my mind, John said, "Franklin figures we can cram at least five or six hundred people out there. He said we'd use the restaurant for the overflow. Selling out won't be a problem, we both know a lot of interesting people, mostly industry types. We'll get a buzz going. I only ask one thing in return, and that is you sign with us."

"Sign with you?" I was incredulous.

"Yes. Don't worry," he waved it off. "It would of course need your final approval, but Franklin has already agreed to it. We're just haggling over the numbers," he said. "You have three months to put together a band and enough material for the record. From what I heard a couple months ago in the store, that shouldn't be a problem. I didn't recognize any of the songs you played, so I'm assuming you wrote them. It goes without saying you'll retain all publishing rights to your own material. But, now I may be overstepping my bounds. Those details will be worked out between you and Franklin. He and I will turn the lawyers loose to wrap up the details after everything is agreed upon."

My head had been spinning for a while. I felt dizzy, like I might even throw up again. The restaurant was a lot warmer than when I'd first sat down. My legs began to feel as if ants were crawling all over them. I reached down and scratched my calves. I got no relief, it seemed like the itching only got worse.

Chapter 38

"IT'S A LONG way from St. Augustine," she purred softly beside me, her perfect breasts exposed in the soft, pale moonlight through the windows of the cottage. The surreal light made her look like a porcelain doll. Our bedroom, the comfortable thought wafted through me.

"We're a hell of a long way from the north woods of Memphis too."

"How did we get here?"

"I caught a bus," I grinned as she playfully poked me in the ribs.

"You know what I mean," she spoke into my neck. I noticed a tiny spider crawling across the ceiling. His was an upside down world, I mused. I wondered if the spider was aware we shared its world.

"Do you believe in destiny?"

I thought about it, unsure how to respond to what had suddenly become a philosophical discussion. "No," I said softly, but with enormous conviction. "I don't believe everything we do, every decision we make, has been decided before we make the choice." I rolled onto my side and looked into Laurie's eyes. Soft, petal-like tears rolled down her cheeks. I drew her closer to me.

"What's the matter baby? Did I say something wrong?"

"I don't want to lose you."

"Who said I was going anywhere? Where's this coming from?" I stroked locks of her hair. They felt like silk to my touch.

"Something is coming at us. It's angry, and out of control. It's out there, like a dark and monstrous hurricane rushing to shore. I'm scared."

I pulled her into me, burying her head into my chest. "I'll look after both of us. I promise you I won't let anything bad happen. I love you, and I always will."

"I know," she said. "It's just that sometimes things happen no matter how much we want them to be different."

I felt my heart break a little. "What we do is up to us. We can choose to love, or we can fill our hearts with hate. There's a lot of pain in this world, but we don't have to let it change us for the worse, like an open wound. When things are at their worst, that's when hope and love shine the brightest."

"Like Venus just before the dawn," she whispered.

I listened as her breathing became more shallow and regular. She finally fell asleep in my arms. Despite what I told her, I knew she was right. Something was coming. I gritted my teeth as I felt its distant presence. Well, come on then, I thought to myself, I'm ready and waiting.

Chapter 39

"IT'S A LOT of work if we want to pull this thing off," I admitted. "We didn't give ourselves a whole lot of time."

"You already have the songs written. I would think that's the hardest part." Franklin cajoled me. "How are the guys doing?" He was referring to the musicians we put together to form the band.

"They're really quite good," I was enthusiastic about the three members we'd chosen a month ago. "I'm pleasantly surprised at how quickly they're learning the new material. Especially Benjamin. I thought he was too young when I first met him. He's nineteen, but he plays bass like a seasoned pro. Wallace and Ben work real well together," I was referring to our drummer now. "The bed tracks are solid. There's nothing to worry about there."

"How about Napoleon?" asked Franklin.

"Bonaparte," I laughed. "That's what we call him because he's so short."

"He must love you for that," Franklin chuckled with me.

"He doesn't seem to mind, I think he likes his new nickname." At thirty-one he was the oldest, and a virtuoso on the keyboards. "Anna, Rita, and Evangelica are simply amazing." They were our backup singers. "We've got another six weeks," I breathed deeply. "With luck and no small amount of divine intervention, we should be ready."

"You'll be fine," he reassured me. "Has John been around?" He changed the subject.

"I haven't seen him in about a week," I replied.

"I'm sure he's busy marketing the hell out of you right now."

"I sure hope so," I confided my nervousness. "Five hundred warm bodies is a lot of people."

"Don't worry," Franklin was matter-of-fact. "By the time August seventh rolls around we'll have to turn away more than we let in. Just keep practicing. There's going to be nothing but heavyweights in attendance. Remember, you're slated for the cross-country tour a week and a half after the concert," he reminded me.

"Thanks, I'd almost forgotten," I rolled my eyes.

"You'll be fine," he said again. "Everyone is gonna love you. Peter Jackson and the Gems," he mused. "The name works."

"Thanks, the band thinks so too." I hesitated

before I asked him, "Have you heard anything?" He knew immediately what I was referring to.

"Murmurs," he admitted. "These kids are fucking good. They're not only ruthless, but the sons of bitches have the patience of Job. I'm not gonna lie to you, they must know about the concert. Half the French Quarter knows about it by now. If they're looking to do anything, we think they might try it that night."

"You mean that's when they'll try and kill me," I said flatly.

"Nobody is going to kill anybody at the concert," I couldn't help but notice the steel in Franklin's tone. The hotel was his backyard.

"Laurie is afraid she's going to lose me." I told him about the conversation we had two nights ago. "She's really scared, I suppose not knowing is the worst."

I heard Franklin's breathing change.

"Let me guess, those murmurs you mentioned earlier. They aren't rumors are they?"

"No, we got word from the street. Unfortunately, the threat is credible," he confirmed for the first time since this thing started. "I just heard from our sources this morning. They're not going to stop hunting for you," he explained.

"So, what then? We keep playing this game of

cat and mouse? What if they've decided to wait me out? Do you really expect me to just stay here forever? And what about this tour that's supposedly coming up this fall? I'll be out on stages across the country. I'll be a sitting duck."

Franklin said, "I think you underestimate our capabilities."

I said, "No, I don't. We're good, but we can't be everywhere at once. We've been on the defensive since day one. I'm tired of it, if I go down I want to do it in a fight, not cowering behind the walls of this hotel. Look, I truly appreciate everything you've done for me, but this is no longer acceptable to me. I guess I'm drawing the line. If it was only me, maybe I could live with it longer. But I'm not alone anymore, and I can't stand hearing Laurie crying herself to sleep at night because she's afraid of me taking a bullet."

I heard Franklin's sigh on the other end of the line. "I was afraid it might come to this," he admitted. Then he said something that surprised me. "I've been selfish Peter. I wanted to protect you from harm, but I have to confess I was guilty of looking after my own assets. I put myself ahead of you. I am truly sorry, and I hope you can forgive me. I should have known that in time the Marigold would become a prison to you."

I felt his sincerity. "There's nothing to forgive," I told him. "When you looked after your own interests, you were also taking care of mine. I got that; I didn't mind. The turning point was when Laurie began to cry herself to sleep. It tore my heart out. Did I know I was being selfish? I never would have thought so, but I was. When she cried like that, I had an epiphany.

"I've never had to think about anyone else before. I like the idea that for the first time in my life, I have someone more important than me. I would give my life for her. You know, when I was in that bus wreck, I was gonna leave that woman," I confided in him. "She meant nothing to me. And yet, I decided to risk my own life to save her. I never would have guessed I had that in me. But I can tell you, I'm very grateful to find out I did.

"We can't go on like this, we can't continue to allow fear to rule us. I was scared shitless in that bus. Somehow I found it in myself to rise above it. We have to go on the offensive and take it on. No more hiding behind walls; now they're going to feel the terror they want us to feel."

Franklin was all business. "I'm coming back there next week. Sit tight until then. I have a few ideas I thought I'd never have to consider. We'll talk, and then we'll all decide which way we want to go with this."

"I understand," I said.

Later in the evening, a little before ten o'clock, the phone rang. I thought it might be Laurie; she'd said earlier she might come over after work. I answered on the third ring. The Wedge's voice on the other end surprised me, and I said as much.

"This couldn't wait Peter. Are you sitting down?"

Chapter 40

IMMEDIATELY I FELT a shortness of breath. My body went cold, like plunging into the creek when I was a kid.

"You're in the bad books of some deadly dudes son," he jumped right in.

"Tell me something I don't already know Wedge. And by the way, how the hell are you?" If he was trying to scare me, it wasn't going to work. I'd had enough of that from everybody: Franklin, Bonnie and Albert, and the thugs outside the hotel. Now I was officially more pissed off than afraid.

"I'm fine," he snapped back. "It's you I'm worried about. I'm sorry for calling so late, but the guys we're dealing with on this thing don't exactly keep banker's hours. Some of the information I'd been waiting for came in tonight. I just finished reading it. Twice. I knew when we decided to dig deeper we might not like what we'd find, but it's far worse than I expected. You're in a great deal of danger son." Wedge didn't sound like his usual, affable self. He spoke quickly, with a quiver in his voice.

"I know they're bad dudes Wedge. Try to calm

down." It felt strange giving him advice, but I could tell he was more than a little rattled.

"All right. Hell, where do I start?"

"The beginning would be the place," I prompted him.

He blurted out, "You landed in a nest of rattlesnakes Peter. These sons of bitches are the worst of the worst. Every last one of them. I am not exaggerating either. Let me explain what's going on so you can understand how bad things really are.

"Everyone's familiar with Hurricane Katrina and its horrifying aftermath. It was utter chaos. No law and order to speak of, death everywhere, and no aid to be had. The Big Easy showed all of us how thin the veneer called civilization really is.

"Eventually they put people onto buses and shipped them to cities they figured could handle them." The Wedge continued, "It wasn't safe for anyone to stay there. The ones who wanted to stay, well, they also got on the buses. A dry Houston with a charged up debit card sounded a lot better than the alternative. But that was nothing compared to what was coming down the pike." The Wedge's voice quivered, "Because what was about to happen next was something right out of a horror film."

Chapter 41

"THE DISPLACED FAMILIES of New Orleans were dispersed into various major cities," Wedge continued. "It was a hard time for those folks. Truth be told, a lot of times they weren't welcome. The Big Easy has a certain reputation, some of it well deserved.

"You see, almost no one can afford to leave. Poverty forces them to stay. After a while the ghetto becomes an evil everyone has to learn to live with. They are largely ignored by the authorities. The police, who they should be able to turn to in difficult situations, become the enemy.

"The youth end up in gangs; some aspire to that kind of life. Their fellow thugs become a surrogate family. These were the children on those buses. They were traumatized and scared, but they couldn't show anyone else how they felt. Because being afraid is a weakness, and being weak oftentimes costs you your life.

"So the children became angry instead, and eventually became overwhelmed with confusion and despair. Finally, when nothing else made sense, the more resourceful of these children fled back to the only life they'd known.

"It started as a trickle at first. Word spread quickly though, and more of them went back to be embraced in the bosom they knew and trusted, the slums of the Big Easy."

"But, there was nothing there," I protested. "The city had been reduced to a toxic wasteland. How did they eat? Where did these kids sleep? Who looked after them?" I found The Wedge's story fascinating, and yet terrifying.

The Wedge heaved a deep sigh. "They went back to their homes," he said.

"You mean they moved back into those trashed houses?" I couldn't believe him. "There was no water, electricity, or plumbing." I was aghast. "How did they live?"

"Like animals," The Wedge said. "They ate food out of cans. By the time they arrived there was plenty of aid to go around. Everyone from FEMA to the Salvation Army was there."

"How did they protect themselves?" I asked.

Wedge said, "There was no one else living there, and those kids didn't need anyone's protection. They had firepower, and they absolutely knew how to use it."

"Are you trying to tell me that ten-year-old children had guns?" I was flabbergasted.

"Yes. They returned to New Orleans with all kinds of weapons. They found their way back, and they occupied and defended their territories from all comers."

"It's unbelievable," I said.

"A book called *Lord of the Flies* was once written."

"Who the hell was the Lord of the Flies?" I wondered out loud.

"The Lord of the Flies is the kid who ended up as the leader of the children of Katrina, the kid who got away with the most murders. Anyone who challenged him ended up dead. Sadly, as these children aged, they recruited more children."

The Wedge's voice shook. "You must leave New Orleans immediately Peter. The kid who became the Lord of the Flies is the same one who is at this moment hunting you. In the book they cut off a pig's head, and put a stake through its neck. The severed head symbolized the power the leader had over the other children. They called whoever held it aloft the Lord of the Flies. That kid came to decide who lived, and who was to be murdered."

Chapter 42

"SO YOU'RE TELLING me I got caught in the middle of a turf war between a couple of gangs trying to kill each other?"

"Yes. There are of course other gangs who roam the streets of New Orleans, but the ones you stepped between are the two most dominant players. They also happen to be the most violent," added The Wedge.

"I didn't step between them," I protested. "They literally drove into my life."

"Be that as it may, the leaders on both teams want you dead," said The Wedge.

"I'm no threat to them, whatsoever," I emphasized the last word to drive home my point.

"Unfortunately, they don't see it the same way." There was an ominous finality to the way The Wedge spoke that wasn't lost on me.

"I take it there's no way we can sit down with them and explain things?" I knew the question was futile, but I asked it anyway.

"There is no reasoning with these savages. They have a bloodlust uncommon even among their peers. I repeat, there is no negotiating here," he said.

"All right," I sighed with resignation.

The Wedge exhaled the breath he was holding, believing he'd finally gotten through to me. "When can you leave New Orleans?" he asked.

I understood, and appreciated the motive behind the question. I was his golden goose. We hadn't yet touched on how my case was moving along. We didn't really have to. It would happen on its own timetable. When it was finished, between the different settlements with Greyhound, Amtrak, and whatever would come from 'The cure,' Wedge and I were likely going to come into millions of dollars. It might take awhile, but in the end, we'd get paid.

"I'm not leaving," I said flatly.

I heard The Wedge groan. "But I thought you agreed," he protested.

"I said all right. That didn't mean I'm giving up, or giving in to these assholes. I'm sorry, but I can't do that. If I left, they would win."

"And you'd still be alive son. There is no shame in – "

"Cutting and running?" I interjected. "No, I suppose when it's all said and done most folks could live with it," I admitted.

"But you're not most folks."

"I think you know that by now," I agreed with him. "I've seen people do similar things. They find a way to live with it, but end up less than they could have been. There's a certain hollowness inside that follows them through life. I don't want to live that way Wedge."

He followed me, "You're not a coward."

"I don't know if that's really the right way to put it," I replied. "I don't think that all the people who won't, or don't, or can't face their fears are cowards. Maybe I'm the fool, and they're the wiser. I just know that, for me, I've to got to stay. There's something at play here that I'm coming to understand is bigger than me. It's bigger than all of us. Look at all the stuff that's been happening to me. Even you have to admit, with all the crazy shit you've seen, lately my life is anything but normal. In fact, these past few months I've felt like a character in a science fiction movie," I paused.

The Wedge mulled it over, and then said, "I can't disagree with you. You've made some pretty good points." He cleared his throat and said, "They'll kill you if they can son."

"I know," I said.

He surprised me with what he said next, "I'm a very rich man Peter. I used to work for the money, I still do. But lately it hasn't been the same as when I was younger. Back then I would have given…" he caught himself, thought for a moment, and then continued, "Back then I gave my soul for a case like the one I have with you right now. I put everything into winning. Now, all these years later, it doesn't mean that much to me anymore. Don't get me wrong, I still do a great job, but I regret some of the things I did and said to win back then. I understand when you say there's something larger than us at stake here. You're right, and I was not being entirely honest with myself about the reason I wanted you to leave. I want to thank you, and I hope you can forgive me. You're something very special. What they call an old soul. Stay, by all means, stay. And I will do whatever is in my power to help you. We'll take on these gangsters together. The good news is we are not alone. Do you remember I told you these thugs were more dangerous than any of us could imagine?" he asked.

I said, "I recall you saying something to that effect." I was amazed at how honest he'd been with me just now.

"As bad as your enemies are, it would appear you have some equally amazing friends."

Chapter 43

"YOU MEAN FRANKLIN and his friends?" I guessed.

"They are not who they would appear to be," The Wedge enlightened me.

"Well, that's just it," I confessed. "I don't have the slightest clue as to who they should be. Please tell me Franklin at least owns this hotel."

"That much is true. From there it gets a whole lot more interesting, believe me. The people you asked me to check on have a history, but not much of one. We can't find any birth or childhood information at all. Their adult lives are just as sketchy. Do a cursory background check on them, and on a superficial level everything fits. They have driver's licenses. There is a title to go along with Franklin's ownership claim to the hotel. They present a façade, but have no foundation. None of the information was fully substantive.

"Let me give you an example," Wedge offered. "Albert Sousa's records went back to him attending high school in Kyle, Texas. Inquiries on those records could not be provided. The high school was real enough, but it burned down the week Sousa left. On the night of his graduation dance. From all accounts most of his fellow classmates perished. By the way, a lightning strike was ruled as the cause of it all. We found that a little strange, but I could live with it. That was, until I started checking on the others.

"We traced Bonnie's background. We got as far back as four years. It led us to an orphanage just across the Texas border into Mexico, not too far from Cuidad Juárez. She'd been a volunteer there. When we went to check on the orphanage, it no longer existed."

"She was bullshitting whoever had those references," I guessed.

"I didn't say the orphanage never existed. At one time, it apparently did. That is until it was swallowed up in a turf war between a couple of the major drug cartels in the area. The six nuns who ran the place, the volunteers, and the twenty-seven children in their charge disappeared. Rumor has it they were rounded up, executed, and then burned and buried in a mass grave. There's no way to confirm it." There was a pause, and Wedge took a deep breath.

"The point is the backgrounds of every one of your newfound associates can be looked into, but only so far. The air of legitimacy is there, but it's as thin as the edge of a sharp knife. To a trained eye, it's downright spooky. What I can't find scares the hell out of me. All of them, John Gant included, can be traced back to some kind of grotesque event that conveniently destroyed past records."

"Even John Gant?" I was bewildered.

"Even him," said The Wedge. "Beyond about thirty years ago, the man doesn't exist. He lived in Brazil before coming to the United States. He had taken up residence upstairs in a hall routinely used for medium-sized concerts. His home doubled as an office. One night he crammed fifteen hundred people into the thousand-seat venue. The band was using pyrotechnics as part of their show. You can guess the rest. Exit doors had been locked, and there were only two front doors. Not enough for fifteen hundred by a long shot. Less than three hundred kids made it out alive. Half a city block burned before they got it under control. Gant left Brazil right after rumors of impending arrests. He comes back onto the radar two years later, in L.A., with what appears to be an inexhaustible bankroll. A few years after that, his good friend Franklin meets him at a concert Gant was promoting in New Orleans. Franklin provided security.

"All of them, including Franklin, have a

dodgy past that starts with a disaster. Where they miraculously escape, but most everyone around them dies," Wedge concluded.

"And they start brand new," I said, "without a scratch on them." An eerie feeling of déjà vu came over me.

"I don't believe in those kinds of coincidences Peter. One, maybe. But this many? There's no way. And then they all end up together in the same place," Wedge said with a slight tremor in his voice.

"There has to be more," I said. "You have to dig deeper. We need to find out more about these people." Then I thought of something. "They're ex-military!" I was suddenly excited. "CIA or some such shit. They sure as hell aren't in the witness protection program. Their profiles are way too high for that. Albert and Bonnie have a fierce, abiding loyalty to Franklin. It's almost as if they are used to taking his orders. You couple this with the complete absence of a reasonable history, and you have ex-military," I repeated. "It's the one thing that could make sense of it all. The only thing I don't get is why they're all here in New Orleans. It would certainly explain how they all know each other, though. What else could account for what we know – and don't know – about them?" I questioned.

The Wedge eased into my theory, "You may have something there." I could tell he wasn't convinced, but measuring what I'd said. "I have to admit it would explain a few things. It hadn't really occurred to me to look in that direction," he admitted. "But now…" he trailed off, lost in his own thoughts.

"Do you know anyone who could look into it?" I asked.

"Maybe I do," he hesitated.

I prompted him, "Well, maybe we should." Then I paused, somewhat puzzled. The Wedge was never this tentative.

"Peter, sometimes – people, very dangerous people – don't want you to know who they are, or were, for some very good reasons. Sometimes the world is a whole lot better off if you leave the past buried."

I listened carefully to his words, I began to believe The Wedge wasn't telling me the whole truth; either that or he was drop dead terrified.

Chapter 44

"WHAT ARE YOU not telling me?" The words slid between my lips like a cottonmouth's tongue tasting the air for the scent of breakfast. "Why are you so frightened by all this?" I blurted out.

"I am frightened," his immediate confession surprised me. "But not by anything I left out. I'm old enough to be your grandfather. Over the years I've seen just about everything. I defended serial murderers, and listened to their stories. In every case, these killers had regrets of some kind or another. Except, there was one who had absolutely no remorse. By his own admission he murdered over a hundred people. His name was Billy Anvil, and he knew he was different from the rest of those killers. I was appointed by the Court to defend him, because he was, of course, indigent and couldn't afford a lawyer. In the course of defending him, I had occasion to ask Mr. Anvil why, after killing his fellow human beings, why was it that he never once felt regret? I supposed he had no conscience. Psychiatrists sometimes call people like Billy Anvil psychopaths, or sociopaths

– catch-all words to explain the atrocities they commit. In Billy's case, none of those descriptions seemed to fit though.

"As far as I could tell, he felt bad about killing all those folks."

"I thought you said he had no regrets," I remembered.

"He did not," The Wedge reiterated. "Empathy and remorse can be two entirely separate matters, as different as day is from night."

I shook my head, the receiver pressed hard against the side of my face. "I don't get it. How could he murder all those people with no regrets, and then feel sorry for them? That makes no sense at all," I said.

He sighed into the receiver. "Billy saw himself as a tool," he tried to explain.

"One of Satan's nasty helpers," I supposed.

"No," The Wedge immediately corrected me. "Billy never confessed to that. He flat-out stated that he neither believed in God, or the devil. He didn't care about such things. He did say some of his victims must have believed because he saw many things in their eyes just before he killed them: fear, loathing, anger, sadness, resignation, and even hope. He always saw something frozen in their vacant stares. He did admit to me though, that on one occasion he observed something that scared the hell out of him. It bothered him until the day he was executed. He saw it in the eyes of one of his female victims. As it would turn out, his last victim."

I felt the hair on the back of my neck stand up. "What did he see?" My voice came out cracked and hoarse.

"He didn't even know the reason he'd been paid to kill her," The Wedge's voice sounded far-off, like he was speaking to me from the end of a tunnel.

"She was the only victim he'd ever physically described to me. The woman he killed was middle-aged, blonde, and of a slight build. Her eyes haunted him until the moment he died. He turned to me while strapped to the gurney, just before he took the needle. It was the only time I ever saw Billy Anvil smile," he remembered.

"What did he see in her eyes Wedge?" I demanded. I suddenly felt my legs begin to itch. At the same time, a cold heaviness ran through my veins, like I'd been injected with frozen mercury.

"He saw his own reflection Peter. It was the only time that ever happened."

Chapter 45

"DID BILLY KILL all those people for money?" I asked. He had alluded to it earlier in our conversation.

"Some," Wedge confirmed. He didn't sound so distant now. I also noticed the chill I'd felt had eased off a bit, and my legs didn't itch so badly anymore.

"When he needed the money, but it seemed to me that for him money was a nuisance. He only needed it so he could kill again. He did mention he was paid to do his job to balance the scales, that he'd been sent to do that. I asked him what he meant, and he would just stare off into space in silence. Occasionally he would mutter something about tools, how they'd get rusty and old if you didn't use them properly, and then maintain them afterwards." The Wedge paused, then continued in a subdued tone.

"But that smile. The last one, the only one. I'll never forget his face. It wasn't a happy smile. It was more like a look of contentment. Like he'd finally finished his job, and now he could move on to whatever he felt was next."

"You said that woman was his last victim," I reminded him. "Why was she the last?"

"She was like a signal to him that it was over. He turned himself in right after he killed her, and confessed to everything. The authorities were puzzled, to say the least. They knew Billy could have gone on killing for a long time. As far as they were concerned, he was clever enough to never get caught," noted The Wedge.

"He never said why he called it quits, or why he turned himself in? Even though he knew he was basically committing suicide by doing so?" I found the entire tale incredible.

"His real reasons, if there were any, he took to his grave. But you can be certain everything he did after that last kill had everything to do with that woman, and what he saw in her eyes as he was taking her life," he said.

"He told you he saw his reflection," I said.

"Like he was staring at his soul in a mirror, I think were his exact words."

"You'll have to excuse me, but I just don't know why you're telling me all this. What does Billy Anvil have to do with these folks I've met in New Orleans?" I wasn't sure if I really wanted an answer. I had a queasy, sick feeling in the pit of my stomach, but I knew there was a point to all of what The Wedge was telling me.

"I guess it's what I can't see that scares me the most. I never understood what drove Billy, just like I can't pin down your new friends. I'm worried they have no regrets, and could shut down like Billy did. He paid with his life for what he did. I don't want you to pay for the actions of others with yours."

Chapter 46

"WE'LL KEEP LOOKING," The Wedge assured me. "I'll reach out to my contacts in the military. It's an interesting angle. Don't hold your breath, though. Someone may have wanted them gone. Like they never were, gone. They might not take too kindly to someone looking to open doors long-ago sealed."

"Do what you can," I encouraged him. "You never know what you might find when you go looking. Until we find out who they are, and where they came from, I won't trust any of them," I added. "What about my mother, and the blonde-haired lady? Have you learned anything new?"

"The blonde-haired lady never appeared on the Greyhound's passenger manifest," he sounded disappointed.

"What about cameras in the bus station?" I asked.

"Greyhound won't release the films until we get a court order," The Wedge informed me. "We need a compelling reason, which I believe we have. But, like everything legal, it's going to take some time. They have an obligation to preserve the footage, sooner or later we'll get those tapes. Then we'll take a look at what's on them."

"How do you know the woman wasn't on the manifest?" I was curious. "I mean, I never did know her name." I wondered how Wedge could look for someone without knowing who she was.

"We're getting a lot of information from different sources right now. I've commandeered a junior partner's office for your case alone. We've already amassed volumes of material. We have both the Greyhound's manifest, and the County Coroner's report of the deceased. I personally cross-referenced the two lists. I'm afraid we found no one matching the description of the woman you rescued from the wreck. That doesn't mean she doesn't exist, though. There are ways people can sneak onto buses undetected. We'll find her, it's only a matter of time. As for your mother," he paused, "She, and other members of your immediate family for that matter, are fast becoming a puzzle wrapped up in an enigma."

"I don't understand. Have you found her yet? By the way, the phone at the house has never been turned back on," I told him.

"I know that," The Wedge said with a hint of exasperation. "There's more."

"That doesn't sound good."

"Did your mother ever speak to you about moving?" he asked.

"No. Absolutely not. That house has been in our family for three generations. We would never sell it. Why?" I was suddenly anxious.

"For now, I'm not having much luck locating her," he said.

"What do you mean?" I was perplexed.

"Linda Lou does not live at the address you gave me."

I felt the hair stand up on the back of my neck. "You mean she moved?" I couldn't see it happening. It wasn't like her to just pack up and leave without at least trying to get in touch with me. If she'd left, I realized she was probably with Senior. Soon enough they would straighten things out, then everything could get back to normal.

The Wedge spoke haltingly, "I had my guy do a search down at the Land Titles Office in Memphis."

"What did you do that for?" I was a little put off. There was no reason for it, and I wondered why he'd done it.

"There was no sign at the house that anyone has lived there for a long time," Wedge pressed on. "The grass is overgrown, and the place has gone to weeds. Some of the windows are smashed in as well. Is there a chance you could have given me the wrong address?"

I thought about it. Maybe he had written down the wrong numbers. I told him the address again.

"That's the house we checked," he confirmed. "There was no sign it's been occupied in recent months," he said again.

"Maybe your guy went to the wrong house. Or maybe he just said he went there." None of what I was hearing made any sense. There had to be a logical explanation. "Maybe she and Senior wanted it to look that way," I volunteered.

"Perhaps. We'll take another look at it. With your permission, I'll ask my guy to go inside this time," he placated me.

"Have him do that," I agreed. "I'm sure he'll find some answers. She may have left a few days after I got here. It would explain why the yard is full of weeds," I said. "Some kids could have thrown rocks through the windows."

"It's possible. We'll look at it again," he promised me.

"Peter, you remember I told you there was more?"

"Yeah, I remember."

"When my guy ran the title, he found a bank owns it," he said.

"That's right," I said. "I think Bank of America holds the mortgage."

"They own the title, that's true," he hesitated. Then he went on, "Your family's name never appeared on that title. I'm afraid no one by the name of Jackson, or your mother's maiden name, ever owned the house at that address. Not now, not ever. Are you certain you've given me the right address?" he asked again.

"I'm certain Wedge. One hundred percent." My heart was pounding like a hammer in my chest. It felt like ice had just replaced the blood in my veins.

Chapter 47

TWO DAYS LATER Laurie joined me in the cottage for lunch. Living on my own for the past few months, I had learned to cook, and I was getting pretty good at it.

"This is delicious," Laurie beamed at me across the small dining room table.

"Thank you," I smiled back. Mac and cheese was not rocket science, but Laurie seemed to enjoy it. Throw in a nice bottle of red, and who knew where things might end up?

As if reading my mind, she said, "I have the afternoon off."

"Is John Gant in town?" I asked nonchalantly.

"I think he's in New York," she shook her head.

"No doubt he's hooking up with Franklin then," I guessed. My tone was flat.

Laurie eyed me across the top of her wine glass. She drank more of it than usual, then set the rest back down.

"I hope there's no problem with us."

"Is it that obvious?" She could see right through me.

"You haven't touched your wine," she observed, "and you've been talking at me since the moment I walked in. Yes, it's that obvious. What's wrong?"

I set my fork down beside my plate; I hadn't been able to eat much of anything since my conversation with The Wedge two nights ago.

"Are you worried about the concert?" she asked.

"No. Not really. It's the one thing I'm looking forward to. I'm a little nervous," I admitted. "Who wouldn't be? But I'm also confident. The band is incredibly professional, and we're getting tighter each time we play. There's something going on that's very special. I can't put it into words, no one can, but we can all feel it."

"So what is it?"

"On Sunday night I had a conversation with my lawyer."

"The guy from Jackson, The Wedge," Laurie said. "He's handling the lawsuits from the crash."

I nodded. "He's doing some other stuff for me as well. He's trying to locate my family up in Memphis."

Laurie's brow furrowed slightly into a question mark. "I wasn't aware they were missing."

"Linda Lou's phone went dead right after the accident," I told her for the first time. "I didn't figure it was a big deal. The Wedge sent someone out to our house to have a look. The guy told The Wedge it didn't seem like anyone had been living there for quite a while. So they checked the county records, and they show we never owned the property. Someone obviously changed them, but why?" I couldn't figure it out.

Laurie said, "Maybe it's something far simpler. Those computers – "

"It's not their computers," I cut her off, wishing she was right. "Somebody altered the Land Title's records to show my family never owned our house. The Wedge is checking into it. He'll find out what happened, and who is responsible. But why the hell would anyone do that? Our house is in the middle of nowhere on the outskirts of Memphis! It isn't worth enough that anyone would ever bother with it. And Linda Lou is gone without a trace. This whole thing is getting creepier by the minute," I stated emphatically.

"What's going on?" asked Laurie. She was as bewildered as I was.

"If I knew the answer to that question, I'd know where my family is right now," I said. "Wedge spooked the hell out of me on Sunday. He told me this story about a serial murderer named Billy Anvil who killed over a hundred different people. I don't know if he was trying to warn me of the possibility that my family has been wiped out, or what? I certainly hope not. But something he told me about this Anvil guy shook me to my core. It was something straight out of The Twilight Zone."

"What did he say?" Laurie's jaw was hanging open.

"Billy Anvil stopped his killing spree right after he murdered a woman in whose eyes he saw his own reflection. He turned himself in to the authorities. But, get this," I spoke in a hushed tone, "The victim Billy described to The Wedge was a dead ringer for the blonde-haired woman."

"That's a bizarre coincidence," she admitted.

I remained silent for a moment, thinking about what she'd just said. Then I replied, "If only I believed in coincidences, but I'm afraid it's gone too far for that."

A second later there was a loud pounding on the front door of the cottage. It sounded like the hollow, muted throbbing of a gigantic heart.

Chapter 48

"DON'T WORRY," I said, getting up. "I know who it is." Even still, I checked through the peephole before opening the front door. I invited Albert and Bonnie inside, and offered them a seat on the sofa. I returned to the kitchen's small table, and saw the surprised look written across Laurie's face. If she'd had other, more carnal plans for the afternoon, they vanished with the entrance of the two assassins.

"If you're still hungry…" I began.

She wore an expression of consternation. "I've lost my appetite," she stated flatly.

I picked up our glasses, and moved my head in the direction of the living room where Bonnie and Albert sat. "C'mon. This involves you as much as anyone."

Laurie remained silent as she followed me onto the couch opposite my two other guests.

"Thanks for coming." I sat down, and looked at Bonnie and Albert.

"It's always a pleasure Peter." Bonnie's smile

appeared genuine. Albert nodded, but said nothing.

"Would either of you like something to drink? Perhaps something to eat?" I offered. I could see by their body language that they were puzzled. I had never invited them to the cottage. Before now we always met in their second floor rooms for private conversations.

"Thank you, no," Albert declined for both of them. "We took an early lunch, and neither of us drink alcohol before dinner."

"You don't know what you're missing," I said. "All right, let's begin," I dispensed with the small talk. "I called this meeting to discuss the new plan."

They looked at each other. Bonnie said, "I'm afraid we're not aware of any new plan." I noticed a slight waver in her voice. Albert stared at me intently. I knew this was going to be an interesting meeting, one no one anticipated.

Albert said, "Do you think it wise to discuss the confidential affairs surrounding our stay here?" his eyes narrowed slightly. I could tell he'd been caught off guard.

"What? Oh you mean you're not sure we should be discussing my future in front of the woman I love?" I asked in mock surprise.

He acquiesced with a simple shrug.

"She knows everything," I assured him.

"I figured as much," said Albert in a fairly subtle, yet obvious reprimand.

"I'm not here to fight over this with either of you. Or Franklin, for that matter. I've made a decision.

"I'm tired of this," I continued. "I can't do it anymore."

"Your music?" Bonnie sounded perplexed.

I shook my head. "My music is how I've kept my sanity these last few months. Aside from Laurie, it's the only thing since I left Memphis that makes any sense to me." Laurie moved a little closer on the couch, and found my hand. She squeezed it reassuringly, in a silent vote of confidence. She had my back, and right now it was damn good to know I wasn't alone in this affair. I squeezed her hand in return to let her know it.

"I feel like I'm in a prison," I complained. "Don't get me wrong, both of you have been great. We've all managed quite well under some very difficult circumstances, but this isn't working for me. I can't hide out like this anymore. No, let me correct that statement. I won't do it anymore. Tomorrow I'm going for a walk in the French Quarter, I'm going to start living my life again."

"I don't think that's a very good idea," said Albert. It almost sounded like a threat.

I shrugged and said, "You might be right, but I'm doing it anyway. And then I'm going to do it again the next day, and the day after that. Look," I stared directly into his eyes, "I know you guys are here to protect me, but I don't think hiding out in Franklin's hotel is really accomplishing anything." I looked from Albert to Bonnie. "I don't think the gangsters are stupid enough to come in here after me. I think they've decided to wait until I come out." I gestured beyond the walls of the cottage. "So my plan is to bait them. With me." Laurie squeezed my hand again, only this time it was an involuntary twitch brought on by what she knew would be a very dangerous course of action.

"I'm going to have to leave here anyway. We're going on tour after the gig in the courtyard. Don't tell me someone who wants to couldn't conceal a weapon and bring it inside one of those venues. It would be a simple matter of going to the front of the stage. A kid could fire off a few rounds before anyone even knew what was happening. In the ensuing bedlam, who knows? He might even get away with it." I drove home my point.

"Your plan won't work," Albert spoke with authority. "It will probably get you killed, and put all of us at risk. We don't have the manpower to watch for the enemy as you walk through these streets."

"Then get more men," I said in a flat tone as I stared him down. "With or without your help, I'm going for a walk. I'll take my chances."

"You're a stubborn man Peter," he replied.

"It got me this far, didn't it?" I smiled.

Albert shook his head in resignation. He knew full well he would accommodate my decision.

Chapter 49

"GIVE US A couple of days to prepare," he asked. "At least then we might be able to think of something to flush them out into the open. If we can get them to make a mistake, it might even give us a fighting chance."

I nodded. "I can wait, but this can't be a stall," I admonished him.

Albert scowled at me. "Give me some credit. We are professionals, and the last time I checked you're still alive."

"I know you're good at your job, but I don't know who you really are Albert. Apparently not many folks do. You and Bonnie have covered your tracks well." I noticed his eyebrows raise ever so slightly. I guess he hadn't considered I might check on them, and must be wondering how much I knew. For now I'd keep him guessing, even though I didn't know much more than I was saying.

Bonnie interceded, "As you have from time to time reminded us, we are not enemies Peter. I'm sorry if you feel we are in some way responsible for your exile. If you insist on this plan of yours, then it must be accommodated. We are simply here to help keep you from being harmed. Please," she implored me, "give us the time we need. Only then can we adequately protect you. Please be flexible."

Hers was the voice of reason. "Of course, I'm sorry. You're right, we need to be careful. It's just that I'm going crazy holed up in this place."

Laurie lightened things up when she said, "You have to admit it's been great for the music. You've gotten a lot of practice Peter."

I looked sideways at her, at her adoring smile, and then back at Albert and Bonnie. I suddenly saw humor in our situation, and I laughed. It was infectious, and the others joined, and together we briefly escaped the seriousness of it all.

I said to Albert, "Take as much time as you need. I'll wait for your permission to go for my walk, but please try not to make me wait too long," I couldn't help but give it one last lament.

Albert and Bonnie were still smiling. He said, "You have my word on it." He rose to his feet, Bonnie followed suit. "We'll go to work on it immediately. I'll make a few calls, and get back to you no later than lunchtime tomorrow. Is that fast enough for you?"

"Now you're making me feel like an asshole."

"Have you ever considered that you might actually be one?" Albert asked with mock seriousness.

I said, "Well if I am, then I guess I'm in good company."

Chapter 50

LAURIE AND I showed them out. When we were alone, and once again sipping wine on the couch, Laurie said, "I'm not happy."

"Yes, you are," I accused her, smiling. "But you are concerned. I would be worried about you if you weren't."

There was a thumping on the front door, and we both looked up.

"They must have forgotten something," Laurie said.

"I'll find out what," I said, getting up from the couch. I opened the door. Instead of finding Albert and Bonnie, two tradespersons stood in the outside alcove. The one in front held onto a solid-looking toolbox of some kind.

"You must be Peter Jackson," the same one stated, taking off his hat in a show of respect. Both of them were black, and close in age to myself.

"I'm Anthony, and this is Coretta," he didn't wait for me to identify myself. "You've probably seen me or some of my crew working in the hotel. We're retrofitting the connections in the electrical terminals, replacing the copper with aluminum. Franklin told me you were staying back here," he explained.

I looked closer at the person behind him, and saw I'd been mistaken in thinking she was a male. "Hi," Coretta smiled as she removed her own hat.

"We can come back if it isn't a convenient time for you."

I glanced over my shoulder. Laurie was already getting up from the couch. I went to her and offered my hand. I led her to the door, and whispered in her ear, "I'm sorry."

She gave me a queer look and said, "I'll call you later." As she left I stepped back to allow the workers to enter.

"It's fine. C'mon in. Franklin never said anything to me about you guys doing work in here though."

Anthony stepped halfway over the threshold, his expression suddenly serious. "We can come back," he repeated. "I don't exactly know when. It's kind of busy, what with the new code enforcement and all."

"No, no. That's okay. My girlfriend was just leaving."

"Only if you're sure now," he smiled again.

"I'm sure. Who knows when you'll get another shot at it, right? Franklin wouldn't be happy if he found out you were here, and I turned you away."

"Well, that'd be between the two of you now, wouldn't it?" he chuckled good-naturedly.

"C'mon in," I invited them in again.

"Thanks. We'll start in the kitchen and work our way through the house to the bedrooms," said Anthony.

"If you or Coretta get thirsty there's some cold drinks in the fridge. Feel free to help yourself. If you need anything else, let me know," I said.

They were already in the kitchen. Anthony unbuckled his tool belt. He set it onto the countertop that separated the kitchen from where I stood in the living room. He grabbed a screwdriver from one of the loops on the belt, and immediately set to work on the first outlet. Coretta, I noticed, cast a glance my way. She saw I was watching, and smiled. I had caught her off-guard. She began to fidget in her own toolbox.

Without looking up, still working on the electrical junction box near the countertop, Anthony said, "Are you some kind of musician? I couldn't help but notice some of the equipment," he looked across the top of the bar to see if I'd heard him.

"I play a little guitar," I engaged him. I saw that Coretta was out of sight, just below the countertop near where Anthony stood.

"That's nice," Anthony was working the small

talk. "I used to play some myself. I found out quickly I wasn't very good at it though. How about you?" he asked. "Any talent?"

I shrugged. "I guess I'll leave that to the people who listen to me. I can play you something while you're working, if you like," I offered.

"That would be cool. How about it Coretta? Would you like to hear some music while we're working?" he spoke to the floor.

"As long as there's no charge," she agreed from below the counter.

"Well, all right then," I said. "Oh – I'll need my lucky pick. I left it near the stove." I walked toward Anthony. "I can grab it from this side of the counter." I was almost there.

"I'll get it for you," Anthony looked me in the eye.

"Don't worry about it," I said. I took one more step. "I know exactly where it is. I can reach it from this side, it's right next to you."

I took one final step and got there just as Anthony glanced to where I said the pick would be, taking his eyes off me for a split-second. It was the break I'd hoped for, and it was the one mistake he made that saved my life.

Chapter 51

WHEN I'D FIRST met with Franklin and his assassins, and Albert slid the weapon under the linen across the table to me, I knew what to do. I could holster it somewhere on my person, but I knew Albert and Bonnie were armed. So I'd hidden the gun inside the cottage, but not just anywhere.

I wanted to have easy access to it if the need arose. But, I didn't want to hide it where it might be found if someone else was looking for it.

I'd noticed there was a two-inch recess under the countertop on the living room side. Thick, expensive granite overhung the plywood base, and hid it.

I asked one of the cooks to buy me three strong key magnets from a hardware store, and I fastened them to the plywood. The handgun, a thirty-two caliber Smith and Wesson, fit perfectly onto the magnets. It was hidden from view, while at the same time accessible in a moment or two should the need arise.

Like now.

I almost dropped it when I felt for it and snatched it off its magnet base. Anthony's head was turning back to me as I swung my arm up and over the lip of the countertop. I pointed it directly into his face. I brought my other hand quickly to my lips, signaling silence.

His eyes were wide and attentive, but held no fear.

"I see it now," I referred to my imaginary guitar pick. "It's there on your left. Actually, you might as well get it for me." My eyes never left his, and neither one of us blinked.

"Damn," said Anthony, still staring into my eyes. His were cold and lifeless, like those of a venomous reptile. "I got the wrong bit. Coretta, you got a medium Phillips you can hand me?"

It sounded rehearsed, like some kind of code they planned earlier in the event something went wrong.

"I found one for you," I heard her voice before I saw the top of her head breaking the edge of the counter, then her shoulders, then the first dark shadow of her own weapon coming up.

Instantly I drew my arm back, swung it toward her, and pulled the trigger. It roared like a sonic boom in the small confines of the cottage's kitchen.

I missed her head, but I got lucky and the bullet tore through the shoulder holding her gun. She screamed, and the weapon flew backwards out of her hand. I used my weapon's recoil to instantly move the barrel back into Anthony's face, a mere three inches from his left eye. The only sound was the screaming from Coretta, who lay sprawled out on the kitchen floor, clutching her already blood-soaked shoulder.

"You fucking white trash bastard! You shot me! You motherfucking bastard! I'll kill you for this!"

I smiled, never moving my eyes from Anthony's. "I honestly don't believe either of you will get a second chance," I hissed. "Move, even a little, and you're gone."

Chapter 52

"PUT YOUR HANDS on the counter," I growled. "Palms down." Anthony, or whatever his name was, complied instantly.

"Where's yours?" I asked him pointedly. "In case you haven't figured this out, one wrong answer is all I need to blow your motherfucking head off. One. Go ahead, asshole. Lie to me," I smiled again.

"In the toolbox." He believed me.

"Put your hands out farther and lean your chest onto the counter." He listened, and moved.

Watching both of them carefully, I circled the counter. Once on their side, I saw the gun Coretta had was out of her reach. She was bleeding profusely, scarlet spreading out across the stone tiles as she writhed in agony. "Stop moving so much or you'll bleed out," I suggested. "Not that I really care," I added with malevolence.

"At least let me get her a towel," Anthony pleaded from where he lay face down across the countertop.

"Keep eating that fucking counter!" I shouted at him. He didn't move.

Now I could smell the acrid, familiar scent of spent gunpowder. All of a sudden, I thought of squirrels. The ones I used to shoot in Linda Lou's garden. I shook it off – now was not the time to get distracted.

I reached into my pocket for my cell phone. Coretta was whimpering in pain, fighting to remain conscious. She had followed my advice, and lay on her back in the middle of the kitchen floor. She stared up at me with wide, contemptuous eyes. I hit the preprogrammed number. Albert answered on the first ring.

"Get back here," I said. "We need to take some suits to the cleaners." Albert didn't ask me what I meant. Minutes later, both he and Bonnie were standing beside me, aiming their own pistols at the two intruders.

I'd actually been startled by their sudden presence, "I didn't hear you come in," I said, giving Anthony a sidelong look.

"You weren't supposed to," said Bonnie.

"We had to be sure you weren't being used to neutralize us," said Albert. "Do you know if he has any weapons?"

"In his tool chest," I replied angrily. A part of me wished I'd hit his girlfriend in the head, and killed her on the spot. It was their arrogance that truly repulsed me. They came into my home to kill me, and I didn't mean jack shit to them. I was just another anonymous hit in what was probably a routine day for these maggots.

Bonnie stepped into the kitchen and retrieved Coretta's gun from the floor.

"She's going to die if we don't get her some help," she observed. Coretta had none of the previous fire in her belly. She was rocking slightly from side to side, blood oozing from her shoulder. She moaned occasionally, her eyes were closed.

"I know," I said. I shot her in self-defense. If I'd killed her, it wouldn't have been murder, but if I let her die now, it would go against what I stood for.

I got two towels from the bathroom, and returned to the living room.

"You can stand up," I ordered Anthony. He carefully raised himself from where he'd been splayed out across the counter. He caught the towels I threw at him. One for the front of Coretta's shoulder, and one for the exit wound. He knelt down on the kitchen floor beside her, and began to work on her to stanch the flow of blood.

"How'd you know?" he asked.

I spoke to his back, "You don't replace copper

with aluminum. It's the other way around. And, no electrician would work on a live junction box."

"Shit," Anthony cursed as he continued to work on Coretta's shoulder. "You got any tape? Something to hold the towels against her wound? She's lost a lot of blood."

"That's what happens when you get shot," I spit out. "An electrician without tape, imagine that!" I moved across the living room and found a half-used roll of tape between a couple of speakers. I handed it to him over his shoulder.

"Thanks," he muttered, taking it from me.

The irony of his gratitude was not lost on me.

Chapter 53

"WHAT DO WE do with them?" I asked Albert.

"First things first," he said as Anthony finished taping off Coretta's wounds. "Put your hands on the counter." He shoved Anthony roughly into it. "Spread your legs," he ordered, kicking them apart.

Bonnie and I watched as Albert patted down the gangster. Satisfied there was no weapon on him, Albert grabbed Anthony by the back of his shirt, and pulled him backwards away from the counter. He then shoved him forcefully into the wall on the other side of the kitchen area. "Have a seat," he directed the man, gesturing toward the floor with his gun. Bonnie moved to a position where she could cover both him and Coretta. Albert bent over the tool chest, and lifted the lid.

"Nice," he said, as he removed what appeared to be a 9mm Glock. The handgun looked all the more menacing with its screwed-on silencer. He scowled at Anthony, and pointed the weapon at his face.

"You're not going to kill him in here with his own weapon?" I was suddenly filled with angst.

"Why not? He was going to kill you," Albert pointed out.

For the first time I could see the fear in Anthony's eyes. He knew Albert was a seasoned killer. I sensed he also knew I was the only thing stopping Albert from shooting him through the head.

"But he didn't," I said with authority.

Albert kept staring at the man on the floor. Finally, slowly, he lowered the gun. "Besides, if you shoot him, you'll also have to kill her," I said.

"The world would not miss them," Albert replied coldly. Something inside me shivered as I realized he really did want to kill them both. "She's probably gonna die anyway," he gestured toward Coretta, who lay moaning just a couple feet from where Anthony sat against the wall.

Looking at Anthony, I was reminded of how much I'd been controlled by my environment back in Memphis. Just as he was by living in the ghetto. It had taken the bus crash, and my survival, to shake that influence.

I liked taking control over my life – being in charge of my own destiny. Now I was responsible for Anthony and Coretta's. The difference between us was I'd learned the difference between right and wrong, despite my upbringing.

"Well then, what do you suggest we do with them Peter?" Albert's tone was caustic.

I looked intently at Anthony, who appeared less a killer now, and more like a bull waiting in a chute for a metal bolt to the head. I could see he was scared. I didn't feel sorry for him, he'd chosen this life. He knew all along how it might end.

"They call your boss the Lord of the Flies?" I asked.

"God for short," he readily admitted.

"Yeah, well there's only one God I know of, and He doesn't order hits on people," I said wryly. "What's your real name kid?"

"Dante Washington. She's really Coretta," he nodded to the woman on the floor beside him. "She's also my wife," he surprised me. "We got married last month."

"Congratulations," I didn't mean it.

"Thanks," Dante nodded. "She needs a doctor."

"We're still trying to decide if we're going to kill you both. If we need to, we will," I spoke seriously. "If we can come up with a way to keep you alive, then maybe we'll talk about a doctor."

He stared at me wide-eyed, and for the moment, speechless.

"How about it?" I prodded him. "Is your boss the forgiving kind?"

Dante's eyes darted around the kitchen. He looked from Albert to Bonnie, and then back to me. I could tell he was confused, and didn't know who among us was the shot caller. He settled on me.

"It's always about the cash. That and respect. They think the kid who died in the car told you who killed him. If those three things can be wrapped into a solution they can live with, then no one has to die."

It was the most honest, succinct plea for all our lives I could ever have hoped for. Seemingly impossible, but I realized I might just have a solution.

Chapter 54

DANTE WASHINGTON HAD thrown out a proposition. Obviously this inferred he had authority, and was in a position to speak on behalf of his gang. Because if he was speaking just to save his own skin, and this was found out by his boss, he'd probably end up dead. He'd basically said so when he brought up how important respect was to them. It was indeed a cornerstone in gangland culture. Disrespect the wrong people, and you often paid the ultimate price.

I looked at Albert, "She needs medical attention. Is there someone you can call?" I negotiated on behalf of our side.

He eyed me intently, no doubt weighing his options. Finally, to my relief, he wordlessly took out his cell phone. Still glaring at me, he punched a number. A moment later he spoke into the receiver, "We have a problem at home. Yes, that's right." He paused. "Now would be good," he continued. "Thirty minutes will be fine. Thank you," Albert terminated the call. His eyes had never left mine.

"Thank you," I said. I turned back to Dante.

"It seems to me we have to make some hard choices," I eyed him suspiciously. To say most of his kind were dishonest would be charitable. But, if there was enough in it for them, I knew they might be persuaded to agree to an unholy alliance.

"We can execute the two of you, in which case we go to war. But, I can't see there will be much benefit to any of us."

"I would definitely go along with that," Dante agreed. He knew what happened in the next few minutes would determine if he, and his wife, would live or die.

"Do you speak for your boss?" I was testing him.

"I have his ear," he quickly shook his head. "But no one speaks for him."

"Fair enough," I said. "But you can talk to him? You can explain our position? If we want it to go that way?"

"Yes, I can. And I'm not just saying it to save my skin. If I lie to you that's one thing. If I lied to the boss," Dante shuddered, "That's an entirely different matter. He would only begin by cutting out my tongue."

"So call him," I said. "You can use your phone. That way he'll know it's you. Help him to understand there's no benefit in killing me.

Not when so many others, starting with you and Coretta, will also die. Those kids that died in their car said nothing to me before they passed. If I knew anything, I would have already gone to the police. Anyone involved would have already been arrested, and charged with murder." I paused and looked into Dante's eyes.

"The contract on my life is cancelled. If we can agree to this, we will prove our good faith by treating Coretta's wound, and then releasing both of you. This shows respect. That's one. You now know neither of those guys said a single word to me. The proof is that no one has been investigated for the murder. That's two. You said number three was cash. I personally don't see we have a problem here. What we may have though, is an opportunity." I had everyone's attention.

Now came my big, calculated gamble. In our last conversation The Wedge and I both found it strange and foreboding that Albert, Bonnie, John, and Franklin, all had dubious pasts. They all seemed to have fabricated themselves into existence. Except everyone has a past.

We logically thought they may have come from the military, quite likely from some form of black ops. We also knew if this was true, then they had at one time or another been involved in some pretty nasty stuff.

In my mind – and probably Wedge's as well – murder, munitions, and no doubt drugs were involved. With this in mind, I pressed forward with my gambit.

"The Lord of the Flies exists on the vices: Prostitution, loansharking, the numbers. They're all part of what you guys do, but what makes you the most money are the illegal drugs," I laid it out for him.

Dante responded, "I'm still listening."

I said, "Good, because I'd be worried about your health right now if you weren't," I put him in his place. "This might be something some of us would like to discuss further. It wouldn't be me," I stressed to everyone. "But after I'm out of earshot, you guys may want to have a conversation about how to help each other out."

The room got really quiet after that, except for Coretta's labored breathing, and a wailing siren somewhere in the distance. I could see they were all thinking about what I'd just said.

I smiled, "Number three – the cash. And that wraps it up, wouldn't you say?"

Chapter 55

IN THE END, greed became the glue that made it all work. Some guy who obviously knew what he was doing showed up, and tended to Coretta. The slug hadn't hit the brachial artery as it made a clean hole through her shoulder. When I thought about it later, I was bothered by how close I'd come to putting one right through her head. I'd been lucky. We'd all been lucky, for that matter. If I'd killed her, the ending would not have been a happy one.

They never told me any details of the deals they made; I didn't want to know. Bonnie told me a few days later that she and Albert would be moving out of the hotel just as soon as Franklin returned from New York. And then, just as quickly as the whole dangerous affair had begun, it was over. The threat to my life had ended.

Still a bit anxious and looking over my shoulder, I celebrated my newfound freedom by taking Laurie out for dinner at a restaurant a couple of blocks from the hotel.

"What would have happened if you had killed her?" she demanded of me. Halfway through the first bottle of an expensive Chardonnay, I told her the story of what happened in the cottage last week. This was the first time we'd been able to talk about it since then. We'd both been busy, she at The Guitar Works, me with putting my life back together. It was something I intuitively knew would be better done alone.

I shrugged, "We'll never know the answer to that question." I could drive myself crazy thinking about the maybes, but it was over now. I much preferred moving forward.

"Doesn't it scare you?" Laurie was stunned at what had happened, and my seeming nonchalance about the whole thing. It had taken no small amount of assurances just to get her to walk out of the hotel and down the street with me. She was more paranoid than I was.

"This thing never scared me. I guess I'm a product of my environment. It's over now; I'm not involved with any of it. How these people want to conduct themselves from here is up to them. The important thing is that everyone involved understands I'm no threat to them. I probably have only one regret about everything that happened."

"And what might that be?"

"I never got a chance to meet the boss," I smiled mischievously as she slapped my arm in mock disgust. She sat back in her chair, and folded her arms across her chest.

"Is this what it's going to be like?" Laurie was sulking. She was pissed off I hadn't told her the story until now.

I sipped some of my wine before I answered. "How do you want it to be? What is it you're looking for?"

"I was never looking for anything, but I found you," she declared.

"We found each other," I corrected her.

She gazed at me lovingly. "Yes, apparently we have," she exhaled a deep breath. "Warts and all, I suppose."

"You have to admit, it hasn't exactly been boring," I volunteered. "I'm sorry. I didn't ask for any of this Laurie. I'm doing the best I can with what I've got. I'm just happy I seem to have gotten to the other side."

"And there's no chance this guy who called himself the Lord of the Moths – "

"Flies," I interrupted her. "He's called Lord of the Flies."

"I could say something about what flies are usually attracted to, but I won't."

"It's fitting," I chuckled. "But probably not a good idea to say it to his face, whoever he is."

She shuddered, like she had a sudden chill. "I'd rather never hear any of their names mentioned again."

"Agreed," I said.

"Seriously. Tell me these people are gone for good. Tell me there's no chance that one day they'll come looking for you," she implored me.

"They're gone," I promised her. "They're never coming back sweetheart."

She looked at me for what seemed a long time, searching my eyes for something only she could find.

"Good," she finally said, satisfied we could get on with things. "What day is the concert?" she changed the subject.

"In about six weeks. We'll play on Saturday night, August sixteenth," I told her.

"Is the capacity still the same?" Laurie asked.

"It started out at five hundred," I sighed nervously, and she noticed.

"What's wrong with that?" Laurie asked.

"The concert is sold out."

"That's fantastic!" Laurie exclaimed gleefully. She saw again that I was less than enthusiastic. "Isn't it?"

"Yeah, it's great. Or at least it would have been great. I found out yesterday that Franklin added another three hundred and fifty seats, at twice the price of the first five hundred. I've never played in front of that many people before. Hell, the biggest crowd I ever had was an open mic one night about a year ago. There must have been a grand total of seventy-five people in the place, and most of them were drunk. I'm nervous. Everyone thinks I can do it, but I just don't think I'm that good. What if I blow it? I hate the idea of letting anyone down, especially after going through as much trouble as Franklin has. Some of these folks who are coming are major-league players in the music industry."

Laurie was shaking her head, smiling. "You have a gift. Listening to you and watching you perform is like taking a magical ride on the tail of a comet. You've truly been blessed Peter. And do you know what makes it all so absolutely wonderful? So incredibly special?"

"What?" I said, not nearly so convinced as she obviously was.

Laurie looked intently into my eyes, searching them once again. She shook her head slightly from side to side, and said almost in a whisper, "You're the last person on earth to know how truly gifted you are. In an innocent kind of way, it's as if you're oblivious to it all."

Chapter 56

I CALLED THE Wedge on the weekend to let him know what had happened since our last conversation. He listened intently without interrupting, until I got to the part where I'd shot Coretta.

"My God in Heaven!" he exclaimed. "You could have killed her Peter." He was mortified.

"Everyone keeps telling me that Wedge. But I didn't. The guy who patched her up said she'd be fine, maybe a little stiff for a few months. But there wasn't going to be any permanent problems for her."

"She must hate you," he stated.

"Surprisingly, no," I said. "In their own way, they're professionals. We may find the code they live by to be strange, but for them it's normal. Getting shot gave Coretta a ton of street cred. She doesn't hold me personally responsible. For them, taking a bullet is viewed as nothing more than an occupational hazard."

"That doesn't make a lick of sense to me," The Wedge said.

"Not to you. But to them, it makes perfectly good sense."

"How could anyone live like that?" The Wedge sounded bewildered.

"In their world, people like you and me are the crazy ones. Fortunately all of us were able to find some ground common enough to meet on."

"Cash would be my bet," said The Wedge.

"I can't say you would be wrong," I admitted.

"Who suggested the deal?" asked The Wedge.

"I gambled on the notion we talked about in our last conversation. I figured our side must have come from the military. They can handle the thugs, and I had an idea they were in business for themselves already. It was risky, but I didn't see as I had very many options. As it turns out, it worked. I guess they're officially in business with each other. If I was cynical, I might even call it a marriage made in heaven."

"And you can swear to me that you do not have a hand in any of this?"

"All I did was make a suggestion. Soon as that was done, I backed off. I told you before, I don't want that kind of life. I just want to make some music," I assured him.

The Wedge exhaled into the phone, "All right, I believe you. I'm incredibly relieved as well. Since it would seem you've wrapped up the whole affair prettier than a Christmas gift, I'll call off that part of the investigation. I think, as is the case most of the time, these barbarians deserve each other."

"Hey, I didn't think they were all bad," I stuck up for Albert and Bonnie.

"They are murderers Peter. Every last one of them," The Wedge adjudicated.

"That may be true, or not. I know Coretta and Dante would have killed me if they had the chance. But remember, if I hadn't missed and had put a bullet through Coretta's brain instead, I'd be right there with them. That would have made me every bit as bad as you think they are."

"You were defending yourself. You're no more a murderer than I."

"Maybe," I acknowledged, "But I don't see much of a difference. A killing is a killing, no matter which way you look at it. The bottom line is I'm glad I didn't kill her, and I'm happy we found a solution. Now I can put all of my attention into the concert next month."

I moved on to the next topic. "How about Linda Lou, Wedge? Have you found out who might have changed the records down at the Land Titles' Office?"

"I'm looking for a motive," he answered

carefully. "That's how it's done. When I find a plausible reason as to why someone would change those records, I'll likely be able to determine who is responsible."

"Do you have any idea where Linda Lou is?"

"Not yet. Something tells me she's with your father. There's nothing concrete, I just feel it in my guts. I'm positive we'll find out all of this is somehow connected," he said.

"I agree with you. The whole damn thing reeks though," I felt a lump in my throat. "I just hope to hell it doesn't have anything to do with the meth business."

"I hope so too son. But don't you worry, we'll find out soon enough. There's probably an innocent explanation for all of this. None of them are in jail; we're checking the hospitals as well. So far we haven't found anything," Wedge admitted. "We're leaving no possibilities to chance though."

"Good," I said. My voice faltered, and then I repeated, "That's good. Thank you for looking after things for me."

The Wedge knew what I didn't have the nerve to ask. "We'll keep looking, we won't stop until we find them," he promised me.

I was doing my best to hold back the tears. "Find her for me, please. I love her. She and Senior did the best they could. They're all the family I have."

"I will Peter. I promise. I'll catch you up on the details of your case in our next conversation." He could tell I was all choked up. We had both danced around it without saying the empty, cold word – death.

Chapter 57

ABOUT A WEEK before the scheduled concert, Franklin brought John Gant around to the cottage to sit in on one of our rehearsals. John brought two A&R guys with him from his record company. They got there late, but we didn't need much encouragement to run through another couple of originals before we wrapped things up.

I was going to stop between songs and introduce the band, but John motioned with his hand for us to continue. The atmosphere was casual, belying the seriousness of what we were doing. It was just the way I liked it. The notes seemed to come alive as we played them, floating like fireflies among our listeners. Even this small audience seemed to inspire the band – we were on fire. When we finished, I was breathing hard. Beads of perspiration dotted my face as if I'd been caught in a light, drizzling rain. Surprisingly, in all this time, neither Franklin nor John had actually heard us play together as a band. Now they and the two record company execs sat and stared at us in dumbfounded silence.

I took my guitar from around my neck and slowly placed it in its stand. The only sound was the steady buzz of the charged equipment that made it seem like we were standing under some high-voltage power lines. Someone behind me turned off the master switch that powered the equipment. The room seemed tiny as it was thrown into complete, utter silence. And still, they stared.

I was overcome with uncertainty. Why weren't they reacting? I thought we were really good. Had I been deceiving myself? I thought of Laurie and became irrationally angry at the thought she'd lied to me. At least, I thought, there was still enough time to cancel the concert and make the appropriate refunds.

One of the execs, the youngest guy, began to clap first. Then everyone joined in. Someone put their fingers to their lips. A loud, shrieking whistle tore through the living room. All four of them began shouting at once, "Bravo! Bravo!" followed by more whistling that was deafening in the small room. Their smiles turned to laughter. The youngest executive pounded Franklin on the back in congratulations. I thought they had all gone mad.

Chapter 58

THEY WERE ALL talking at once, like a group of giddy schoolchildren. I couldn't understand any of what they were saying. It was mayhem.

"Gentlemen, please!" John Gant's booming voice quieted them to a somewhat tolerable level. "At least allow Peter to introduce his band."

"Maybe they should introduce themselves," I said, still shaking with anxiety. As the band shook hands, and met the execs, I realized I was immensely proud of all of us. We'd all worked hard to get here.

We'd be ready when the time came. Hell, we were ready now, a little voice inside me spoke with an unaccustomed bravado.

"I'm Clifford Johnson," one of the record execs leaned forward, and held out his hand.

"I'm Peter Jackson. I'm very pleased to meet you. I hope we've put some of your fears to rest," I added earnestly.

"You guys were great," Clifford smiled at me warmly. I liked him instantly, and I could tell the feeling was mutual.

"This is my associate," he yielded to his colleague, who was plainly also pleased with what he'd just heard. He shook my hand enthusiastically.

"I'm Roger Penner. It's a real pleasure to finally meet you Peter. I can see now everything they told me about you was more than true. You guys were really tight on those last two songs. I didn't recognize the tunes though."

"That's because you've never heard them before. I wrote them three weeks ago," I admitted. "I'm relieved you like what you heard."

"So those last two songs are yours? I kept wondering where they came from. Now I can't get them out of my head. They're going to be big, but you're going to be a lot bigger. We need to get you guys into the studio right away," said Roger. There was urgency in his tone.

"Calm down Roger," Franklin said. "Every one of us knows what we need to do." He turned to me and said, "What do you think? Are you guys ready to record? By the way, tell them the name of the band," he added. He sounded like an excited schoolboy.

"Peter Jackson and the Gems," Napoleon Daniels, our keyboards player, had sidled up beside us to join in on the conversation.

"Hmm," Clifford was thinking out loud. He

became aware we were listening to him. "Oh, sorry," he instantly apologized. "I love it."

"But…" I filled in.

"I'm just thinking in terms of marketing right now. You might want to think about shortening it."

"To what?" I asked pointedly, unoffended.

"That's up to you," Roger Penner chimed in. "The Gems?" he suggested.

"How about just plain old Peter Jackson?" Clifford made the suggestion in a subdued tone.

For a few moments nobody said anything. I looked at my band mates, into their eyes. I knew they were here because of me, but I always believed a band should be a democracy.

I took a deep breath. "How about it guys? What do you think?"

"Your call Peter," Napoleon spoke for all of them.

I looked at each one of them, pausing briefly and silently to show them my respect. Anna, Rita, and Angie smiled at me encouragingly. I looked back at Clifford Johnson.

"What's your title at the record company Mr. Johnson?" I asked him politely.

"The record company is an offshoot of John's parent label. It's called Emblem Recording Artists, ERA for short. You may have heard of us."

I had. They were the real deal. "My official title is Executive Vice President. Mr. Penner here – Roger," he corrected himself, "is the President of the Artists and Repertoire department. He's the head gatekeeper for ERA. Usually we take a great deal of time to consider any new act, but you're different from anything I've seen in a very long time Peter. John insisted I come here today, and well… he does sign my checks." He winked at me, and laughed. "But he trusts me, and I make some very important decisions for him." I could see the affection he had for John as the younger man squeezed the elder statesman's shoulder. "And by the way Peter, why don't you call me Clifford?"

"Okay," I agreed. "I've got a question for you, Clifford."

"I hope I can answer it," he smiled.

I saw that John and Franklin were watching me closely. "This all seems to be happening very quickly. I've only been here a few months. I tried out a guitar the day after I got here. Not only does John turn out to own the place where I buy my Strat, but he's also a big-time promoter who just happens to know the heavyweights of the music industry. All I did was pluck a few strings on a guitar, and suddenly everyone knows about me. Based solely on what John told you, because none of you guys actually heard us play our music until now, you show up and offer the band a recording contract. Not to mention we're doing our first gig next week in front of a packed house. It all seems very surreal. It's not really supposed to happen this way, or is it? Don't get me wrong. I'm flattered. I really appreciate your guys' enthusiasm and all, but this whole thing seems like a dream. I'm just wondering when I'm going to wake up in my little home in Memphis, and have to feed the chickens."

They all chuckled. "It's no dream Peter," Clifford assured me. "But you are right about one thing; it doesn't usually happen this way." He took a deep breath before he continued, "In this industry we dream that one day we'll discover the next superstar, the next Elvis Presley. The guy who has so much God-given talent that he only comes along once in a lifetime."

"I don't for one second believe I'm that guy," I interrupted him. "I'm just not that good."

He shrugged, "Maybe not. But what if? You have something that touches people to their core. It takes them somewhere where they can forget about all the negative things in their lives. You've been blessed with an incredible gift. It's up to you what you do with it. You can make a lot of people's lives better if you use it judiciously. A good piece of advice I can give you going into this thing is to use what God has given you wisely, and never confuse the talent with who you are as a man. Think of it simply as a possession. It's part of you, but it's also separate. You own it. Don't ever make the mistake of allowing it to own you."

"That's good advice. Thanks," I said quietly. I was silently wondering to myself if I could live up to everyone's expectations.

Chapter 59

IT WAS A couple of days later. The band had left about an hour earlier; we were practicing every day now.

I lay sprawled across the sofa in the living room. Tired, but feeling good about what was coming ever closer. I basked in the rare silence until I heard the key in the front door. I forced myself into a sitting position, and smiled in anticipation. Laurie entered the cottage. Oddly, I noticed how tired she looked. I bounded off the sofa, and grabbed the two plastic bags she struggled with while she extracted her key from the door.

"I've got them," I said, hearing the telltale chimes of the wine bottles as they bounced off one another when I grabbed the bags.

"Thanks," she was breathing hard.

I turned her toward me after she had closed the door. I held her by the shoulders as I searched her eyes. "You look tired. Are you okay?"

"I'm fine," Laurie assured me. "Those bags got heavy on me. I've been carrying them from the Creole Marketplace. It's a bit of a workout."

"That market's got to be two miles from here!"

"I needed the exercise," Laurie seemed to force a smile. I kissed her long and hard.

"Hmm," she purred. "What's the occasion? Not that I'm complaining, mind you."

"I'd be worried if you did," I teased her. "It's nothing special. I'm just happy to see you." We sat down together on the sofa, and I popped open a bottle of red and poured us both a drink to get started.

Handing her a glass, I said, "At least John's not making you work nights anymore." I hadn't seen the need to let her know, but I'd talked to him about it after practice two days ago. John had seen to it immediately, there would be no more working late for my girl.

"I noticed that. All my shifts suddenly changed, as if I knew people in high places," Laurie said with a lifted eyebrow. "I got a raise too. Imagine that?"

I changed the subject, "I have a confession to make. It's serious. Of course you know that John and Franklin, and a couple of the guys from the record company came by to hear us rehearse on Wednesday?" She nodded for me to continue. "Well, there was a moment right after we finished the last set when there was this eerie silence.

Everyone just sort of stood there and stared at everyone else. All my insecurities suddenly rushed to the surface and took over. I'm not trying to excuse myself from what I'm about to tell you, but I don't want to ever hide anything from you. So this is my confession of sorts."

"I'm listening," she looked at me intently.

"I haven't quite been able to accept everything that's happened to me over the last number of months. None of it is supposed to happen this way. It's very confusing to me. There have been times when I've felt my life isn't in my control."

She cocked her head at me. "You left Memphis for a better life. Why is it so surprising when that begins to happen? I think you deserve it, you've worked hard. You made a decision to leave a life behind that was obviously going nowhere fast. It took courage to stand up to your father, and your uncle."

I thought about it. "Maybe you're right. But I still can't escape this weird feeling I'm living someone else's life. Sometimes, a lot of times, I don't feel like I'm me, if that makes any sense. The other day, when everyone was standing here staring at me, it felt like I was me again."

"What do you mean, it felt like you again?" She was trying to understand me. How could I expect her to when I wasn't sure what I was trying to say myself?

"I felt like, no, I was certain in that moment that you had lied to me. Like I'd been exposed for the fraud I've always been, the fraud I still am. In that moment of total despair, I blamed you for taking me there. The one person I've met in this godforsaken life who truly loves me, and trusts me to never betray that love. I look into your heart and all I see is something as pure as the driven snow, and that makes me feel ten times worse about what I did. I'm sorry for it, and I hope you can find it in yourself to forgive me."

She looked into my eyes, and I felt it again. Like a charlatan, asking for blessings that I could never deserve.

"That is the sweetest, nicest, kindest apology anyone has ever given to me." She shocked me to my very soul. I was stunned into complete silence. I realized in that moment she'd given me another chance.

Chapter 60

"THEY TOLD YOU how great your talent is," Laurie helped me to understand. "Not you. The two are as different as night and day."

I wiped the tears from my cheeks. I felt as if a tremendous weight had been lifted from my shoulders. To be forgiven was truly one of the more amazing virtues of love.

"I know. Clifford Johnson warned me about getting lost in myself. If that ever happens, I want you to promise me something," I said.

"All right," Laurie didn't hesitate.

"If I get full of myself you'll kick me so hard I won't be able to sit down for a week," I said seriously.

"You have my word on it," Laurie agreed. She smiled and stroked my cheek. "I love you."

I searched her eyes. "I'm a long way from perfect," I sighed.

"No one is perfect," she spoke softly.

"I love you too." I leaned over and kissed her on her cheek. "I think I always have," I confided. "Thanks for forgiving me."

She nodded. "You're welcome. Are you worried

about the concert next Friday?" She moved on to a different subject.

I said, "I'm not concerned about our ability to play my music. I think the lyrics will strike a chord with people, and the arrangements are better than good. The Gems have the potential to be some of the best musicians in the country."

"Is that what you decided to call yourselves? It's good. I like it, but I thought your name was going to be out front," she said.

I shook my head. "Just The Gems. We're all in this together, I need them."

"They need you more," she stated.

"I don't know if that's true or not, but we're a group. Perhaps later on we'll change it. I'm not quite ready to call it the Peter Jackson Show. They told me they wouldn't mind if I went ahead and used my name. It just doesn't quite feel right, though. I liked The Gems more. Besides, it has a nice ring to it," I concluded.

"It sounds like there's no stopping you now."

"We'll know a lot more next week, after the show. I may not be worried about the band, "…but I'm terrified of the people who are coming to hear us play."

Laurie sipped some wine. She looked at me over

the rim of her glass. I could tell she was thinking hard about something.

She finally spoke, "They all hear something different. I saw it in their eyes when you played in The Guitar Works. No two pairs of ears are alike, and music will always be a personal thing to whoever is listening. And most everyone who hears it, loves it. That is something extremely rare. There's no real explaining it either. It's enough to know that some sounds, and the way they are arranged and blended to form a song, have a mystical quality. Like thunder, for example," she was excited now.

"Thunder?" I didn't follow her.

"You see it in little kids when they first hear it. They're scared. Have you ever stopped to consider why? Thunder is just another sound, like tens of thousands of other noises. No one teaches those kids to be afraid of the sound of thunder. The point I'm trying to make is, although everyone hears music differently, there's a certain universality to it all.

"Thunder scares most people. That sharp crackling noise that seems like it's about to rip the sky open right down the middle upsets us. Other sounds, like a babbling brook or a soft rain seem to comfort most of us in some inexplicable way.

"The music you create does this. It brings out an emotion in people. Whether it soothes them, or makes them angry, or whatever. Anyone who listens to your music, feels your music."

I said, "It's the one thing every musician on earth yearns to accomplish. To be able to make people feel what you feel."

"And you've somehow captured it. You have it sealed in a bottle called your soul," she whispered with reverence. "And no one, no matter what, can ever take that away from you Peter. It just is." Her eyes lit up now, like a twinkling star.

I sipped some of the ruby red wine from my glass. "I think you must be my biggest fan," I finally said. I had to admit, her praise made me feel uncomfortable.

"It's easy to get a little carried away when you just might be sitting on the sofa beside the next Elvis," she teased. "I am one hundred percent your biggest fan, but you missed the other part."

A question mark registered across my face.

Laurie laughed, "I will always be your number one fan. Always."

Chapter 61

IN THE WEEK leading up to the concert, I became absolutely consumed with my music. I paid attention to every last detail. If there was such a thing, I wanted every single note to be perfect. I deemed anything short of this goal to be unacceptable.

Interspersed with our marathon practice sessions, we also spent time in a state-of-the-art recording studio owned by John Gant. By the time the morning of the big concert rolled around, I felt we were ready. It hadn't come easy. Everyone in the band worked very hard, and the process wasn't without its share of frayed nerves.

I had seen very little of Laurie during the lead-up to the show. When we did talk on the phone she seemed tired, almost listless at times. I noticed, but wasn't overly concerned. I probably sounded the same to her. We were all working harder than we had ever worked before in our lives, and it felt great to be a part of something we sensed was very special. We all agreed. We didn't just want to wow tonight's audience, many of whom would be the who's who of the industry's heavyweights, we wanted to blow them all right out of the water.

I was talking with Laurie on the phone. "So you'll come by tonight then, about an hour before the show starts?" I was nervous and excited. This was it, the final few hours before we put it all on the line.

"I wouldn't miss it for the world," Laurie stated emphatically.

"I've missed you," I said honestly. "It's been more than a week."

"I know," she said. "But that's okay. We've both been busy. John had me helping with inventory. I never would have dreamed that he sells as much stuff as he does."

"That stuff, as you put it, has in part made John into a very wealthy, and influential man," I noted. "That isn't all he's doing either. You'd be surprised at all the things he's got his fingers into."

Lately I'd been hearing bits and pieces about some of John's other holdings. The recording studio was just one more in a series of successful ventures.

"John has done a lot of nice things for us," I acknowledged. "I'd like to pay him back, starting tonight."

"You don't owe him anything. He believes

in you, which means he believes you're about to make him a fortune," said Laurie.

"That may be true," I said, "but without John, I would never have gotten this shot at my dream. At least not now."

"I think the world would have found you sooner or later. Don't ever think you owe any of these guys anything. Without talent like yours, they'd be nowhere. You're the gas that runs the engine."

"I'm still grateful," I said. "I guess it's the way I was brought up. There's nothing that says they have to do it," I pointed out.

"No there isn't," Laurie agreed. "And it's nice that John and Franklin do help certain people. Always remember though, there's always going to be something in it for them. When was the last time you saw them buy lunch for a homeless person?" she asked pointedly. "They probably never would," she answered her own question. "Therein lies the difference. You would buy someone lunch if you saw they were hungry."

There was a sharp knock on the cottage door. "Someone wants me. I can hear them at the door. I think we probably have to do the sound check. I'll see you later tonight then."

"Break a leg," she said. "I'll see you before the

show, and remember, after all the pictures and autographs, you're mine for the rest of the night."

"Laurie?"

"Yes?"

"Thanks."

"For what?"

"Everything, love. Everything and more."

Chapter 62

WE STAGED OURSELVES in the cottage to wait for the crowd to gather outside. The grand entrance would stamp an indelible signature on the rest of the night.

I looked around the living room, crowded with the band. There was a palpable, nervous determination in their eyes. More importantly, I could also sense an almost child-like exuberance. Come what may, we could not be more ready.

The stage had been set up on the far side of the courtyard, directly in front of the fountain. The steady hum of the cottage's air conditioning could not altogether drown out the buzz from beyond the front door. A half hour ago I'd stolen a peek from behind the bougainvillea vines that smothered the front of the cottage. Franklin had set up six mobile bars, three on either side of the nine hundred seats. Workers put in a dance floor immediately in front of the stage. The seating was split into four sections, with an eight-foot wide aisle running straight up the middle to the dance floor. Not one of those chairs, I realized in awe, would be empty tonight.

John and Franklin had done an inspiring job in getting out the crowd. I got even more nervous when I spotted a couple of local television stations' cameras near the stage. I already knew we would be doing our own promotional filming, but hadn't heard about these local broadcasters. Our management was serious all right. I wondered wryly if John also owned a piece of the television stations.

I still hadn't heard from Laurie. I was worried, but forced my mind back to the music. I couldn't let anything, even Laurie, interfere with my concentration.

Silently fingering the imaginary fret board of my Strat, I looked around the room. Anna, Rita, and Angie huddled in the back corner, talking together in animated, hushed tones. Angie caught me looking at her. She smiled, brimming with confidence. I nodded, and returned her reassuring smile.

Napoleon looked serious as he sat off in a corner by himself. Bonaparte may have been short in stature, but he was a giant when it came to character. We had developed a solid beginning to an excellent friendship. I liked him immensely, as I did each of them. I had nothing but confidence in what lay ahead for all of us.

Ben, our bassist, was naturally conferring with Wallace, the drummer. They sounded great in the studio, laying down irrepressible bed tracks for me to carouse on top of with guitar licks that sprang from my mind. Sometimes – most times – I wasn't even really aware of what I was playing. It was as if I'd go into a shaman-like trance. Everyone just kept telling me to keep doing whatever I was doing, because it was definitely working. Their only complaint was how hard it was to keep up with me at times. I kept telling them to just keep playing.

And then there was Raymond Beauchamps, the guy I was fast thinking was going to end up being our road manager.

Ray was a quiet, unassuming black man, born and raised in the Lower Ninth Ward of New Orleans. He'd started hauling garbage for FEMA right after the Army Corps of Engineers plugged the holes in the levees and pumped the water out of the City. That's how he'd first met Franklin. Franklin had seen past the dirt of an honest day's work and discerned a man with integrity.

Mainly his job was to keep the hotel clean from top to bottom. Ray had been equal to the task. He had proved to be both reliable, and responsible. He'd embraced the trust and position Franklin offered him, and never looked back. When I had come along, Ray was the first staff member to whom I'd been introduced. At first I perceived Ray as somber and brooding. I had never met anyone like him before. He seemed genteel enough, but I intuited that if someone pushed the wrong buttons, Ray just might come unhinged. That initial assessment, much to my relief, could not have been more wrong. I learned after he began to open up to me that he was intelligent, articulate, and possessed an undergraduate degree he'd gotten on a Pell grant from Tulane University. He was as stable as they came, but it never hurt that people thought he might go a little crazy if things didn't go his way.

When Franklin suggested that Ray might be the perfect guy to help out when we went on tour, I immediately warmed to the idea. For his part, Ray thought it would be great. He confided in me that he'd been considering a change for a while. He just hadn't worked up the nerve to tell his friend Franklin about his plans to move on. We agreed that God did indeed work in mysterious ways.

The cottage's front door opened, and Franklin walked into the living room. He looked around at us in silence. The door was slightly ajar, and the din outside was clearly discernable.

"It's time." His voice resonated with authority. He knew what was at stake. He smiled then, disarmingly. He winked at me, and shouted, "Let's kick some ass!"

Chapter 63

RAY LED US through the front door in a line behind Franklin. No one saw us as we took an immediate right in front of the cottage. We headed for the side entrance near the back of the hotel. We made our way through the hotel in stolid, determined silence.

When we finally exited the restaurant and climbed the stairs onto the stage, it was like walking out onto the surface of a world in a different universe.

We rehearsed our entrance during the sound check until we had it perfected, but nothing could have prepared me for the bedlam when the crowd noticed us taking the stage. They went absolutely crazy. Close to a thousand people cheered and screamed as I plugged my guitar into the amp. Some people got up and rushed the stage. Immediately they were blocked by security.

"No, no. Let them come closer," I found myself speaking into the microphone. "We're here to have some fun. Anyone who wants to come closer, come on up. That's what rock'n'roll is all about." Several hundred cheered, and left their seats to cram in closer to the edge of the stage.

"Thanks for being here," I said with sincerity. "I know you probably had better things to do," I added, tongue-in-cheek.

"I heard about this party at the hotel tonight. I heard it was going to be huge!" I screamed. "So I decided I'd better get my ass down here and see what all the fuss was about." I looked around from side to side, as if I was searching for someone. The crowd was hooping and hollering. I pointed to myself, and they cheered even louder. I nodded my approval, and waved my hand out across the top of the crowd, pointing to all of them.

"I think I found the party! I hope you all enjoy the show!" I looked back of me, to the members of the band. They were grinning from ear to ear. I whirled back to the crowd.

"Let's get it on!" And we began.

I struck the first note on my guitar, and was transported through time and space to another dimension. My thoughts were immediately of Lynette. She and her family lived about a half mile down the dirt road from where I'd grown up. Mr. and Mrs. Carter had eight kids, so it was no coincidence one daughter was close to my age. Lynette and I became good friends on the awkward road to puberty. Life was more difficult for her, because Lynette was born without the gift of sight. She once asked me to describe colors to her. I tried, but couldn't do it at first. Sensing that I was embarrassed, she helped me, and in so doing made me see the world a little more as it must have looked through her eyes.

"Tell me how they feel," she instructed me. "It's easier that way." She was twelve, I was eleven.

"Hasn't anyone told you what a color looks like? Haven't you asked anyone before?" I was bewildered.

She was smiling, with that vacant, unfocused stare peculiar to the blind. She shook her head, and explained, "It's never come up. But I'm glad I thought to ask you."

"Why me?" I asked.

"Because you're kind, I can trust you. Some of the other kids make fun of me. They call me Blind Betty. They can be really mean sometimes."

"You must hate them," I said.

"No, I don't hate them. Mama said they just don't know what it's like to be blind and they feel bad about it. So they make fun of me instead."

"I guess I can try," I said tentatively.

"Tell me what black feels like Peter. It seems odd that's what they call us. By the name of a color. I've always wondered what it must look like. How is it so different from what they call you?"

I sighed. We were sitting on a log at the back of her house, side by side. I had fallen in love with Lynette the year before, in grade five, but had never worked up the nerve to tell her. She went to a different school. They said it was a special school because she was blind. After I was dropped off I'd wait for her bus to arrive at the end of the gravel road. She would hold my hand so I could walk her to where she lived on the edge of the woods.

I played in the dirt at my feet with a stick I'd found near the log. The sounds of the woods came to me in the silence that had somehow slipped in between our conversation. The different birds called out to one another. Something, probably a squirrel, rummaged in the thick undergrowth to my left, near where we sat. Frogs croaked behind us, down by the creek that ran behind the clearing at the back of Lynette's happy home.

"Black feels like your favorite ice cream right after church on a blistering hot Sunday. It tastes like ripe watermelon later in the afternoon, as the sun sinks low in the sky, and the crickets begin to sing. Black feels like everything good that has ever happened to you. It feels like when your mama takes care of you when you fall and skin your knee, and she makes all the pain go away."

The screen door at the back porch swung open. Lamar, one of her older brothers, peered out into the backyard and spotted us on the log.

"Lynette, you gotta come in for supper. Hey Peter," he nodded at me. He was fifteen. I liked him. I liked everyone in Lynette's family.

"Hey Lamar," I waved at him with my stick.

"I'll be there in a minute," Lynette called back to him.

Lamar went back inside.

"I guess I better get going," I said, not really wanting to.

"Thank you Peter." She reached out and found the side of my face. Then her warm lips found my cheek. In that moment, I was glad she was blind. Otherwise she would have seen how red my face became.

She died later that same year in the fall, when I'd been sick and hadn't been waiting for her when the bus let her off at her stop. She turned the wrong way after getting off. The driver didn't see her. Later, he told them it was because he'd been looking the other way, for me.

Chapter 64

YEARS LATER I realized that Lynette's world must have been every bit as vivid, and quite likely even far more so, than that of those who could actually see. Her mind made up for that lost sense of sight. Her imagination and insight had created that which she could not observe with broken eyes.

I went to the place in my head where Lynette lived. A world above what we call reality. Full of imagination and insight beyond the mere physical. It seemed to last forever while I was there, and then was over in the blink of an eye.

I struck the last note of the last song. It twirled through the air like a dancing marionette. It grew dimmer and dimmer, and finally, reluctantly, disappeared into nothingness.

It seemed I was briefly suspended in time, in a moment between realities. In that no-man's-land, I was filled with incredible angst. Then, as if someone flipped a light switch, I heard the screaming of the audience as they appeared again in front of me. I found myself standing on the stage, once again in the courtyard of the Marigold.

My breath caught in my throat, because for a brief moment in time I saw the back of myself silhouetted in the lights at the foot of the stage. Quickly the flash of this image vanished. It was me now, standing in front of the mic, and the fans who were screaming and clapping in a roar that sounded like thunder.

I shook my head, knowing that somehow I'd just been looking at the back of myself. I was spooked to the core of my being. It was a miracle I managed not to let it show. I looked down at my fingers; they were shaking uncontrollably. If anyone saw my hands I sincerely hoped they believed I was trembling with the excitement of such an amazingly successful debut.

Chapter 65

I'D COME BACK to the stage like a prizefighter knocked to the canvas, not knowing how long he'd been unconscious when he finally came to. It was the same as when I'd first tried out the guitar in the music store. I had no awareness of the passing of time.

As the courtyard came back into focus, I fought off the sudden urge to vomit. In spite of this, I felt exhilarated. It was as if I drew strength from the emotions that surrounded me. The people were screaming for more; the applause seemed to go on forever. Some of the younger people were literally jumping up and down. They'd lost all control. To my relief, I felt my earlier nausea fade as I soaked up the love that poured out of them. It was like a huge, emotional tsunami. I felt what seemed an actual physical energy wash across the stage.

"Thank you and good night!" I screamed back at them. "We'll be back!" I followed the band members as they headed back toward the restaurant doors. I noticed the old clock above the door, and realized we started playing an astonishing two hours ago. Instinctively I knew that what I'd just been through was tied to the collective emotional state of the crowd. This time it had been exponentially stronger than the first time at The Guitar Works. It must be magnified by the sheer number of people, to the point it almost made me sick. As the door of the restaurant slid shut behind us, it muted the noise from the courtyard. Suddenly, but not surprisingly, I thought of Laurie. As we retraced our steps toward the cottage, it felt like I was walking through a dream. In my mind I walked down this hallway only a few minutes earlier, not two hours ago.

I corralled Franklin at the end of the hallway.

"It was unbelievable Peter," he was ecstatic. "In all my years I've never seen anything like tonight," he was bubbling over.

"Have you seen Laurie?" I tried to hide my desperation. I knew something was wrong, she had promised to be here.

"No, I haven't," said Franklin, suddenly sympathetic.

"She was supposed to be here. There's no way she would have missed this. There's no way," I repeated, more to myself. "We need to find her. Can you call Ray and ask him to help us?"

"Have you tried calling her?"

"I would have, but I can't find my damn phone. I must have put it down somewhere. My mind's been on the show, it was all I could think about," except for Laurie, I thought to myself.

"Where was she supposed to be before the concert?" Franklin asked, now also concerned.

"She was working at the store," I quickly informed him. "Something's happened to her." I could feel myself beginning to panic.

"All right. We'll find her. Don't worry."

"We'll find her," he said again, this time with a steadier assurance. He took out his phone and quickly dialed a number.

At the same moment John Gant appeared with a small crowd at the other end of the hallway. They were happy, and boisterous.

"C'mon," I grabbed Franklin's arm. I didn't want John to see us. "Let's get out of here before we can't."

We dashed toward the exit on the other side of the building.

Franklin cursed under his breath. "No one's answering."

"Who were you calling?" We conversed on the fly.

"The store," he said.

"And no one answered?" I was really scared

now. "It's Friday night." I checked my watch. "The Guitar Works doesn't close for another hour."

"Tell me something I don't know," Franklin said. We hustled down the stairwell and out to where Franklin parked his car. We ran at least twenty stop signs and half a dozen red lights on the way to The Guitar Works.

The moment we pulled up I saw why no one had answered the phone. The place was jam-packed full of people. As we quickly walked from the car to the front entrance we had to dodge a crowd milling about on the front sidewalk.

I glanced at Franklin as we approached the door. He shrugged. I was surprised to see a beefy guy wearing a security t-shirt controlling the store's entrance. I didn't know him, but he immediately recognized Franklin.

"Don't tell me – this is John's doing," Franklin spoke to the man.

The big guy smiled, nodding. He looked at me then. "This be the man," he accused me.

Franklin introduced us, "Errol, meet Peter Jackson."

"I recognize you from your album cover. Congratulations on your release. We got quite a turn-out. Are you here to sing, or just sign autographs?"

"Neither," I said, bewildered. "I don't know

what you mean. We're here for my girlfriend Laurie. Is she inside?"

Errol's brow furrowed. He looked quizzically at Franklin and asked him, "He doesn't know?"

"Hell Errol. I didn't even know," Franklin was confused too. "I was busy with the concert down at the hotel. John never said anything about this to me. Well, he may have mentioned something a couple weeks back," he corrected himself. "But he didn't say anything about all these people being here tonight."

"What the hell is going on?" I was getting annoyed. "What are all these people doing here? Where's Laurie?"

I glanced behind me as I heard my name mentioned in a conversation among five or six teenaged girls. They were giggling and pointing at me.

Errol said to Franklin, "Tell me about it. We didn't exactly expect this kind of turnout either. It caught all of us off guard." He looked at me again. "It's your release party. It's been insane all night. These are all the kids who couldn't get into the concert."

I stared at Franklin. He began to explain. "John pressed a demo from your recording in the studio."

"What?" I couldn't believe it.

"I remember him mentioning it a while back," he continued, "but in all the work leading up to the concert, it slipped my mind. Or maybe I just didn't take John seriously. You know, in one ear and out the other. He must have been promoting this on social media. I guess we were just too busy to notice."

"That's exactly what he was doing," Errol grinned. "And we're just about sold out," he added with satisfaction.

Right now I didn't care. "Where's Laurie?" I was pissed off I had to ask again.

"Who's Laurie?" asked Errol.

"She's my girlfriend," I shot back. "She works here. She's an assistant to the store manager."

"Uh-oh," Errol suddenly turned serious.

"Uh-oh?" My heart was suddenly in my throat. "What do you mean, uh-oh?"

"Is she a blonde? About five-seven? Gorgeous?"

"All those things and a whole lot more," I said. "Have you seen her? We called here right after the concert. No one answered." I stated the obvious.

Errol replied quickly, "She fainted Peter. She collapsed a few hours before your show. We… someone called an ambulance. They took her to the hospital."

"My God! Are you serious? What hospital?" I demanded.

Franklin already had me by the arm, pulling me after him. "Come on. I know which one. It's close to here. We can get there in ten minutes, tops."

I didn't argue as we pushed our way through a small crowd that had formed near us as more people began to recognize me. Once clear of them, we sprinted towards Franklin's vehicle. Later, I could not even recall the harried, panicked drive to the hospital.

Chapter 66

THE HOSPITAL ROOM was bathed in an ethereal, bluish twilight. Laurie lay on the bed, unconscious. I moved to the side of the bed. Her breathing was shallow, but also regular, which was a good sign. Franklin shuffled in beside me. He put his hand on my shoulder.

Tears welled up in my eyes as I looked at her. I felt helpless and small. Her eyes were closed. She seemed peaceful. If she was dreaming, I hoped she was in a serene place.

More tears spilled down my face as I understood just how deeply Laurie and I had fallen in love over the past few months. What had happened? I still had no idea why Laurie was here.

I heard something behind us, the almost silent creak of a door being pushed open. Light spilled into the room. I turned and saw a nurse as she entered.

Her eyes were kind, but the hospital had rules.

"I'm sorry, but I don't think you can be in here," she whispered an admonishment. "Visiting hours are over. Are you family?" She quickly threw out a line of hope.

Franklin was a stretch; he was, of course, a black man. She obviously spoke more to me.

"I'm her fiancé," I whispered through the tears. "I'm staying," I added with finality. "And he's her uncle," I lied again, motioning to Franklin, who smiled and bowed slightly.

The nurse scrunched up her face, then relaxed. "I'll let you stay for a little while longer," she spoke quietly and respectfully, leaving the time open-ended. "She needs rest," she quickly added.

"Come and see me before you leave," she wanted to speak with us, but clearly not here.

Laurie moved slightly in the bed, but did not awaken. I looked at Franklin and nodded. There wasn't a lot to be accomplished by staying, even though I wanted to. I needed to know why Laurie was here. I motioned for Franklin to follow the nurse outside. I took a last look at Laurie's beautiful face, and then left the room too.

Chapter 67

"WE WON'T KNOW anything until her tests come back. No matter how much you stomp your feet, clench your fists, and demand answers. I'm sorry," the doctor was firm.

"How long will that take?" I was exasperated.

"It will take as long as it takes." The doctor was becoming irritated with my barrage of questions.

I took a deep breath, and fought to maintain my self-control. After all, this guy was technically not even Laurie's doctor. Franklin and I had spoken with the kind nurse who we met in Laurie's room. She filled us in with what little information she could provide. The time Laurie had been admitted, and the fact they had given her a mild sedative to help her sleep. She'd been conscious when the ambulance had first arrived. She'd been able to provide the staff with the details of her insurance provider, and the name of her personal physician, who would attend the hospital in the morning. And that was about it. Of course, I wanted to know more.

"Look," I said, attempting to be more congenial. "I'm not trying to be a pain in the ass here."

The doctor's eyes narrowed in disbelief.

"How would you be acting right now if the person you cared most about in the world was in there," I pointed down the hallway from the nurse's station for effect. "That's my girl in there. I think I can be forgiven for being more than a little concerned about her."

The doctor seemed to relax a bit as he sized me up. He held out his hand. "I'm Dr. Murray." He smiled for the first time since the nurse had summoned him to the station.

"Peter Jackson," I shook his hand firmly. "I apologize for being an asshole," I added.

Dr. Murray quickly shook his head. "You weren't. If you're guilty of anything it would be caring a great deal about that young lady in the room down the hall. You need to let us do our jobs. The truth is we don't know what happened to your girlfriend tonight."

"Laurie. That's her name. And she's my fiancée Dr. Murray. Only I haven't exactly asked her to marry me. Not yet, but I will. As soon as everything gets back to normal. I can't stand to see her so vulnerable, and I don't ever want her to be alone again."

"Now she has you to look after her," Dr. Murray said warmly.

"Yeah. That's right. Now she has me, and I don't intend to ever leave her."

"She's a lucky woman," Dr. Murray said with conviction. "Don't worry. We'll take good care of her. I'm on duty all night." He looked at the chart he held in his hand. "Dr. Gordon will see her in the morning. He's her personal physician. I know him; he's an excellent doctor. Results of the blood work we've done are on their way." Dr. Murray looked up from Laurie's chart, and then back at me. "We'll find out what happened, and treat her accordingly.

"Go home. Both of you. There's nothing to be accomplished by spending the rest of the night here. Get a few hours sleep, and come back tomorrow."

I started to object. He stopped me. "She's been sedated, and will sleep through the night. Come back in the morning. You can see Dr. Gordon then," he said.

I sighed. The fight left me. I knew he was right. If we stayed, by the time Dr. Gordon arrived in the morning, we'd both be exhausted.

"Agreed," I capitulated. "Thank you Dr. Murray."

"Rest assured, she'll have the best of care. Now both of you. Please." He smiled reassuringly. "Go home."

Chapter 68

LAURIE HAD BEEN exhausted for much longer than she let on. But, she improved steadily over the weekend and on into the next week. Her stay in the hospital proved a blessing in disguise, as we spent hours of quality time together. For the most part we were uninterrupted. Beyond the walls of the quiet hospital room though, a firestorm raged out of control.

John was at its center, and he was proving to be a master of the game. He had been working quietly and efficiently behind the scenes. Moving five thousand albums by an unknown musician was no small feat. I'd done all of one concert. John managed to press, distribute, and promote our music to coincide with it.

He also managed to get local broadcasters interested enough to show up and film parts of the show. Now snippets of our concert were being aired on the local television stations. Social media was all over it. It was a marketing campaign to kickstart sales of our full album before next month's tour. I wondered which one of five or six mega-bands would select The Gems to be their warm-up act. I hadn't seen any of the band since the concert because I'd been at the hospital with

Laurie. I could only imagine how they felt about the way everything was unfolding.

Franklin told everyone that Laurie and I needed some time alone together. He drove me to and from the hospital, and also kept me abreast of the details for the upcoming tour.

Then came Wednesday, and the end of things that had been.

I was in the room with Laurie when both doctors walked in, which was unusual. They wore poker faces; it wasn't a good sign. I swallowed hard, trying to get rid of the sudden lump at the back of my throat.

Laurie stared solemnly first at Dr. Murray, and then at Dr. Gordon.

Laurie immediately sensed something wasn't right. She preempted any misgivings they may have had with regard to privacy. "Peter is staying," she said with surprising strength.

"Laurie, we – " Dr. Murray began.

"I'm staying," I cut him off, leaving no room for debate.

They nodded. "Okay" said Dr. Gordon. He continued, "I hope you don't mind Dr. Murray being here Laurie, we've both had a hand in this. I hoped he could sit in on this consultation. Is there anyone else you would like to be here?"

Laurie shook her head as I squeezed her hand.

She searched my eyes. "Everyone important in my life is already here," she smiled nervously.

Dr. Murray looked at Dr. Gordon, who nodded. Dr. Murray looked back at Laurie, and continued.

"Your test results came back." He paused, "How long have you been feeling this way?" he asked.

"What way?" she laughed nervously. "I've been a little tired lately, but that's probably because of the inventory assignment at work. We've been putting in some long hours."

"This isn't a recent thing, is it? My guess would be you've felt poorly for at least a couple of months. You've been tired, and experiencing nausea. You've been throwing up quite a bit, haven't you?"

I looked from him back to her. "Laurie?" I was alarmed now.

She stared at me in silence for what seemed a long time. She finally returned her gaze to Dr. Murray.

"At first I thought I had a cold," she confided. "That was about three months ago. It didn't go away, though," her bottom lip trembled. I began to massage her arm. The tiny room seemed to close in on us, getting even smaller. "It got a little better, then a little worse, like a seesaw. When it got really bad, my stomach would hurt. I'd sometimes throw up during the night."

"Why didn't you tell me?" I spoke softly to her.

She smiled. "There was nothing you could have done."

"I could have taken you to the doctor. We could have gone together."

She looked at Dr. Gordon. "I should have – I know," she sighed. "It's just that life was so busy, and I didn't think it was serious."

She looked at me again. This time she looked incredibly sad. She spoke quietly with resignation in her voice. "I guess I know now," she said.

"Know what?" I looked frantically from her to the men on the other side of the bed. "Know what?" I implored them. I was shaking my head. Tears were filling my eyes. I looked back at Laurie.

"My condition is critical – isn't it Doctor?"

My legs suddenly felt like they were on fire.

Chapter 69

LIFE AS I had come to know it ceased to exist. When pressed, Dr. Gordon had given Laurie about twelve precious weeks to live. They left us alone in the room, and we cried in each other's arms for over an hour. I climbed into bed with her. Exhausted and emotionally spent, we finally fell asleep in a warm embrace. I never felt so helpless in all my life. There was simply nothing we could do.

No mistake had been made. Still, I didn't believe it. I could not accept that in a couple of short months Laurie would be leaving me. My denial continued when they discharged her from the hospital the next day. Aside from managing the pain that would come, there was no way they could help her.

Her frail body, they said, was riddled with a rare, terminal cancer. It was everywhere. They could not cut it out. There was no radiation or chemotherapy that would kill it.

She came home with me, back to the cottage. Word of her illness quickly spread. Everyone who'd come to love us was deeply affected by the sudden and unexpected news. Some were saddened; others became angry. No one could quite accept it. At least not yet.

For the first couple of days we avoided even mentioning what was happening. This came to a head on the morning of the third day after Laurie checked out of the hospital. As had been my habit when she stayed overnight with me, I awoke first. I watched her face as she lay sleeping.

I suddenly felt terrified. The truth was sinking in, and I didn't want her to leave me. Now that I had someone I loved, everything was different. Before I'd met Laurie, it had always been about me and my past. Since we got together, I looked only forward – not at what I left behind.

And now my biggest reason for living, my very future, was wasting away right before my eyes, and there wasn't a damn thing I could do about it.

Tears welled up in my eyes. My nose began to run and itch at the same time. I sneezed and Laurie opened her eyes. She peered up at me, and then I really began to bawl.

She gently reached up to my face to wipe away the tears. "Don't cry Peter," she whispered softly. "Please don't cry. I couldn't bear it. Let's just enjoy the time we have left. There are people who don't get even that. At least we know what's coming."

I massaged my eyes, and regained some degree of composure. "Do you mind if we talk about it?" I asked solemnly.

She smiled. "Everyone dies Peter; it's natural." Her smile broadened. "Who knows – you might even go before I do."

I shook my head, unable to stop myself from smiling along with her. "I've always loved your sense of humor. Are you hungry?" I asked her. She had eaten next to nothing since leaving the hospital.

"As luck would have it, I'm starving," she stated.

"Good," I said. "What would you like for breakfast? I make a great omelet."

"That's the only thing you make well," she teased me.

"Who are you trying to kid?" I admonished her. "I can boil water better than anyone I know."

"See if you can make us both a decent cup of coffee while I jump in the shower. I'll meet you in the dining room in fifteen minutes."

"One more thing," I said. I leaned close to her face and kissed her passionately on the lips. Still close to her, I spoke softly, "I love you more than you'll ever know."

"I do know," she whispered.

"I'll make breakfast," I said.

She smiled, and agreed, "You'd better get started before I change my mind."

Chapter 70

A FEW MINUTES later we were sitting at the dining room table. I watched with satisfaction as she took another large bite out of the vegetarian omelet in front of her.

We finally agreed to talk about what was coming. I was nervous as hell. I fought through it. This wasn't about me, I wasn't the one who wouldn't be here in a few months. I knew now was the time to say the things that needed saying. I drew a deep breath. "I guess I'll start."

"Okay." She said, as she played with the food on the plate. I was glad she'd finished at least half of it before she'd lost her appetite. She needed nourishment now more than ever.

"How does it feel Laurie?"

"Probably a lot like getting kicked in the guts by a horse on steroids," she said in a nonchalant way. She put her fork beside her plate, and looked directly into my eyes. "I'm scared. I've never been so scared in my life. I don't want to die, I haven't really lived yet. It isn't fair. I just got through some really shitty stuff in my life, and then I meet you. We had what I thought was going to be a wonderful future together. What did I do that was so terrible to deserve this?" She fought back the tears. I began to get out of my chair to go to her.

"No," she stopped me with a quick motion of her hand. "That isn't how it's going to be." She wiped the tears from her eyes with the back of her hand. "It can't go this way," she said as she fought to regain control of her emotions. I could only dream of the strength she possessed. She forced a smile. "We don't have the time for it."

"What can I do?" I felt helpless.

"Exactly what you've been doing since the first day we met. Be yourself. Now isn't the time to change just because I got a shitty hand."

"We both got a shitty hand," I corrected her. "None of this is going to mean anything without you: the music, the concerts, all the accolades. I used to think my music was everything. I guess maybe because I didn't have anything else. You're what I've looked for all along, I just didn't know it until now. I'm scared too, I don't want to be alone in this life.

"You're damned right it isn't fair!" I became aware I was rambling. I stopped talking, even though I knew there was a lot more to say. This wasn't going to be easy.

Laurie looked down at her half-eaten omelet

in despair. "Don't think poorly of me for what I'm about to say," she almost muttered.

This time I got up from my chair, and walked around the table. I stood above her and she looked up at me. I held out my hand. She smiled and reached for it. Silently I led her into the living room. We sat down on the sofa.

"I could never judge you," I assured her. I could see she was really shaky.

"When I found out I'm dying, I thought it must be God's way of punishing me for having the abortion," she sighed. "I murdered that child. I made that decision. She never got the chance to know me, go to school, or fall in love. No marriage. No growing old with someone. I guess it's only fair that most of the same things are now being taken away from me."

"You can't say that," I protested. "And I'll tell you why. How many people did I hurt when I was cooking meth?"

"That's different than what I did," she said.

"How is it different?"

"They took advantage of you. You didn't know any better," she said.

I shook my head. "I was never that naïve. I knew I was manufacturing death. Even as a kid, I had a choice, same as you. In fact, I'm a lot more guilty than you could ever be. I don't think you were given much of an option. You weren't ready to raise a child. Your boyfriend was just a kid, like you were. Having that baby would have been a disaster for everyone."

"How do you know that?" she shot back angrily.

We were silent then. The sound of our breathing punctuated the uneasy silence between us.

"I don't," I stated. "I'm sorry. I never should have said that. But think about this – If what you say is true, then I should have been dead a long time ago. And what about redemption? If everyone who made a mistake when they were young and didn't know better was killed off by a vengeful God, there wouldn't be one single human being left. There'd be no forgiveness, because everyone would have already been condemned. I cannot and will not believe that. Your getting sick doesn't have anything to do with your abortion. Believe me, God isn't that vindictive."

She stared at me, digesting what I'd said.

"Have you always been such a sweet talker?" she finally asked.

I leaned over and took her into my arms. I held onto her tightly, as though my embrace could stop the cancer from taking her away.

Chapter 71

NO ONE WAS saying anything about the fact we weren't practicing for the tour. For my part, I tried to care, but it just wasn't there.

It was five days after Laurie was discharged from the hospital. We talked about her cancer here and there, but there wasn't a lot to add to what had already been said. Feeling so powerless and vulnerable was frustrating. I could only imagine how Laurie felt, with the fear and uncertainty of her impending death hanging over her like an omnipotent clock winding itself down. Only there was no way of winding this one back up.

We stopped cooking our own meals. I added up the time I'd have to spend doing it and decided not to. I didn't want to waste a second we had left together. In less than a week, Laurie was showing further signs of the end nearing. In the evening she was retiring a few minutes earlier, and waking up every morning a few minutes later. The cancer was sucking her life away, and relentlessly closing in on her.

"I'll have coffee for you in five minutes," I said, seeing she was awake.

Laurie yawned, smiling. "What time is it?"

"Time for you to rise and shine," I smiled with her. "How are you feeling?"

She frowned. "Tired. It's nothing a half dozen cups of strong coffee won't cure though. For a while, at least."

I looked at the floor, wishing beyond all hope that I could do something to stop this madness. Why was this happening to us? Hearing her talk about how little time she had, the first thought of the day, was almost more than I could bear. I smothered these feelings. There was no way I was going to feel sorry for her. Laurie deserved more, much more.

"I know," I said softly. "I'll be back in five minutes."

"Peter?"

I turned back to her.

"Two cream, no sugar please."

"As you wish," I said, and headed for the hotel's kitchen.

I ran into Raymond as I walked down the cobblestoned pathway in the courtyard. The stage was gone now, everything was gone. This past Friday night flashed through my mind. It was as if everything was a dream then, and a nightmare now.

"Hi boss," Ray greeted me. "You okay?" he was concerned, but didn't want it to show too much.

"I'll live," I said in a flat tone.

Ray's glance flirted with the ground between us. I reached out and put my hand on his powerful shoulder. It was a conciliatory gesture.

"Don't act so damned self-conscious Ray. Let the others know too. I'm not a porcelain doll," I chided him.

Ray looked back at me. There was understanding in his eyes.

"Are you handling things?" I asked.

He nodded. "We're with you on this thing. If there's anything we can do – "

"You're already doing it. Tell the band not to worry. Everything's up here," I pointed to my head. "Everything will be fine. I'll be ready for the tour."

Ray nodded again. "Franklin and John were asking about things. I'll let them know."

"It's a fucking race Ray," I suddenly lost my composure. "Is she going to die before the first show? Or is she still going to be hanging on? If she is..." I trailed off.

Now it was Ray who put his hand onto my shoulder. "We'll work it out, we have your back. However it goes. If we have to cancel…"

"We can't do that. The Gems will do the shows. We'll find a way through this fucking mess. We have to. Life goes on, right?" I fought back tears. Ray stepped into me and gave me a big, burly hug. When he stepped back I felt a lot better.

"Thanks man, I appreciate it. Tell the guys that we're meeting tonight about this," I suddenly decided. "Ignoring what's happening isn't going to make it go away. Tonight at eight, in my cottage. Franklin, and John too."

"Won't Laurie be there?" he asked as if I had forgotten.

"You're damn right she'll be there. This involves her more than anyone. She'll have something to say, no doubt. She's not dead yet."

Ray said, "Peter, I was just – "

I cut him off. "What'd I tell you in the beginning of this conversation?"

"Don't be so damned self-conscious," Ray smiled.

"That's right," I agreed, smiling too. "Now I better get over to the kitchen. Laurie's hungry."

We hugged again, both of us feeling a sizeable

weight lifted from our shoulders. I headed for the kitchen in what was now a hurry. I was moving less cautiously, and faster than I should have been. In that same moment, other seemingly innocuous random events were unfolding. Everything around me suddenly began to come together to form a disaster.

It was like driving into a fatal car crash. How many miniscule details happen over a person's lifetime to put them in the exact place and time to die in the middle of a horrible wreck? The chances of it happening exactly that way are a billion to one, and yet it happens all the time.

Chapter 72

I WOULD FIND out later that when I bumped into Ray there was a young couple having breakfast in the hotel's restaurant. They were with their three-year-old daughter; she was playing with a toy they brought with them to keep her occupied. The little girl's tiny, awkward fingers explored the large plastic wheels on the base of a brightly-colored clown's body. She had already dropped it twice, not quite enough times for her mother to take the toy away.

The restaurant was busier than usual. The couple had been waiting for more than twenty minutes for their order. The baby was hungry, restless, and fidgety.

The day before, a pigeon had been chased away from a meal by a small dog, one of those breeds that make the most noise. The shrill yapping drove the bird up over the hotel and into the courtyard. In its instinctive panic it aimed for a dark opening near the ground. Only the dark opening was one of the glass windows adjacent to the exit door of the restaurant. The bird died instantly from blunt force trauma, its fragile neck broken in two places. The window cracked along its entire length.

Two workmen finished extracting the damaged window from its frame. Ray was telling them to work as fast as possible to install the replacement window. The glass was heavy. One of the men had a lot of trouble lifting it. He'd been drinking a lot lately because he'd broken up with his girlfriend. Now his back was sore. He blamed it on the weight of the windows, but secretly knew his kidneys were telling him to ease up on the booze. He cursed under his breath as beads of sweat from his brow spilled freely down the surface of the glass near his hand. The uncomfortable hot air from the courtyard gushed into the dining room through the large hole where the window had been removed. That guy Ray had been right; if they didn't work fast the people in the restaurant would start complaining.

The little girl's toy clown slipped from her fingers, and for the third time fell to the floor. It clattered onto the ceramic tiles, and was instantly kicked by a harried waiter bringing the family's breakfast to the table. It tumbled across the walkway, and righted itself onto its wheels after rolling over a couple of times.

I was giving a bit of a berth to the worker with the hangover. His back was to me as the toy clown, a frozen smile across its face, rolled under the guy's foot as he carefully backpedaled. His foot came down, and immediately flew out from under him.

The hangover guy's foot twisted abruptly. He screamed in agony, heroically trying his best to hang onto the sheet of glass. The window was slipping from his grip, and he was going down. I was half a step away from him. Without thinking, I lunged toward the glass as the worker's knees buckled, moving to where his gloved hand was slipping from its purchase. My hand made contact with the bottom edge of the heavy window, just as his slipped from it, and as the window began to fall. I went with it, realizing too late I'd misjudged its weight. All of this took only an instant. I began to snatch my hand back as the pane contacted what I knew had to be the floor.

Instantly it felt like I'd been stung by a handful of angry wasps. From an outstretched arm's length, I watched in horror as the makeshift guillotine performed its grotesque handiwork.

My right arm came back without my fingers as the glass exploded into a million tiny pieces. I held my hand up in front of my face in total disbelief. All of my fingers were gone. My thumb remained intact, still where it ought to have been. I screamed as the blood began to spurt from the top of my outstretched palm with every beat of my heart, like some adolescent kid's obscene Halloween joke.

Chapter 73

AT FIRST THE pain was intense, like a flash of lightning. But within a few seconds there was only a dull throbbing sensation. I could feel the blood coming out through the edges of my palm, where the appendages used to be.

I suddenly noticed Ray beside me. He would tell me later that he'd become nervous, and returned to personally supervise the window's installation. "My God," he gasped, and then his instincts took over, and he flew into action.

The patrons were all looking at us from the tables throughout the dining room. Their gasping and fainting spells weren't going to do me a damn bit of good. Ray was a different matter though. He put the picture together in an instant, and took control.

"Look at me Peter," he commanded. "Don't look at your fingers."

"I don't have any fingers Ray," I looked up from my hand to his face.

"You're going to be all right," his admonition sounded completely absurd given the circumstances. "It's a clean cut." He turned to the waiter beside him who was the integral link in this macabre chain reaction. Ray calmly grabbed the white linen napkin draped across his shoulder.

"I need an ice bucket, with ice," he added. "Now Arnold! Not tomorrow!" he snapped. The waiter darted toward the kitchen as Ray wrapped the napkin around the end of my palm as best he could to stop the bleeding. He motioned with his head to the installer who'd tripped on the clown.

"Give me your belt!" he ordered. "Quickly," he urged him.

The guy offered his belt in two seconds flat.

"I need your help to stop the bleeding," said Ray. "Wrap it tightly around his wrist while I hold on to this rag."

The worker nodded. His eyes were bulbous, but he limped forward and wrapped the belt around my arm, tightly cinching it.

"Now yours," Ray barked his order to the other installer.

The man quickly removed his own belt. Seeing what he needed to do, he already had the belt in a loop as he stepped forward.

"This might hurt Peter," Ray warned me. I nodded nervously. I was going into shock, because as they cinched my hand I felt very little, only the pounding of my heart in my eardrums, and in my hand.

"All right, that's good. Hold the belts steady. I'm going to have to find his fingers. If Peter faints, don't let him hit the floor."

I began to feel hot all over just as he said it. My legs began to tingle and itch, like insects were crawling all over me. Ray moved toward the large pile of broken glass on the floor. Not in the least concerned about cuts to his own hands, Ray began to hurriedly sift through the glass, scattering the shards this way and that.

I watched him from the other side of a dark tunnel. He snatched them up as he found them, one at a time. He had a bit of trouble finding the fourth finger, but he finally located it just as Arnold reappeared with a bucket of ice. Ray stood up, grabbed it, and gently placed my four fingers into the ice. Arnold said nothing as he handed Ray the lid to the bucket. Ray calmly placed it over my fingers, and snapped it shut.

"We'll use your van," he nodded to the installer who'd handed him the second belt. "It's out front, isn't it?"

He nodded. "Follow me. I'll get us there fast," he referred to the hospital.

"Let's move," said Ray, turning to the other

installer. "Try to keep his arm as high as you can without hurting him. I'll call Emergency and tell them we're on our way." He turned to me. "Can you walk to the front of the hotel?"

I nodded, even though I couldn't quite think straight. The bugs were crawling higher up my legs, painfully stinging me now. It didn't make sense – if anything my hand should be screaming in pain.

"Put your good arm around my shoulder and hang on Peter. You'll be fine," he repeated. "Keep his arm as high as you can," he admonished the other installer again. "Let's do it, let's go."

We moved forward as one. I took one slow step after another, feeling as if I was treading through a dark, murky thickness. All I could think of was that I had no fucking fingers on my right hand.

Chapter 74

THEY CALLED IN four orthopedic surgeons, one for each finger. They assessed me, and immediately prepped me for surgery.

I woke up in the same hospital Laurie had been discharged from. The room was bathed in the ebbing warmth of the Big Easy's setting sun. The day was dying, the same thing I felt like doing.

I swam up from the murky depths of the strong anesthesia, and finally opened my eyes.

"Peter?" It sounded like a gasp.

"Laurie," I tried to say her name as she came into focus. It came out closer to something like Rory. She was standing right above me; I could tell she'd been crying.

I tried my best for a smile. My lips felt fat and almost lifeless, barely able to function. I fought through what was left of the anesthetic. "How are you feeling?" I managed, as a small amount of clarity returned. The room seemed to shift slightly on a weird axis and then return to itself.

She shook her head, and tears spilled freely down her pale cheeks. All I could think of was how beautiful she looked. "Not me," she moaned. She leaned over and put her hands on both sides of my face. Her tears spilled onto my lips.

"Don't cry," I quietly beseeched her. "Please don't cry. It means you feel sorry for me. I need something else right now. Something better than pity."

I glanced at my right hand. My arm was in traction, completely immobile. Everything was covered in white cotton bandages. I didn't know if the doctors had been able to reattach my fingers, if not I was useless. I shook off the notion in disgust. I was guilty now of the very thing I'd just asked her not to do. I resolved that no one, myself included, was allowed to feel sorry for me.

Laurie removed her hands from my face, and retrieved a Kleenex to dry her eyes.

"That's better," I encouraged her as my head continued to clear. "I'd hold your hand, but unfortunately I don't think I can move mine right now." I shifted slightly in the hospital bed to get more comfortable. At least my legs felt okay. There were no fire ants feasting on them anymore.

Laurie laughed, in spite of herself. Then she became serious. "The doctor will be here in a few minutes. Probably more than one of them. They were here about two hours ago."

"How long have you been here?"

"Franklin told me what happened. I waited in the cottage for you to come back with the coffee. After about twenty minutes, I got up to look for you. He was already pounding on the door. He was super upset, almost crying. He gave me a ride. A bunch of people came to the hospital. The entire band came down to see if there was anything they could do. John showed up too. A lot of people care about you Peter."

I was touched by their outpouring of love. They had come for me, and to comfort Laurie. I was almost overcome by this knowledge. I barely stopped myself from losing control. Poor Laurie. I would have given both my hands if there was some way to save her. She didn't have much time.

I was suddenly angry. We'd been given little enough time to say goodbye. And now this. Laurie needed me to see her to the end. I was pretty sure I wasn't going anywhere soon, now that I'd lost my fingers. Since she hadn't told me otherwise, I had to conclude the doctors failed to reattach them. Outwardly, for Laurie's sake, I remained calm. Inwardly, I was seething at the pathetic injustice of life.

Senior told me not long after Lynette had been tragically killed by the bus, that everything happened for a reason. Still, I had remained inconsolable. That cold autumn in Memphis seemed to last forever. I became as empty, and devoid of spirit as the old oak tree down the road that had been struck by lightning the same day Lynette died. There was a blackened, charred hole right through it. That winter the cold winds made a haunting, howling sound every time they came in from the northwest and blew through that hole. I always imagined it was Lynette, lamenting the life she'd lost before she'd had a chance to live it.

I looked up at Laurie. "I'm sorry," I said.

She immediately shook her head, denying me that. "It happened. We'll make the most of it."

I barely nodded. She looked exhausted. "I want you to go back home soon," I managed. "To the cottage."

She began to protest. I stopped her, "Please, you need rest. Ask the doctors for something to help you sleep if you need it. They'll have no problem with that. I know you love me, but this isn't about me. I'll get through this, I need you to be strong for me though. That means you have to look after yourself. You'll drive me crazy with worry if you stay here. Come back in the morning. I'll be all right without my fingers, I'll be just fine."

She looked at me with a question mark across her face. The color seemed to return to her complexion.

"You don't know," it was a quiet observation.

"Know what?"

She smiled. "They called in two teams of specialists, some of the best doctors in the country. It will take time, and you'll never have the same movement, but they'll work. You have your fingers back Peter."

Chapter 75

I BEGAN TO feel pain in the early morning hours. It woke me up around three am. The first thing that came to my mind was an image of the window exploding and the glass cascading onto the floor in a crystal shower, the shards devouring my hand. I held it up, and voilà – no fingers. I remembered the emotions. First, there had been shock. That had quickly turned into a panicky fear. Finally, an incredible angst, as I realized everything I'd worked so hard for was gone in that instant.

Right before I'd gone under the anesthetic one of the doctors asked me why I didn't let go of the window. I told him that my reflexes, the very thing that caused that moment, had betrayed me with their quickness. There was no real answer or logic to explain what happened. Whatever my intentions, the end result was a horrible tragedy.

I pressed the call button for the on-duty nurse. My throat was raw and sore from the surgical breathing tube. My tongue was dry and swollen.

I looked to the table beside the bed for something to drink. There was nothing. I glanced up at the wall clock again. Ten minutes had passed since I hit the call button for the nurse. The pain had gotten worse; I impatiently hit it again. I rolled my tongue inside my mouth, hoping to moisten my throat. Everything was dry as a desert. Where was the nurse?

The door to my room was closed. The clock on the wall in front of me was the only light source. It glowed green, and gave off enough light to see around me. The bathroom was a few feet to my right, its door slightly ajar. The pale nightlight inside threw a soft, muted glow of its own through the opening.

I decided I couldn't wait for the nurse, who obviously wasn't responding to my summons. I sized up my situation. My arm was suspended in a sling hung from a metal bracket above the bed, but nothing was holding it in place. I tried lifting it from where it rested and found I could do so without too much discomfort. My hand up to my elbow was completely wrapped in familiar white gauze.

I was able to carefully extract my arm from the sling. I knew I had to keep it above my heart; I didn't want to compromise the integrity of the surgery. But my thirst was growing by the minute, overriding common sense. Where was the damn nursing staff?

My arm free and stretched out in front of me, I swung my legs over the edge of the bed and sat up. Immediately I felt the fire ants return, as if they were consuming the flesh below my knees. My head was spinning, and I fought to keep from passing out. Somehow I managed to stay conscious. The pain in my legs was absolutely horrible – almost as bad as my thirst, which had driven me to this desperate act.

It took every ounce of my willpower to finally stand at the side of the bed. I stood there, battling with the urge to give up or pass out. My thirst was more compelling. I grabbed onto the familiar IV pole and began to steer it, and myself, the few feet toward the bathroom door. My legs were on fire.

It seemed to take forever to slowly and painfully move the short distance to the bathroom door. I managed to push it open. Painstakingly, I shuffled into the bathroom and over to the sink. I supported myself on the edge of it, gathering my strength. I finally looked up to find a cup so I could get relief from this damnable thirst. In the dim glow thrown off by the nightlight, I caught my reflection in the mirror above the sink. I screamed when I saw what I knew had to be me. The sound I made was a horrible, dry inhuman rasp. It was like the hiss of a wounded snake.

The thing that stared back at me was an abomination. My face was blackened and grotesque – flesh melted off in some places, particularly around my jawbone. The logical part of my brain said this isn't real, just like the last time. But the vision in front of me of blackened flesh hanging from my shoulder blades and ribs was real to the rest of my mind. I screamed again in abject horror at the monster I saw in the mirror. I blinked hard, opening my eyes this time to myself, my normal self, staring back at me. My gauze-wrapped arm was held out in front of me like some twisted, broken branch. I was shaken to the core. My other arm – my good arm – trembled uncontrollably, and I was hyperventilating. The scorching pain I'd felt in my legs changed into a horribly familiar, maddening itch. I wanted to bend down and tear at the flesh with my fingernails. I remembered with utter clarity the first night spent in the hospital in Jackson after the bus crash. I recalled every terrible detail. Now I was experiencing the same nightmare all over again.

The room seemed to move, as if I was swimming underwater, and looking up through it. My knees began to give out from under me. I was losing consciousness. Right before I collapsed, I made every effort to roll onto my left side, to protect my reattached fingers. Then everything went black.

Chapter 76

I REGAINED CONSCIOUSNESS sometime later. The room still glowed with a soft light, but immediately I noticed it was green, and not the pale yellow of the bathroom's nightlight. I glanced around me as things came into focus. Somehow, either with someone's help or through my own efforts, I was back in the hospital bed. The clock on the wall read 3:10 am. It had been a nightmare.

I was breathing hard, and my legs were itching like hell. My entire arm felt uncomfortably hot. It wasn't quite painful, but it was close. My hand throbbed like a bass drum with each beat of my heart. The door to the room eased open, and a nurse entered as quietly as she could, the rubber soles of her shoes squeaking only when she rounded the corner of the bed. She wore a concerned, kind expression as the light in the hallway washed across her face. She approached me, and saw I was awake.

"How are you feeling Mr. Jackson?" she whispered, warmth in her voice.

"The painkillers are wearing off," I managed

hoarsely from somewhere behind my swollen tongue. At least I didn't sound like a snake. The nightmare had seemed as real as the first time, back in Jackson. "I'm thirsty as hell," I added. "Do you think you can bring me some orange juice?"

"Yes, of course," she said.

"Call me Peter," I corrected her. "Miss…?"

She smiled. "It's been Mrs. for twenty-two years. Are you in pain?" she was suddenly serious.

"My legs feel like they're being gnawed on by hungry rats. Surprisingly, my hand isn't that bad though."

She frowned. "I'll get you something for it."

"My throat is drier than a dying cactus," I complained.

"That would be from the breathing tube," she confirmed.

"My hand feels hot, and like it's the size of a watermelon," I added.

"But no real pain?"

"I can't say there is, but I think it's on the edge. I don't want to wait until it's too late – I did lose four of my fingers."

She nodded. "I can only go so far with the dosage of the painkiller. There's a limit to what I can do without a doctor's order. I'll give you the maximum though. It should put you out for the rest of the night. At least one of your surgeons will check on you in the morning."

"I'm very grateful," I expressed my relief. "To each and every one of them. I'm looking forward to thanking them. I imagine things could very easily have gone the other way."

"Fortunately they didn't," she smiled. "I'll be back in a few minutes with something to ease your discomfort."

"Thanks." She turned to leave, and I stopped her. "You never told me your name."

"Doris Anderson," she said.

"Thanks Doris."

I looked at her more closely. She had a certain, odd familiarity about her. "Have we met? You look familiar to me."

The smile never left her face. "Perhaps we have," she humored me.

"Have you ever been on television?" I asked her.

She chuckled good-naturedly. "Not that I'm aware of. I'm definitely not an actor, if that's where you're going with this."

Much later, I realized that she never really did answer my first question.

Chapter 77

WHATEVER DORIS GAVE me, it worked. When I finally woke up, it was daylight. That was the first thing I noticed. The second was Laurie, asleep in the chair beside my bed.

The warm sunlight from the room's partly-drawn curtains washed gently across her face. It was pale, and I could see she'd lost weight, no doubt from the cancer. It was only a matter of time before she would finally succumb to the relentless, unforgiving illness. She looked so innocent, and so beautiful.

I slowly shook my head from side to side. Tears welled up in my eyes. Such a pure heart did not deserve this. There was nothing fair about it. If this wasn't enough, I was now incapacitated. I brushed the bead of a tear away, determined not to make this about me. As limited as I was in my ability to help Laurie, help her I would.

Suddenly my right hand felt as if it exploded. Unable to control myself, I screamed out in agony. Laurie was immediately awakened.

"Peter! What… "

"Call the doctor!" I screamed. "For God's sake!" I stared at my gauze-covered hand, fully expecting to see a crimson tide spreading across the white cotton bandages. It was obvious something had just gone horribly wrong.

I threw my head back into the pillow behind me, writhing in agony, my teeth grinding to the point where it felt like they would shatter. "Hurry!" I screamed again. Laurie bolted for the door, and disappeared beyond it into the hallway. I screamed again, this time cursing aloud. I'd never before felt such excruciating pain.

It seemed to take forever for the medical staff to arrive, but in seconds the room was filled. As I contorted in pain, one of them fought with me to cover my face with some sort of mask. With the help of another, they finally managed to keep it in place. The light in the hospital room began to dim. The room shrunk to a single point of awareness, and then that too vanished.

Chapter 78

"PETER? PETER? CAN you hear me?" A strange voice called to me through the darkness. It seemed to come closer each time it called my name, as if it was crawling toward me from the other side of a long tunnel. The voice got louder with each utterance.

When at last I forced my eyes open, I stared into a harsh penetrating light. It was taken away, leaving small explosions of colored twinkling lights. As they faded, I found myself looking into the face of an elderly man.

"Ah," he uttered, seemingly satisfied. "You're awake. Welcome back."

"Laurie…"

"She's fine Peter. She's in the waiting room down the hall. You gave us quite a scare."

"What happened?" I asked, fighting to remember.

"First allow me to introduce myself. My name is Dr. Bruce Evans. I was the lead surgeon on the team that worked on you to reattach your fingers."

He looked at me quizzically then, which I found odd, and a little bit disturbing.

"How long have I been – "

"Not long," he interrupted me. "Enough time for us to have a closer look at you, and your hand."

We were interrupted as the room's door swung open and three other smock-attired men entered the room.

"Ah. The team has arrived." Dr. Evans noted with satisfaction. The three men sidled up to the hospital bed. They stared down at me, like Aztec priests examining their latest sacrificial candidate. I groaned inwardly, certain I was due for some really bad news.

Dr. Bruce Evans introduced them in turn, each nodding upon hearing his name. "Dr. Keith Pickering, Dr. Nigel Crossfield, and Dr. Stewart King." They all watched me silently. I guessed they were a bit embarrassed, having failed, not really sure how to apologize for an unsuccessful procedure.

"Hell guys," I was the first to speak. "You did your best. That's all anyone can ask for. It was a long shot, we all knew it. And none of us are God, are we?"

They exchanged unreadable glances.

"It's okay," I addressed them with a conciliatory tone. "I seriously want to thank each of you for trying your best. Please don't feel bad about the way things turned out." I gazed down at the mound of gauze around the end of my right arm. They must have used a mile of the stuff.

I sighed. "At least it doesn't hurt anymore," I conceded. I was sad; I knew I would never play a guitar again. That part of my life was officially over.

Dr. Evans cleared his throat. The other doctors looked at him expectantly, deferring to him.

"Peter," he began tentatively. "Something extraordinary has happened. We have no explanation for it. None of us have ever experienced anything quite like it."

I looked carefully at him, not quite sure what he was getting at.

"Did something happen to my hand?" I asked. "Did you have to do something to my hand?" Adrenaline coursed through my veins. I stared back down at the gauze, terror mounting inside of me.

"Nothing happened to your hand," Dr. Evans, seeing my panic, was quick to step in with a professional assurance. "At least nothing bad." He looked over to Dr. King, who happened to be standing closest to my hand. "Doctor, can you help me with this please?"

Dr. Evans turned back to me and said, "Peter, what's happened can only be described as a miracle.

We… well, we consider our part in what happened to be something of a gift. What I'm attempting to explain to you…" he glanced in the direction of his associates. "Hell," he said, somewhat frustrated. "A picture's worth a thousand words." He nodded to Dr. King, who produced a pair of surgical scissors.

I must have twitched. "There's no need for you to be apprehensive. Go ahead Doctor," he directed his fellow surgeon.

It took Dr. King only a few seconds to cut away the yards of gauze. I stared down at my hand, and was astonished by what I saw.

All my fingers were there, present and accounted for, attached to my hand. There was no discoloration, no scars, and no sutures holding them onto the top part of my palm. There was only a slight redness where they had been severed from my hand.

I gaped at my hand and fingers in shock and disbelief. I willed them to move. I slowly clenched them into a fist, and then straightened them out again.

The only reminder of the gruesome accident two days ago, was a slight stiffness in the joints of my fingers.

Chapter 79

THEY DIDN'T WANT to let me go, but as I'd told the surgeons who operated on me, I wasn't in prison. Short of kidnapping me, there was no way they could hold me against my will.

"Please," they begged for what seemed the hundredth time. "Let us examine you, if only for a few days."

My eyes narrowed as I slipped the hospital gown off, and put my own clothes back on. "Not possible," I made it clear to Dr. Evans. I wasn't being rude, I was just stating a fact. "I'm afraid I don't have a few days."

As I fastened the buttons on the front of my plaid shirt, I marveled at the dexterity in the fingers of my right hand. Unbelievably, they seemed to move more fluidly now than before the accident.

The Doctor continued as I sat down and began to lace up my sneakers. "Peter, think of the people who could benefit from what has happened. There is no scientific or medical precedent here; no possible explanation for such accelerated healing. It has to be something internal, something entirely unique within your physiology. You must allow us to find out how this happened," he said. It was almost a demand.

I finished lacing my sneakers, and looked up at him, deciding whether or not to tell him. I sighed. He should know.

"I've been here before Doctor," I looked evenly at him.

"Where?" he asked. "You mean here, at this hospital?"

I shook my head. "It was the Jackson Baptist Medical Center in Jackson, Mississippi. Eight or nine months ago, I was on a Greyhound bus. We got hit by a train. I was the sole survivor. Well, there was someone else, but that's another story." I didn't want to get into it with him. "The bus was crushed under the wheels of the Amtrak. It caught fire, and I was very badly burned."

Dr. Evans' eyes grew larger. "I heard about that!" he suddenly remembered. "There was one survivor. That was you?" he seemed astonished.

I nodded.

"I remember seeing it on the news. It was a miracle anyone got out of that wreck alive, but you did. They spoke about your miraculous healing. At one point they said you were so badly disfigured that they were likely going to have to amputate limbs."

He stared at me then, as if he was looking at a ghost. "That was you," he repeated to himself, almost in a whisper. "And now this. Peter Jackson, who the hell are you?"

At least he hadn't asked me what I was, I thought ruefully. If he had, I don't think I could have blamed him. Truth be told, I was beginning to wonder that myself.

"Let us do some tests," he implored me again. "There's something in you that accelerates your natural healing capacity beyond anything anyone has ever experienced. For the second time! Let us have a closer look. I'm begging you Peter."

I shook my head, "I'm sorry Doctor. Besides, Jackson Baptist is almost a year ahead of you."

Even as I spoke with him, I knew I had to call The Wedge. The doctors in Jackson had been working on this for a long time, and they had the samples these doctors so coveted. Surely the lawyer must know something by now.

I flexed my fingers in front of me, looking down at the fist I'd made. There was nothing visible to indicate that only forty-eight hours had passed since I'd lost my fingers. It was impossible, and yet I stared at them now, unable to deny the facts.

Obviously, I'd make the tour now. I suddenly realized that none of the band knew what had happened. Everyone still figured I'd lost my fingers. I would tell them of course, but not just yet. There were other, far more important things I had to do while there was still time.

These more pressing thoughts brought my mind back to Laurie. She only had a few weeks. Soon it would be days, and then just a scant few hours. I clenched my fist, angrily opening and closing it.

Then it suddenly hit me like a blinding flash of lightning.

I jumped up and extended my right hand to Dr. Evans. "Thank you Doctor, for all your help." I was excited now. I felt light-headed with the prospect. It was a crazy idea – insane – what I was thinking, but everything around me was crazy. More importantly, I had absolutely nothing to lose, and the whole world to gain.

The Doctor's hand closed around my own. He knew I had to go, and nothing was going to change my mind. I felt the sincere energy and power in my fingers as we shook hands. "I will never forget you. Please tell the others how grateful I am."

Dr. Evans smiled in resignation. He spoke from his heart when he told me, "I wish you well Peter. Keep in touch."

I nodded. I hurried out the door. I knew I didn't have much time if I was going to pull it off.

Chapter 80

LAURIE'S JAW DROPPED when she saw me. I held my hand in front of her, waving it slightly from side to side like a windshield wiper. She just stared at it, and me.

I smiled. "At first, I didn't believe it either."

"How…" she fought for words that didn't come.

"I don't know," I stated. I sat down in the chair beside her, where she'd been waiting until the doctors sent for her to come and see me.

"It's a miracle," I began.

All Laurie could think of to say was, "You'll be able to make the tour! The band won't believe it!"

I laughed, flexing my hand in front of both of us, but the last thing on my mind was the tour. I stared at her, a goofy smile across my face.

"What?" she asked, bewildered. She was recovering from her initial shock of seeing my hand perfectly healed.

"This," I beamed, holding up my hand and twiddling my fingers. "The doctors put them back onto my hand, but something else healed them so quickly. I can't say what it is, but it all started with the accident. Not only do I heal at an absolutely incredible rate, but I also heal perfectly." I looked at my hand again. My fingers danced to a silent tune only they could hear. "They move differently now. It's subtle, but I can tell the tissues have a certain memory – knowledge they never had before."

"You're scaring me Peter," Laurie said.

"I know I sound crazy, but I'm not," I assured her. "I'm just trying to describe to you how my fingers feel to me. It's like they're not really a part of me anymore. They're something more. You have to admit, it might explain a few things. Sure, I could always play guitar, and I was really talented at it. But after the crash everything changed, there's like a tide of emotion now. I wish you could have been at the concert, you would have seen what I'm talking about. I'm sure it's got something to do with how my body heals itself. You saw it in The Guitar Works the first time we met. You remember how those people reacted to me playing?"

She nodded, wide-eyed.

"Don't you see it's all somehow connected?" I said, more to myself. "It's some kind of gift. I can feel it." I grabbed Laurie's hands in mine. She trembled slightly from my touch.

"We're going to Mississippi." I announced.

"Peter, I can't!" she shook her head slowly to accent her words, no doubt wondering what I was thinking. "You go, I'll be fine. I'll wait for you here." She was resigned to her fate.

"You're the reason we're going there," I softened the tone of my voice, in spite of the excitement that coursed through every fiber of my being. "Don't you get it? I'll call Wedge and tell him to expect us. We'll take your car. We'll pack light and leave first thing in the morning, right before dawn."

"Are you okay?" I could see she was worried about my sanity. I took a deep breath before I began again. I hoped this time I would speak more coherently, so she could understand.

"I'm sorry, I got ahead of myself. The way the burns on my body healed in Jackson wasn't normal. Just like what happened with my hand. Look at me," I commanded. "I've never been more serious in all my life when I say this. I believe with all my heart there is something inside me, something running through my veins that can cure your cancer. But, you're going to have to trust me.

Think about it, and ask yourself the same question I did. What do we have to lose?"

She started to cry. She said, "Oh Peter, I want to believe you, but just listen to yourself."

I grabbed her by the shoulders. "I know how this must sound." I looked down in frustration, shaking my head. I looked back at her, searching her eyes. I took my right hand from her shoulder. With the tips of my fingers I delicately brushed the tears from her cheeks as she closed her eyes. I brought my hand back a few inches from her face and held it there so she could see the moistened fingertips. She looked at them, and then back into my eyes. I raised my eyebrows in a question mark.

"What have we got to lose?" I whispered softly to her. "Please Laurie. I love you. Do this for us. Let's go to Jackson to see those doctors."

She looked at me for what seemed an eternity. Finally, mercifully, she nodded and collapsed into my arms, weeping softly.

Chapter 81

THERE WERE A few things I had to do before we left New Orleans. I called The Wedge first, right after I took Laurie back to the cottage so she could pack some sundries for the trip. I held my breath until his assistant picked up after the third ring. I introduced myself and said, "Please tell me Mr. Harding is in."

Relief washed over me when she asked me to hold. In less than a minute, Wedge's voice boomed across the line.

"Peter, my boy. How are you son? It's very good to hear from you. I was actually going to call you at the end of the week. We've had some developments," he immediately volunteered. He was cheerful, which was a good sign.

"Is it about my family?" I asked him hopefully.

"We're still looking into that. It's the damnedest thing. I'm afraid I have very little to report to you on that subject. Having said that, I do have some other interesting news for you."

He sensed immediately I hadn't phoned him

for small talk. I was grateful for his understanding, and perceptive mind.

"With your permission, we'll get back to your family afterwards," he was being sensitive.

"That's fine. What I really need to know is how the rest of it has been progressing."

"By the rest of it you must mean what's been going on with the doctors and scientists who have been working non-stop to find out how the hell your burns healed so quickly?"

"That's why I'm calling."

"They found something very unusual in your blood Peter. They found it a month ago, and they've been analyzing it ever since."

"What is it they found?" I was keenly interested, for obvious reasons.

"That's just it," he replied. "None of the researchers seem to know. Let me correct myself, they have a pretty good notion what it can do, but they don't have a clue as to what it is."

"That's the way of the world isn't it? Today's science is yesterday's voodoo."

The Wedge chuckled, "It wasn't too long ago that you would have been burned at the stake. Luckily we've come a long way since then. Still, no one has ever seen anything like the stuff that's swimming around in your bodily fluids. It's special, whatever it is."

"It's my blood," I said.

"Maybe," said The Wedge. "It's definitely something *in* your blood. Right now they can't even determine whether it's organic or inorganic. They're becoming more and more interested in you though."

"Why's that?" I wondered.

"So far they haven't been able to replicate it," he explained.

"I don't understand."

"They're running out of the samples they took from you when you were at the hospital. They need more."

I absorbed what he said.

"There's more," The Wedge lowered his voice. "Since you're obviously the only source of whatever it is, the military has developed a sudden and keen interest in you. Have they contacted you in any way?"

"No they haven't," I was suddenly worried. "But, of late I've been pretty hard to find." I'd go into the details of my accident with him later.

"Some Colonel phoned me looking for you. I told him to go screw himself, that I was your lawyer and whatever he had to say to you he'd have to do it through me. He didn't much like it, but he went away. At least for now. Rest assured though, he'll be back." It was a foreboding prediction.

"You did everything right. You're a great lawyer Wedge, and I consider you somewhat of a friend as well."

"In my experience someone always says that to this old southern gentlemen right about the time they need a big favor. Whatever it is you want, I sincerely hope I can oblige."

"You haven't heard what I want yet," I said with an edge to my tone.

"It doesn't matter son. My life has become somewhat lethargic of late. Some might even suggest it has taken an ugly turn toward boring. I would welcome any prospect that would spice it up. How may I be of service?"

I warned him, "By the time I'm done telling you, you may regret saying that."

"Why don't you let me worry about that," he replied with kindness in his voice. "Now tell me what's on your mind."

"I've got to get some of what's inside me into Laurie. I'm talking about my blood. Obviously I can't do it alone. I need the doctors who first treated me in Jackson to help me with this. If they choose not to help me, I'll offer what I have to someone else. I need you to broker this deal Wedge. After we finish, I'll stay and work with them. I'll supply them with whatever they need so we can all make this a better world.

"Laurie is dying. This is the only way we can save her. I'm sorry about using the leverage, but it's the only way. It's this, or nothing."

"I see," The Wedge mused. Unexpectedly he asked, "What did you mean when you alluded to the doctors who treated you first? The ones here in Jackson? That would seem to imply there's been a second time."

The Wedge was better than good. "I had an accident at the hotel yesterday morning," I confessed. "The fingers on my right hand were cut off. All of them," I said flatly.

"I'm sorry, did you say you cut your fingers?"

Even though nothing about it was funny, I had to force myself to keep from laughing. I said, "You heard me right the first time. They were severed from my hand."

"My God!" he exclaimed.

"They were able to reattach them," I continued. "And last night, at the hospital, something strange happened. They were somehow able to heal themselves."

There was a short pause before he asked me, "What does that exactly mean, they healed themselves?"

"Exactly what you think it means," I said.

"My God," he repeated. Then again, this time in an awed kind of whisper, "My God in Heaven."

"I'm bringing Laurie to Jackson with me. We're leaving in the morning. She needs what's inside me, she doesn't have much time. Tell them they have one crack at this. If I hear one peep about why it can't be done instead of all the reasons how it can, they'll never see me again." I hesitated. Then I said, "No one will, I'll take it down the road with me. I'll find others who will help me. Is that clear?"

"Leave it with me," a stolid conviction of purpose resonated in his voice. "Come straight over to my office when you get here. I'll be waiting for both of you."

I let out a deep sigh of relief. "I was right about you Wedge."

"About which part?" he asked.

"Do you really have to ask? I'll see you tomorrow my friend."

Chapter 82

THAT NIGHT I said goodbye to everyone in New Orleans I had come to know and love. John, of course Franklin, and the entire band as well. Sooner or later everyone I knew dropped by. They'd all heard about the accident, so when they saw my hand with their own eyes, they were truly amazed. I'm sure some of them thought it was a bad practical joke, but there had been witnesses. Raymond was a no-nonsense kind of guy. If anyone was thinking it was a joke, and that he was in on it, they thought better of saying it to his face.

I assured everyone that three weeks from now, I'd be good to go. Right now, I explained to them, Laurie and I needed some time alone in Jackson. I told them Laurie had people there. At least for a few days, or maybe even a week; then I'd come back to New Orleans and we'd get ready for the tour. Finally, Laurie and I said goodnight to the last of our friends. As promised, we took off early the next morning, right before dawn.

Driving north on Interstate 55, I couldn't escape a strange sense of foreboding. As we passed it, I glanced in the rearview mirror at the bullet-riddled road sign welcoming everyone to the Big Easy. A dreadful feeling came upon me that I wouldn't be coming back, that somehow this was going to turn into a one-way trip.

I shook off the uneasiness, thinking I was just being foolish, wondering where these thoughts were coming from. I glanced over at Laurie. She'd fallen asleep in the passenger seat, curled up under a pink wool blanket we'd decided to bring with us at the last moment. The bones of her face were more pronounced now due to her continued weight loss. Her pale skin stretched across her high cheekbones much too tightly for my liking. I gritted my teeth, and faced the concrete ribbon in front of me, fighting back tears. Somehow we'd find a way. Together, Laurie and I would beat this monster.

We got into Jackson three hours after we left New Orleans. It took me another twenty minutes in light morning traffic to arrive at The Wedge's office. His secretary was waiting for us in the cozy reception area. We were introducing ourselves to her when Wedge appeared. I could see he was happy to see me, but also very serious.

As the three of us sat down in his office to talk, he said, "Welcome back to Jackson Peter." He smiled warmly at Laurie. "How on earth did this young man talk such a beautiful woman into falling in love with him?"

Laurie smiled back. "Thank you, Mr. Harding, but be careful with your assumptions," she sounded strong and confident.

"Why, whatever do you mean?" Wedge asked in mock surprise. His eyes twinkled. Clearly, he was enjoying himself.

Laurie engaged him further, "Maybe I talked Peter into love."

"Touché," he chuckled. "Doesn't matter who started it, you are here together." He exhaled a large breath, and turned his focus back to me.

He leaned back in his large, mahogany-colored leather chair, and looked solemnly at me.

"They said they wouldn't do it Peter," he informed us.

It felt like I'd taken a shot to my guts from a heavyweight fighter.

"All right," I quickly recovered. I'd promised myself I'd be strong for Laurie, no matter what. "Thank you for your time Wedge," I started to get up to leave.

"Wouldn't doesn't mean can't," he stopped me.

I sat back down, and waited for him from across his big oak desk.

"Something in your bloodstream is unique to you. It's something brand new."

"You mean it's a different blood type?" Laurie spoke up, her brow furrowed.

"Words," The Wedge pointed his index finger upward in front of his face to emphasize his point, "are important. I said your bloodstream. Whatever you have inside you can't really be called blood. You have the veins and arteries of a normal human being, but what runs through them is not what anyone in the medical profession would call blood."

"Well, what the hell is it then?" I didn't really believe him, or the damn doctors for that matter.

The Wedge actually shrugged. "No one knows," he admitted frankly. "But it is irrelevant for what we have planned."

I saw Laurie flinch, and went to her. I never took my eyes off her. I took her hands in mine. They were weak, and trembled in my grasp.

"Don't be afraid," I spoke softly, reassuring her. "Do you trust me?" I whispered in her ear.

She hesitated, and then nodded.

"I'm going to save you, sweetheart."

Tears welled up in her eyes. She opened her mouth to say something. Then she closed it, and slowly nodded her understanding. No one had ever accused Laurie of being stupid.

Chapter 83

LATER THAT SAME afternoon, a solemn group of people convened in a stark boardroom on the second floor of the hospital. A group of Jackson Baptist Medical Center executive administrators and doctors were present. A young woman's life was at stake.

"We can't allow it. There is no way this can be permitted," one of the doctors was objecting. He spoke in a droll tone. Arrogancy oozed out of him like pus from an infected wound.

"We can't *not* allow it," a man in his forties who wore a white smock pointed out matter-of-factly, like it should have been the most obvious thing in the world. It escaped him why his older colleague was arguing the point in the first place.

"That will be sufficient gentlemen," a dignified man at the head of the table intervened. I remembered the white-haired man had been introduced earlier as Dr. Irfan Virk, the hospital's current President.

There were twelve of them in all. They had been speaking among themselves, back and forth, jousting now for close to an hour. It was tedious, and I realized that none of the banter was accomplishing a damn thing. They went around and around, like a stupid hound dog chasing its own tail.

I looked toward the end of the table. The Wedge had been surprisingly silent for the most part. I watched him carefully as he studied those who sat around the table. I wondered when he would make his move. I figured he was simply waiting them out, carefully listening to their discussion. Occasionally he would prompt those in attendance with an offhand comment, or a well placed question, trying to determine how best to influence the outcome.

Another doctor whose name was Anne Sterling, and who had been introduced as a member of the hospital's Board of Directors, was speaking. She was a fit sixty or so years of age and wore a snow-white head of closely-cropped hair. "I will have to agree with Joseph on this one. God forbid something went wrong. We have to think of the liability. We would surely be sued, and we cannot afford to take the risk. It is gambling on the very future of the Medical Center, pure and simple. The very idea we're even having this discussion is absolutely absurd," she finished.

"You have finally articulated the one thing we can all agree upon." The Wedge's voice spilled out across the table like a tipped-over glass of expensive wine. All eyes turned to him. He was allowed to continue; they must have realized they really had no choice. We owned everything. What had The Wedge told me all those months ago? Everything derivative of me was mine. Every sample they'd taken from my body had belonged to no one but me. Some of them seemed to have forgotten that, and were acting as if it was theirs. I had a feeling The Wedge was fixing to straighten this notion out in no uncertain terms.

"You are most certainly being asked to gamble on the very future of this fine institution. However, it is blatantly obvious to me that none of you understand *all* the implications."

The Wedge continued, "There is a great deal at stake here today. In a word, the future is what I am referring to. And aside from a couple of extraordinarily gifted and enlightened souls among you," The Wedge smiled at young Dr. Norman Radcliffe, who couldn't help but smile back in acknowledgement, "No one else here seems to have picked up on that yet.

"Our situation is unique. We have the opportunity to change the world. This is not about me, you, liability, or loss mitigation. Anyone stupid enough to think it is, is most certainly lost in the details. Or maybe I should leave it at just lost, because you're only thinking about yourselves.

"Imagine for a moment, a world without disease. Think about an existence where we could remove the physical pain most of us live with each day of our lives. No cancers, common colds, or influenzas. A world without the horrible disease and pain that for many people is a part of everyday life.

"I'm not suggesting in any way that we conquer death. Oh no. That is not for any of us mere mortals to decide. That one we will leave to God. The same God, by the way, who has so benevolently given us this opportunity we now find ourselves considering. There's one for all you churchgoers to think about," he added. "Not that any of you are hypocrites. Far be it for me to suggest this. Because everyone here is perfect, aren't we?" He stared at each of them in turn. I noticed that a few of them could not meet his gaze, electing instead to look down at the table.

Disregarding them, The Wedge soldiered on. "We have a chance to do something great here today, something historic. We could go elsewhere. Eventually we would find a small group of people courageous enough to write such a future. But why not you? Why not now? And here? If the only thing that's stopping you all from agreeing to this is, as you say, the future of this hospital, then you are a bunch of asses. One of the things we are addressing here *is* the future. Not so much of this distinguished Medical Center, but of this world, and of humanity itself.

"If you don't believe me," The Wedge charged forward, "then surely you must believe history. Do you not recall how insulin came to us, and what it has done for the world? It was a doctor who experimented with it on the first patient, a dying fourteen-year-old child. Of course everyone was afraid. Think about this for a few moments. That doctor risked what little was left of that poor boy's life so that for centuries to come our children could live. The only difference here, I suppose, is that he wasn't going to be sued if he failed. Make no mistake about his risk, however. If he'd killed the child, what then? He would have probably spent the rest of his days tortured by what he'd done. But fortunately for us, that huge gamble didn't stop him.

"With the signed, legal documentation put in place here, it is my opinion none of you need worry about such consequences. We can legally structure the agreement so there can be no reprisals. You'll all have the luxury of that immunity. Dr. Banting and Dr. Best, who risked everything and changed the world forever on that afternoon in 1922, did not. What they accomplished, however, was to take away the pain of millions of their fellow human beings. Forever. Risks? You're damned right this thing is risky. And we cannot – we must not – " he banged his fist onto the table. It sounded like the boom of a cannon. The Wedge forced himself to calm down before he said the last thing he'd come with me to say. "We will not allow this gift to foolishly slip through our fingers. There is not one among us who could ever pay the price to answer for such an arrogant travesty."

Chapter 84

"THAT WAS WITHOUT doubt the most powerful summation I have ever had the pleasure of presenting to a jury," said The Wedge.

He, Laurie, and myself were seated in the lounge down the hall from the conference room. His eyes twinkled with a strange, and beautiful passion as he spoke.

"It's as if every case I've been a part of for my entire life led me to this moment. Thank you for allowing me to be a part of this Peter," he spoke with reverence.

The doctors and hospital officials had asked us to wait while they decided if they would agree to our conditions. They remained in the conference room to talk things over. They'd been in there for over an hour.

"You have to admit, it's an uncommon jury," I said.

"They all are," The Wedge agreed. "But yes, this one is more uncommon than most. We are dealing with life and death issues, but not like your typical murder trial."

Up until now Laurie had been mostly listening. "How do you feel about the death penalty?" she wanted to know what he thought.

"I'm all for it," his immediate reply surprised me. "There are some very bad people out there doing some very bad things. But I have one caveat," his mischievous grin seemed at odds with the subject matter.

The Wedge continued, "If the murderer is found guilty of the crime and subjected to the ultimate penalty, then fair enough. But afterwards, if he or she is found to be innocent, then round up the rogues who played a part in the new murder and hold them accountable in exactly the same way."

"You mean – " Laurie began.

The Wedge suddenly became deadly serious. "They would all be guilty of the same crime: the Judge, the jury, the cops who gathered the wrong evidence, and last but not least, the Prosecutor. Especially the Prosecutor. Try them all. And if they're found guilty, hang them from the nearest tree."

Laurie and I were silent as we thought about it. I finally said, "If that was the case, then no one would ever be executed."

The Wedge's smile returned as he stated the obvious. "I guess if you held them accountable for such a terrifying mistake, there would be no more death penalty. Better a thousand guilty go free than one innocent be murdered. Throughout the ages, a countless number of innocents have suffered horribly because of the conduct of some very unscrupulous people. History proves time and again that you can't always tell the good guys from the bad ones. Personally, I would never condone anything that can't be reversed.

"Those men and women in that conference room have a serious, important decision to make. They can't know the outcome; that part troubles them the most. If they refuse us, they are condemning an innocent."

I glanced at Laurie. She smiled, suggesting I could talk freely, giving me her tacit approval to do so.

"Laurie is dying," I said. "She only has a few weeks left. Can't they see that?" I asked with a broken heart.

The Wedge sighed deeply. "Give them just a little more time to sort it out. There are deeper things afoot they must consider."

I said, "I guess this is as good a time as any to ask you about my parents. Have you learned anything about the whereabouts of Senior and Linda Lou?"

He looked at me blankly. I couldn't tell what he

was thinking. He finally said, "We haven't been able to find them. In fact, it's as if they were never born."

"I guess they're hiding," I said. "They've done it before. Can you just keep looking? Sooner or later they'll turn up."

The Wedge never stopped looking at me, but said nothing.

"What?" I asked.

His brow furrowed. "Peter, either they received the assistance of every known government agency from the very hospitals that you guessed they were born in, to the IRS, or they never were."

I chuckled at the very idea. "I may have been mistaken about them being born in a hospital. Maybe they used midwives; home births were common back when they were young. So it wouldn't be out of the question that their births were never registered. As far as the IRS is concerned, I don't imagine they ever filed any tax returns. Not with how Senior and his brother made their living."

"How about prison?" The Wedge asked.

"What about it?" I was getting frustrated.

"Your father was sent there."

"That's correct," I said.

"There's no record of it, your father must have lied to you. There's no record of any of them having a driver's license, no utility bills in their names, and no school records. Not even a mortgage on the house you claim to have lived in."

"The home I claim to have lived in?" I strongly objected. "I grew up in that home! We owned it. Someone must have erased all the records."

"If that's the case, then they have been able to accomplish what no one else has ever done," he replied. "I'm not saying it would be impossible. But the idea that multiple and independent government agencies would somehow manage to get together and erase someone's identity is virtually incomprehensible. What possible reason would these agencies have for going to all that trouble?"

I glared at him. "Do you think I've been lying to you about my parents? Why would I do that?"

"Do you think it's at all possible that you are confused?" The Wedge asked gently. "Could the bus crash somehow have affected your mind?"

"I was burned, there's nothing wrong with my head. Did you really look into all those records?" I was beginning to doubt his integrity.

"We looked Peter," he said. "If you like, I can assemble the team who worked on it, and you can meet with them. You can ask them any questions you wish. We kept records of every agency, and every interview."

"So what then? I made it all up?"

"I'm not suggesting that at all, but the facts remain. It would seem that none of the people you asked me to locate for you have ever existed."

Chapter 85

THINGS CAN BE weird living in the backwoods of Tennessee, and I guess this proved it. Laurie squeezed my hand. She smiled at me. "I believe you, there has to be an explanation for it. No one can simply vanish with no trace they ever existed."

"That is something we can agree upon," The Wedge concurred. "That, and the fact there is an explanation for it. Perhaps not one that's immediately obvious to us, but an explanation nonetheless."

There was noise down the hallway in the direction of the conference room. We looked up as the door opened, and the room's occupants spilled into the hallway. The verdict was in.

It was my turn to squeeze Laurie's hand. I could see she was scared as some of the doctors moved up the hallway toward where we sat. I took solace in the fact that if they turned us down, we'd find someone else who'd say yes, but I also knew we were running out of time.

We stood to greet the three doctors who

approached us. The nine others had gone the other way, back to their offices, I supposed.

Dr. Radcliffe led the charge, flanked by two equally young doctors. Their expressions were severe, so I expected the worst. They stopped in front of us and they stared at me as if I were a lab rat.

Dr. Radcliffe cleared his throat. "Peter, there is something we need to tell you. I'm afraid it isn't good news."

"We kind of expected it," I conceded with a sigh. "I'm sure you did your best with them Doctor. I guess they just don't have your vision. You tried, and we'll always be grateful to you for that."

A trace of bewilderment flashed across his face. "No, no. That's not at all what I mean," he quickly objected. He glanced at Wedge, and continued, "Your friend Mr. Harding is an extraordinarily gifted orator. The conference got a little heated, but you were successful. We voted, and the majority agreed with your proposal."

"What proposal?" asked Laurie. "Everyone has talked around it. You haven't told me specific details." She looked directly at me. "I need to know what is so revolutionary that no one can talk about it. What exactly do you and all of these doctors have in mind? Why didn't you tell me more before we left New Orleans Peter?"

Laurie was upset, and I needed to reassure her. I said, "I didn't go too far into it because nothing was for sure. I didn't know if…" I glanced at the three doctors, "the hospital would step outside of protocol, and risk everything for the future. We got lucky." I turned my gaze back to her. I stepped toward her, and gently held her shoulders. "Whatever it is that runs through my veins could cure you if we transfer it to you."

Laurie looked at me, searching my eyes. She saw I was serious. I felt her knees begin to buckle. I held her up as my grip tightened around her shoulders. "Listen to me now," I urged her. "You've seen how my fingers recovered, and you know about my burns healing. These things are nothing short of miracles. Somehow I received a gift in that horrible accident." I shook her gently. "I lived so we could meet and I could save you. Because I love you, Laurie, more than life itself. Like The Wedge said, none of us has the right to squander such a gift. Least of all you and me.

"We're going to do this thing, and if it works, then we're going to do it again for others. It all begins with us." I continued, "Out of all the people in the world, I have no idea why this happened to me; it just did." I shrugged. "I want it to be used to help you, and then others, too. It can change the world for the better."

"I'm scared Peter," she trembled.

"I know," I said. "So am I."

"What if something goes wrong?" she asked quietly.

"We have to at least try. Please say yes. For all our sakes, agree with this, we're running out of time."

Dr. Radcliffe cleared his throat. We all looked at him. He looked at the floor, as if he was summoning the fortitude to say what he obviously had to. We waited patiently. Finally he spoke, "There's the matter I alluded to earlier Peter. I'm afraid there is something rather important we didn't tell you about."

I was suddenly filled with overwhelming angst, because I knew what he was about to say was definitely not good news.

Chapter 86

HE CONTINUED, "IT'S the main reason the people in the conference room objected to this transfusion."

Laurie couldn't help herself. She was angry. "I'm dying. I have a few weeks left to live. Look at me. I've lost twenty percent of my body weight in three months. I sleep for eighteen hours a day, and the rest of the time I can barely keep my eyes open. What the hell does anyone have to lose?" She turned to me. "I'll do it Peter. If I don't make it," she turned back to the doctor, "it doesn't matter. It won't change a thing. I'm already dead." She was breathing hard from the exertion of her emotional outburst.

Dr. Radcliffe looked at her, empathy written large across his face. He moved his gaze in my direction.

"We haven't been able to replicate the substance in your body Peter. I can't say bloodstream, because you no longer have one. Or rather, you no longer have what can be called blood running through you."

"I don't get it," I said.

"I think I understand what Dr. Radcliffe is saying," The Wedge interrupted. "Allow me Doctor. There is no more where that came from, is there?"

One of the other doctors answered. "No, there isn't," he said. "We don't think it can reproduce itself once it leaves Peter's body."

"You don't know that for certain," charged The Wedge.

"That's true," he agreed.

"Because you have never tested this theory," Wedge pressured him.

"Yes, that's true, but the fact remains that we cannot reproduce what runs through Peter's veins. This, coupled with the fact that as far as we know no other human possesses it…well, you can guess the rest." He said to me, "Peter, when a person gives blood to save another it is truly an act of grace, but we can do this because we know the human body can regenerate more blood. In your case, we have no such guarantee. We don't at this moment know that this will naturally occur." Ominously, he concluded, "The body can lose only so much of its blood before it begins to shut down and eventually dies.

"With you, there are two main concerns. If we take too much of what you have, you will likely succumb. This would probably leave you in a vegetative state, or you could die," he repeating his earlier warning.

"We have no idea how much of your, shall we call it sustenance, might be enough to cure Laurie, and we don't have any idea how much of it we can take before you may expire. You may already be nearing this point from how much you bled when you lost your fingers. I'm afraid the risks are off the charts. Both of you could die." He glanced at his associates before he continued. "I'm sorry," he apologized to me. "You must know the risks."

After a moment the other doctors nodded their agreement.

"We may lose this gift Peter. If you don't survive the transfusion, then whatever this is will leave with you. If you remain alive, we can still extract small samples that we can study."

"What about the samples you already have?" I asked.

"They have degenerated," he said with finality.

I slowly shook my head in disbelief. "What the hell do you mean, degenerated?" I asked him.

"We've learned that once your sustenance leaves your body, it quickly decays. Every seventy-two hours or so, approximately half of the sample dies."

"It's my blood!" I almost shrieked. "What you're talking about is part of me!" I proclaimed.

The third doctor spoke for the first time. "We're not so sure about that. We really don't know what we're dealing with here. We do know that whatever lives in you, is something no doctor has ever seen before. Whatever you have is somehow able to send the body's normal healing process into warp drive. Not only that, but your sustenance seems to mimic the process of creation. Your fingers didn't just reattach themselves to your hand. It was more as if they grew back onto your hand at an accelerated rate that would defy any scientific explanation.

"The bottom line here is that if we remove some of your bodily fluids and transfer them to Laurie…" he paused to carefully consider what he would say next. "There's ample evidence at this point that you would likely not live through the procedure. The substance in your veins would, in our professional opinion, not be able to replace itself in time. We can't even be sure it would heal Laurie. We could lose both of you." He finished his speech.

I became aware of my breathing as we stared at each other in silence. I finally said, "I'm alive and I shouldn't be. That's something now, isn't it? I respect all of you, but the only sure thing is that none of us really know about my, what did you call it? My sustenance." I took a deep breath. "I'll take my chances Doctor, because that's the only chance that Laurie has. I've made my decision. If it costs me my life, then so be it. At least we tried. It's all we've got," I muttered.

I turned to Laurie, "I'd rather pass on a life with you not in it." I smiled. "It just wouldn't be the same without you sweetheart."

I faced the doctors. "We're in agreement then. I don't need to tell you we have to move quickly. I've only one last question. When can your team be ready?"

Dr. Radcliffe nodded, looked back at me and said, "It will take three days to get everything prepared."

"Good," I said.

"Are you a religious man Peter?" he asked hesitantly.

I shrugged. "Sometimes, most of the time not, it depends. Why?" I was hedging, but then again, I wasn't prepared to dismiss help from anyone or anything.

"Now might be a good time to call in a priest for both you, and Laurie."

Chapter 87

THREE DAYS LATER, as I lay on the hospital gurney, I thought about what Dr. Radcliffe had asked me. I asked Laurie how she felt about it, and if maybe she wanted to call someone in. Up until that point, I hadn't even thought to ask her if she even belonged to a church, or whether she was Catholic, or Protestant, or maybe even Jewish. It turned out she was none of the above, but that never stopped her from believing in God. Praying to God eased the guilt of her abortion. So she had kept praying. Somehow that faith helped make more sense out of life, gave it order. It also explained a few things that were otherwise difficult to understand. Like what was happening now, for instance.

I looked from side to side, examining the room we were in. Laurie was lying comfortably in a bed beside me, about six feet away. This gave room for the doctors and hospital staff to move freely between us. I gave her a reassuring smile, which she returned, making an effort to blink her eyes. I mouthed the words, I love you. We were both sedated, readied for what was to come, and barely hanging onto consciousness.

I looked up at a nurse who was checking the IV lines that ran between us. The nurse turned, and saw I was looking at her. She smiled. I could swear I recognized her from somewhere. I fought to dismiss the thought, but couldn't get rid of it. I decided I had probably seen her earlier somewhere in the hospital. Besides, the mask she wore covered most of her face.

"Peter?" My vision was suddenly filled with the masked face of Dr. Radcliffe. The ceiling light behind him made it look as if he had a halo. "Can you hear me?"

I tried to speak, but my lips would no longer move. I barely managed to blink my eyes in a sign I could still hear him.

"Good," he said. "We're going to put you and Laurie to sleep now. We need to lower your blood pressure so that we can begin the process."

I blinked again. They had told me all of this yesterday, along with their plan to mix the fluids inside my body with the blood inside of Laurie's body. That way, they reasoned, they could maintain a static volume in what they described as a closed system. It was a gamble, but everything we were doing was a risk. No one had ever tried anything remotely similar to this procedure before.

I stole one last sideways glance at Laurie. Her eyes were closed now. Her breathing was soft and regular. I felt a great sense of relief at the peacefulness etched across her thin face.

The IVs ran into a large machine that would mix our fluids together, and then move them back through both our bodies. If whatever resided in me was incompatible with her blood, well, they had warned us.

Dr. Radcliffe was talking again. "Whatever happens," he hesitated before he continued, "All of us have a great deal of respect and admiration for your courage. We'll do our best to bring you back, I promise you. Both of you."

Tears filled my eyes. I managed to blink one last time. The doctor turned and nodded to someone out of my view. Almost instantly the room began to dim. The last words I heard him say were, "Come back to us son," and then everything around me started to shrink. Like the picture on our old black and white television when Senior switched it off, and told me it was time for bed.

The halo above the Doctor's masked head grew smaller and smaller until only a tiny pinpoint of light remained. It looked like a faint star in a distant constellation.

Chapter 88

THE TINIEST ESSENCE of light exploded into a million blinding shards of color. I had a sensation of floating in a vastness that went on without end. The colored lights exploded outwards, quickly filling the void, like they were being sucked there, rather than pushed by the initial blast of energy from the first tiny point of light.

As I watched the lights moving at an incalculable rate of speed, they started to change. Giant tails spewed out from behind them. Billions of them, of every imaginable color, with hues I'd never seen before. There was something on the very edge of my mind, something about…I struggled to latch onto a memory that seemed older than the mountains. I had it! I recalled a life a long time ago; a young girl who died never seeing anything at all. She may have been blind, but her life had been as brilliant as the cascading shower of infinite lights that now surrounded me. Her soul as infinite as the very essence of what I was experiencing.

Try as I might, I could not remember the girl's name, or where the memory had come from.

One of the lights streaked toward me from so far away that distance no longer had meaning. I thought to move as the fiery orb headed straight toward me.

Before I could think beyond this instinct, a blinding blue light hit me. It exploded into a million pieces, all of which cascaded on past me, or perhaps even through my body.

My senses reeled from the blast. Sounds assailed my consciousness that I never knew existed. They were beyond anything I'd heard before. They were indescribably beautiful. Music, but not.

There were also smells. Odors seemed to float through me, weaving a tapestry among the sounds, lights, and a myriad of other things I couldn't identify. Yet the entirety of it in no way overwhelmed me. It began to dawn on me that I'd become something much more than I'd been.

Everything seemed to start fading then. As I noticed this, another more brilliant light expanded across a distant horizon. It grew extraordinarily larger as it quickly moved across the vast space between where I was and where it had originated. It wasn't moving forward, but expanded purple and then orange, until it was about to engulf me, like a huge atomic explosion. The other lights, colors, and comet tails continued to collapse all around the periphery of my consciousness.

The energy expanded across the infinite void in what seemed to be mere moments, yet I had no concept of how long it actually took. It could have been seconds, or it could have taken eons. As it reached me, the huge wall of energy suddenly stopped a mere foot from my face. I gingerly reached out to touch it. It was then I realized I had no hands, and no body. Even so, whatever I had become made contact with the infinite thing anyway. Because I willed it to happen, and because I wanted to know more.

Chapter 89

THERE WAS AN intense flash of all consuming, all expansive power.

I saw my hand then, in front of my body. It was stretched out toward a figure lying on a bed beneath me. There were tubes going into and coming from this prone figure. There was a breathing machine next to what I now surmised must be a hospital bed. I couldn't recognize whether the person lying there was a man or a woman, because whoever it was appeared to be horribly burned.

Then a question formed in my mind. "Why am I here? And just exactly where is here?"

"You," a soft voice whispered. It appeared to come from all around me. I wasn't certain if someone spoke, or if the voice originated inside my own head.

The room seemed to move then, everything tilted. The bed with the person in it seemed to revolve on a hidden axis, and I found myself standing beside it now, rather than floating above it. For the first time I became conscious of a third person, or entity, in the room. I turned my head sideways, and stared in numb disbelief at a woman beside me.

I knew her! At least I recognized her. She was the nurse who tended to me when I severed my fingers. She was also with the doctors who were trying to save Laurie. Far more significantly, I now recognized her as the blonde-haired lady I rescued from the raging inferno in Jackson all those months ago.

"Me," I stated what had now become obvious.

She smiled, and slowly nodded.

We looked in front of us at the man lying in the bed.

He – me – was burned beyond recognition. I had seen myself before, in the bathroom mirror as a horribly disfigured creature, in this same room right after I'd been brought here from the train wreck.

I watched my body, examining it closely for any signs of life.

"I'm dead," I said flatly, turning to the woman.

"Still and always Peter," she spoke softly. I could tell she was trying to comfort me.

I felt an incredible sense of loss. Pain tore through my soul.

"I'm sad," I said. "More sad than I've ever been."

"I know." She looked at me in sorrow.

"I don't understand any of this." I fought to remain calm, in spite of the overwhelming angst of it all.

The blonde-haired lady sighed deeply, sensing my despair and grief, wanting to somehow take it away.

"I know that too," she tried her best to soothe me.

"Who are you?" I asked. "And what did you mean when you said still and always?"

She smiled radiantly and said, "There is no greater love than what you showed on that bus. You could have just saved yourself; you thought about it. Do you remember?"

I nodded, "Yeah, I do. I thought about it all right," I conceded.

"But you couldn't just leave me there, could you? To die with the rest of those people."

"No ma'am, I couldn't do that, it wouldn't have been right. I couldn't have lived with myself."

"You would have found a way."

"Maybe," I agreed. "Then again, maybe not. I didn't really have time to think about it."

"Yes, you did," she contradicted me. She looked me in the face again, this time a hint of mischief on the edges of her lips. "I was there. Remember?"

I smiled too. "I guess you were," I said. "Did you know what I would do? Before I saved you, I mean? Or did I? Save you?" She and everything around me, I knew, was beyond my comprehension.

"I owe you an explanation, about everything. And no, I didn't know what you would decide to do before you did it, but I can say I was very happy with the decision you made."

"What was it? Some kind of test or something?" I asked. "I must have passed."

"What makes you say that?" she wondered.

"I'm here, aren't I?" I pointed out.

She nodded again. "No one can argue that."

I glanced around the hospital room again, and then back to her. "Do you have a name?"

"You can call me Mary, if you like. It doesn't matter, it's only a name."

"Are you going to tell me where we are Mary?" I asked politely.

"Your will to continue the life you were living was far stronger than most Peter," she began. "This, in and of itself, is sometimes enough.

"In your case though, the injuries were much too severe to sustain your corporal form." She gestured to the bed.

"But I survived the accident," I objected. "The

doctors saved me. I got better." Even as I said it, I knew different. Because there I was, right in front of us, looking more like a charred and blackened piece of wood than anything human.

"Your will to live was strong," she repeated. "But there's something else inside of you that's even stronger. Every time you could, you put others ahead of yourself. Me, for instance. You made the decision to save another, a stranger. Even though you were young, and desperate to live the life you believed you could, you wouldn't at the expense of another. As a result of the decision you made, you moved into a kind of limbo. Let's say you got stuck in transition. You were not quite dead, but you weren't really alive either."

"Are you saying I imagined everything after that train hit the bus, that it was all a fantasy? Some kind of a weird dream?"

"Sort of," said Mary. "A soul as old as yours is able to move through, and into other realms of consciousness. Human beings call it enlightenment. Do you recall when you ran out of the music store, and chased after me?"

"Of course," I remembered.

"You saved that baby in the stroller."

"Anyone would have done that," I stated emphatically, not wanting to believe otherwise.

"Not very many would have done that. Most would have watched it happen, and convinced themselves there was nothing they could have done to stop it."

"I don't want to believe that," I said.

"I know," Mary spoke in a soothing tone. "But, I believe you know otherwise."

"What makes the difference Mary?" I asked, bewildered. "What made me so special?"

"You've led your many lives differently than others Peter. Compassion led you to this place. Even when you were young, you cared so much. You didn't have to wait every day for that bus with the blind girl on it. You didn't have to walk her up that gravel road back to where she lived. She loved you for that, they all did. Her family never forgot your kindness."

"But she got killed." I lamented.

"It was out of your hands. That's what it means to be human," she patiently explained. "That, and what we do with the time we are given."

"So I died in the accident?" I was beginning to accept it.

"That life ended shortly afterward, yes."

"And everything after that was some weird illusion?" It came out as a kind of accusation.

"Laurie wasn't real either, then?" I got to what was bothering me the most.

"She was the love inside you Peter. She was as real as real can ever be.

"In fact, everything you experienced after the crash was your reality. Who you are made all of it possible. Do you remember watching the back of yourself when you were playing in the band to all those people? Was that not real?"

"It seemed real enough, but I don't understand it. How was it possible that I was able to watch myself? Were there two of me?"

"There are as many of you as there are stars in the universe. Those colored lights, sounds, and everything you sensed were all the infinite possibilities of the countless lives we all live. Your life force grows stronger and stronger with each existence. One builds upon the ones that came before. Every soul has a unique trajectory. Yours has begun the period when all lives become one."

Chapter 90

I WAS FINALLY able to force open my eyes, but only to allow a tiny sliver of light in. It seemed like lead weights were attached to my eyelids. I fought hard to focus, but everything around me was murky, like peering through a dense fog. I couldn't think of where I was, or where I'd been. I could hear a rhythmic sound.

For a reason not known to me, I envisioned a cemetery with two opened graves. One for a small, innocent girl who'd been crushed to death beneath a school bus, so long ago now that it must have been another life. The other, my own, because I'd tried to save her and was also crushed beneath it.

The clacking sound of the pump forcing air into my lungs grew less and less audible. It was all but gone now, replaced by the steady, high-pitched tone that indicated the flat line.

Requiem for a Life

THE STIFF, COOL breeze that snapped at his shoulder-length blonde hair had an uncustomary bite to it for this time of year.

It was late September in San Francisco as he stood on the east side of the Golden Gate Bridge. He stared out across the estuary, and found the haunted island of Alcatraz.

He looked down to the water below, and shuddered involuntarily. *It was a long way down.* He took a deep breath, and gusted it back out. He checked from side to side. Good. There was no one coming that he could see. Hesitating only slightly, he nervously climbed up over the railing and onto the ledge that ran along the other side of it. He turned around to face Alcatraz, his arms twitching as his slender fingers held onto the orange railing with a tenuous purchase.

"How old are you?" a female voice interrupted his final reverie, reflexively causing him to grip the railing more tightly.

He chanced a sideways glance to his left. She must have come from the north, the Sausalito side of the bridge. She was dressed in a sweat suit, and was breathing heavily. She'd been on a run across the bridge, he thought, which explained her sudden appearance on the walkway.

"What? I'm a little busy right now!" he was flustered, caught up in the absurd moment, yet couldn't help but notice how beautiful she was. This was not at all what he planned.

"I was wondering how old you are?" she spoke above a sudden blast of cold wind. Her hair flew backwards like the tails of a black cat-of-nine whip.

He shook his head in disbelief.

"That isn't…" he began. "What do you mean, how old am I?" the flash of anger he felt came from nowhere. He instantly regretted it. "I'm sorry."

"I'm sorry," she also apologized. "I didn't mean to intrude on your…" she trailed off. She continued, "You're not going to believe this, but I…" she searched for the right words, "I came out here to… I was actually thinking about doing what I think you're about to do. But, I'm not so sure about it now. I'll come back another time. I'm sorry I bothered you." She made a move to leave, but stopped. She turned back to him and said, "This is awkward. I feel like I should say something. I'm not sure what." She began to leave.

"Wait!" he blurted out.

She turned back, unsure of herself.

"Please," he spoke softer this time. The cold wind had picked up. His blonde hair snapped across his face as he carefully turned around on his purchase. It had been drizzling all morning. Even now a heavy shroud of fog rolled in across the Bay. As he began to climb back over the railing, he lost his footing and slipped on the wet metal. He almost went over, but caught himself by grabbing onto the handrail. He climbed over it and onto the sidewalk. His heart was racing as he stood on solid concrete a few feet in front of her, breathing hard.

"That was close," she said.

He looked back over his shoulder to where he'd been. "Yeah," he agreed. "It was a little too close." He looked back at her. "Why'd you come here? I mean," he hesitated, "I guess I know why, but I'm curious as to the reason. You're a beautiful woman, you look like you could write your own ticket. What happened in your life that things got to this point?"

"I could ask you the same thing. You're young and not hard to look at."

He shivered. He was wearing a lighter jacket than he would have, had this been a normal day. He hadn't seen a need for something warmer when he'd decided to come here and do this. Now, he regretted it. It was funny how quickly things could change, he thought to himself, at the same time wondering how to respond to her.

"It's all right if you don't want to talk about it," she said.

"No, it's not that," he said. "It's this place. I'm cold."

She shivered. "So am I."

He looked at her closer then. She was incredibly beautiful. He remembered reading about such a suicide when he'd been younger. He'd concentrated on the picture beside the story and wondered why someone with her beauty had been driven to such a desperate act. Now a similar thing was being played out right in front of him.

"Do you want to go somewhere?" he asked. "To talk, I mean. Suddenly I don't want to be alone. My guess would be you feel the same way right now. Maybe we can help each other."

"I… Why not?" she gave in. "We can always come back another day." It wasn't a joke, nor was it meant to be.

He smiled tentatively. "That's the spirit. Who

knows? We may find some common ground, other than this."

"Stranger things have happened," she admitted.

"C'mon then, let's go back. Let's try something new." He suddenly laughed.

"What's so funny?"

"I was about to say, what do we have to lose?"

She laughed too. It was wonderful and light-hearted, like the sound birds' wings made on the wind.

Together they began to walk back down the bridge in the direction of San Francisco. After walking on the pathway in silence for about five minutes, she said, "I thought there was no love in this world."

He took a deep breath of the fog. "I know."

"Do you believe in fate?" she asked him.

He thought about it carefully before he answered. "I never used to. Now?" he stopped, and turned to face her. They were near the bottom of the bridge. For the first time in forever, things felt different for him. The world was still very much confusing, but something happened up there on the bridge that by his reckoning wasn't supposed to.

"Have we ever met before?" his eyes examined hers. "I feel like I know you from somewhere."

She stared at him. "Normally I'd say no, but these days I haven't been too sure of much. I have to admit there is something..." she trailed off. She began again. "Not too long ago someone told me that we are all bolder than the heavens, brighter than the stars. I didn't believe them. Now I don't know what to think. Something deep inside me changed just now when I saw you about to jump. I can't explain it; I just know it happened. It's crazy. This whole thing is crazy. Me and you meeting this way."

"Imagine if it works, and something comes from it. Years from now they'll be asking us how we met?"

She searched his eyes. She thought she may have found some hope. It was only a tiny thread, but she'd felt it nonetheless. And like he said, *What did they have to lose?*

"Maybe you were wrong," he said thoughtfully.

"About what?" she wondered.

"That there's no love in the world," he said.

"I meant for me. I've seen a bunch of happy people in my life. Not much of it came my way."

"Things can change."

They walked on in silence. The fog began to lift, and the first rays of warm sunshine spilled onto the streets of the Embarcadero.

He turned to her as they stopped in front of a diner.

"Lunch?" he smiled with the offer.

"I don't even know your name," it suddenly occurred to her.

He held out his hand, smiling. He bowed slightly and said, "I'm Peter."

She laughed that laugh again, and it warmed his heart to hear it, and to see her this way.

She took his hand in hers. "I'm Laurie, Peter. I'm very happy to make your acquaintance."

END

Ghosts of our Lives

James Falkener

It is hard to detach from the present tense
When other worlds seem so far away;
Different lives, other paths, redefines our sense
And redeems our thoughts and how they play.
What we often wish for in our life –
Our cherished hopes, and how they unfold,
Can sometimes hurt, often pain with strife –
Leaving one's emotions out in the cold.
Dubious accounts make for doubtful cases
As one questions the underbelly of our lives.
What we did, where we went - all of the places;
We trade our heroes for the ghost that survives.